The

Past

and

the

Punishments

Fiction from Modern China

This series is intended to showcase new and exciting works by China's finest contemporary novelists in fresh, authoritative translations. It represents innovative recent fiction by some of the boldest new voices in China today as well as classic works of this century by internationally acclaimed novelists. Bringing together writers from several geographical areas and from a range of cultural and political milieus, the series opens new doors to twentieth-century China.

HOWARD GOLDBLATT

General Editor

Yu Hua

Translated from the Chinese

by Andrew F. Jones

General Editor, Howard Goldblatt

University of Hawai'i Press   *Honolulu*

The

Past

and

the

Punishments

Printed in the United States of America

01 00 99 98 97 96   5 4 3 2 1

Library of Congress Cataloging-in-Publication Data

Yü, Hua, 1960–

    The past and the punishments / Yu Hua ; translated by Andrew F.

Jones ; general editor, Howard Goldblatt.

        p.   cm. — (Fiction from modern China)

    Translation from Chinese.

      ISBN 0–8248–1782–6 (cloth : alk. paper). — ISBN 0–8248–1817–2

(pbk. : alk. paper)

      I. Jones, Andrew F.   II. Goldblatt, Howard, 1939–   .   III. Title.

IV. Series.

PL2928.H78J66   1996

895.1'352—dc20   96–5143

               CIP

Designed by Richard Hendel

Contents

The

Past

---

and

---

the

Punishments

On the Road at Eighteen

The asphalt road rolls up and down like it's pasted on top of ocean waves. Walking down this little highway in the mountains, I'm like a boat. This year, I turned eighteen. The few brownish whiskers that have sprouted on my chin flutter in the breeze. They've only just taken up residence on my chin, so I really treasure them. I've spent the whole day walking down the road, and I've already seen lots of mountains and lots of clouds. Every one of the mountains and every one of the clouds made me think of people I know. I shouted out each of their nicknames as I walked by. So even though I've walked all day, I'm not tired, not at all. I walked through the morning, now it's the tail end of the afternoon, and it won't be long until I see the tip of dusk. But I haven't found an inn.

I've encountered quite a few people along the road, but none of them has known where the road goes or whether there's an inn there. They all tell me: "Keep walking. You'll see when you get there." I think what everyone said was just terrific. I really am just seeing when I get there. But I haven't found an inn. I feel like I should be worried about that.

I think it's weird that I've walked all day and only seen one car. That was around noon, when I'd just begun to think about hitchhiking. But all I was doing was thinking about hitchhiking. I hadn't started to worry about finding an inn — I was only thinking about how amazing it would be to get a lift from someone. I stood by the side of the road waving at the car, trying my best to look casual. But the driver hardly even looked at me. The car or the driver. They hardly even looked at me. All they fucking did was drive right by. So I ran, chasing the car as fast as I could, just for fun, because I still hadn't started to worry about finding an inn. I ran until the car had disappeared, and then I laughed at myself, but I discovered that laughing too hard made it difficult to breathe, so I stopped. After that I kept walking, happy and excited, except that I started to regret that I hadn't picked up a rock before I started waving at the car.

Now I really want a lift, because dusk is about to fall and I can't get that inn out of my goddamned head. But there haven't been any cars all afternoon. If a car came now, I think I could make it stop. I'd lie down in the middle of the road, and I'm willing to bet that any car would come to a screeching halt before it got to my head. But I don't even hear the rumble of an engine, let alone see a car. Now I'm just going to have to keep walking and see when I get there. Not bad at all: keep walking and see when you get there.

The road rolls up and down from hill to valley, and the hills tempt me every time, because before I charge up to the top, I think I'll see an inn on the other side. But each time I charge up the slope, all I see is another hill in the distance, with a depressing trough in between. And still I charge up each hill as if my life depended on it. And now I'm charging up another one, but this time I see it. Not an inn, but a truck. The truck is pointed toward me, stalled in the middle of the highway in a gully between two hills. I can see the driver's ass pointing skyward and, behind it, all the colors of the approaching sunset. I can't see the driver's head because it's stuffed under the hood. The truck's hood slants up into the air like an upside-down lip. The back of the truck is piled full of big wicker baskets. I'm thinking that they definitely must be packed with some kind of fruit. Of course, bananas would be best of all. There are probably some in the cab, too, so when I hop in, I can eat a few. And I don't really care if the truck's going in the opposite direction as me. I need to find an inn, and if there's no inn, I need a truck. And the truck's right here in front of me.

Elated, I run down to the truck and say, "Hi!"

The driver doesn't seem to have heard me. He's still fiddling with something under the hood.

"Want a smoke?"

Only now does he pull his head out from under the hood, stretch out a black, grimy hand, and take the cigarette between his fingers. I rush to give him a light, and he sucks several mouthfuls of smoke into his mouth before stuffing his head back under the hood.

I'm satisfied. Since he accepted the smoke, that means he has to give me a lift. So I wander around to the back of the truck to investigate what's in the wicker baskets. But they're covered, and I can't see, so I sniff. I smell the fragrance of apples. And I think: Apples aren't too bad either.

In just a little bit, he's done repairing the truck, and he jumps down from the hood. I rush over and say, "Hey, I need a ride." What I don't expect is that he gives me a hard shove with those grimy hands and barks, "Go away!"

I'm so angry I'm speechless, but he just swings on over to the driver's side, opens the door, slides into the cab, and starts the engine. I know that if I blow this opportunity, I'll never get another one. I know I should just give up. So I run over to the other side, open the door, and hop in. I'm ready to fight if necessary. I turn to him and yell: "Then give me back my cigarette!" The truck's already started to move by now.

He turns to look at me with a big, friendly smile and asks, "Where you headed?"

I'm bewildered by this turnaround. I say, "Doesn't matter. Wherever."

He asks me very nicely, "Want an apple?" He's still glancing over at me.

"That goes without saying."

"Go get one from the back."

How am I supposed to climb out of the cab to the back of the truck when he's driving so fast? So I say, "Forget it."

He says, "Go get one." He's still looking at me.

I say, "Stop staring at me. There's no road on my face." With this, he twists his eyes back onto the highway.

The truck's driving back in the direction I just came from; I'm sitting comfortably in the cab, looking out the window and chatting with the driver. By now, we're already the best of friends. I've found out that he's a private entrepreneur. It's his own truck. The apples are his, too. I hear change jingling in his pockets. I ask him, "Where are you going?"

He says, "I just keep driving and see when I get there."

It sounds just like what everyone else said. That's so nice. I feel closer to him. I want everything I see outside the window to be just as close, just as familiar, and soon all those hills and clouds start to bring more friends to mind, so I shout out their nicknames as we drive by.

Now I'm not crying out for an inn anymore. What with the truck, the driver, the seat in the cab, I'm completely at peace. I don't know where the truck's going, and neither does he. Anyway, it doesn't matter, because all we have to do is keep driving, and we'll see when we get there.

But the truck broke down. By that time, we were as close as friends can be. My arm was draped over his shoulder and his over mine. He was telling me about his love life, and right when he'd got to the part about how it felt the first time he held a woman's body in his arms, the truck broke down. The truck was climbing up a hill when it broke down. All of a sudden the squeal of the engine went quiet like a pig right after it's been slaughtered. So he jumped out of the truck, climbed onto the hood, opened up that upside-down lip, and stuffed his head back under it. I couldn't see his ass. But I could hear the sound of him fiddling with the engine.

After a while, he pulled his head out from under the hood and slammed it shut. His hands were even blacker than before. He wiped them on his pants, wiped again, jumped down, and walked back to the cab.

"Is it fixed?" I asked.

"It's shot. There's no way to fix it."

I thought that over and finally asked, "Now what do we do?"

"Wait and see," he said, nonchalantly.

I was sitting in the cab wondering what to do. Then I started to think about finding an inn again. The sun was just falling behind the mountains, and the hazy dusk clouds looked like billows of steam. The notion of an inn stole back into my head and began to swell until my mind was stuffed full of it. By then, I didn't even have a mind. An inn was growing where my mind used to be.

At that point, the driver started doing the official morning calisthenics that they always play on the radio right there in the middle of the highway. He went from the first exercise to the last without missing a beat. When he was finished, he started to jog circles around the truck. Maybe he had been sitting too long in the driver's seat and needed some exercise. Watching him moving from my vantage point inside the truck, I couldn't sit still either, so I opened the door and jumped out. But I didn't do calisthenics or jog in place. I was thinking about an inn and an inn and an inn.

Just then, I noticed five people rolling down the hill on bicycles. Each bike had a carrying pole fastened to the back with two big baskets on either end. I thought they were probably local peasants on their way back from selling vegetables at market. I was delighted to see people riding by, so I welcomed them with a big "Hi!" They rode up beside me and dismounted. Excited, I greeted them and asked, "Is there an inn around here?"

Instead of responding they asked me, "What's in the truck?"

I said, "Apples."

All five of them pushed their bikes over to the side of the truck. Two of them climbed onto the back, picked up about ten baskets full of apples, and passed them upside down to the ones below, who proceeded to tear open the plastic covering the top of the wicker and pour the apples into their own baskets. I was dumbstruck. When I finally realized exactly what was going on, I made for them and asked, "Just what do you think you're doing?"

None of them paid the slightest bit of attention to me. They continued to pour the apples. I tried to grab hold of someone's arm and screamed, "They're stealing all the apples!" A fist came crashing into my nose, and I landed several feet away. I staggered up, rubbed my nose. It felt soft and sticky, like it wasn't stuck to my face anymore but only dangling from it. Blood was flowing like tears from a broken heart. When I looked up to see which of them had hit me, they were already astride their bikes, riding away.

The driver was taking a walk, lips curling out as he sucked in deep draughts of air. He had probably lost his breath running. He didn't seem to be at all aware of what had just happened. I yelled toward him, "They stole your apples!" But he kept on walking without paying any attention to what I had yelled. I really wanted to run over and punch him so hard that his nose would be left dangling, too. I ran over and screamed into his ear, "They stole your apples." Only then did he turn to look at me, and I realized that his face was getting happier and happier the longer he looked at my nose.

At that point, yet another group of bicycles descended down the slope. Each bike had two big baskets fastened to the back. There were even a few children among the riders. They swarmed by me and surrounded the truck. A lot of people climbed onto the back, and the wicker baskets flew faster than I could count them. Apples poured out of broken baskets like blood out of my nose. They stuffed apples into their own baskets as if they were possessed. In just a few seconds, all the apples in the truck had been lowered to the ground. Then a few motorized tractor carts chugged down the hill and stopped next to the truck. A few big men dismounted and started to stuff apples into the carts. One by one, the empty wicker baskets were tossed to the side. The ground was covered with rolling apples, and the peasants scrabbled on their hands and knees like ants to pick them all up.

It was at that point that I rushed into their midst, risking life and limb, and cursed them, "Thieves!" I started swinging. My attack was met with countless fists and feet. It seemed like every part of my body got hit at the same time. I climbed back up off the ground. A few children began to hurl apples at me. The apples broke apart on my head, but my head didn't break. Just as I was about to rush the kids, a foot came crashing into my waist. I wanted to cry, but when I opened my mouth, nothing came out. There was nothing to do but fall to the ground and watch them steal the apples. I started to look around for the driver. He was standing a good distance away, looking right at me, and laughing as hard as he could. Just so I knew that I looked even better now than I had with a bloody nose.

I didn't even have the strength for anger. All I could do was gaze out at everything that was making me so angry. And what made me the angriest of all was the driver.

Another wave of bicycles and tractors rolled down the hill and threw themselves into the disaster area. There were fewer and fewer apples rolling on the ground. A few people left. A few more arrived. The ones who had arrived too late for apples began to busy themselves with the truck. I saw them remove the window glass, strip the tires, pry away the planks that covered the truck bed. Without its tires, the truck obviously felt really low, because it sank to the ground. A few children began to gather the wicker baskets that had been tossed to the side a moment before. As the road got cleaner and cleaner, there were fewer and fewer people. But all I could do was watch, because I didn't even have the strength for anger. I sat on the ground without moving, letting my eyes wander back and forth between the driver and the thieves.

Now, there's nothing left but a single tractor parked beside the sunken truck. Someone's looking around to see if there's anything left to take. He looks for a while and then hops on his tractor and starts the engine.

The truck driver hops onto the back of the tractor and looks back toward me, laughing. He's holding my red backpack in his hand. He's stealing my backpack. My clothes and my money are in the backpack. And food and books. But he's stealing my backpack.

I'm watching the tractor climb back up the slope. It disappears over the crest. I can still hear the rumble of its engine, but soon I can't even hear that. All of a sudden, everything's quiet, and the sky starts to get really dark. I'm still sitting on the ground. I'm hungry, and I'm cold, but there's nothing left.

I sit there for a long time before I slowly stand up. It isn't easy because my whole body aches like crazy every time I move, but still I stand up and limp over to the truck. The truck looks miserable, battered. I know I've been battered too.

The sky's black now. There's nothing here. Just a battered truck and battered me. I'm looking at the truck, immeasurably sad, and the truck's looking at me, immeasurably sad. I reach out to stroke it. It's cold all over. The wind starts to blow, a strong wind, and the sound of the wind rustling the trees in the mountains is like ocean waves. The sound terrifies me so much that my body gets as cold as the truck's.

I open the door and hop in. I'm comforted by the fact that they didn't pry away the seat. I lie down in the cab. I smell leaking gas and think of the smell of the blood that leaked out of me. The wind's getting stronger and stronger, but I feel a little warmer lying on the seat. I think that even though the truck's been battered, its heart is still intact, still warm. I know that my heart's warm, too. I was looking for an inn, and I never thought I'd find you here.

I lie inside the heart of the truck, remembering that clear warm afternoon. The sunlight was so pretty. I remember that I was outside enjoying myself in the sunshine for a long time, and when I got home I saw my dad through the window packing things into a red backpack. I leaned against the window frame and asked, "Dad, are you going on a trip?"

He turned and very gently said, "No, I'm letting you go on a trip."

"Letting me go on a trip?"

"That's right. You're eighteen now, and it's time you saw a little of the outside world."

Later I slipped that pretty red backpack onto my back. Dad patted my head from behind, just like you would pat a horse's rump. Then I gladly made for the door and excitedly galloped out of the house, as happy as a horse.

I

Willow walked down a yellow highway on his way to the civil service examination in the imperial capital. He wore a dark green cotton robe over coarsely woven pants, a faded cap, and a dark green silk belt strung around his waist. He looked like an emerald green tree walking down the yellow highway. It was the height of spring, and stands of peaches and willows flourished amid the mulberry and hemp fields as far as the eye could see. Thatched cottages, enclosed within bamboo fences, were strewn sparsely across the countryside. The sun hung high above, its innumerable rays like golden filaments threading through a silk loom.

Willow had been walking down the highway since dawn, and in that time the only people he had encountered had been a pair of government messengers hurrying down the road and a few soldierly men on horseback urging their mounts on with whips held high. The storm cloud of dust stirred by the horses' hoofs had obscured Willow's view of the road ahead. He had not encountered any other travelers since.

Several days earlier, when he first left his village home and stepped onto the yellow highway, desolation had welled up in his heart. The heavy clatter of his mother's cloth loom had continued to pursue him long after he had left their thatched hut, searing his back like a burn. And his father's eyes in the moments before his death bore vividly down on him. He had stepped onto the yellow highway to win glory for his ancestors. The brilliant colors of spring unfolded before him like a scroll, but he had no eyes for the scenery. He saw what seemed to be the fluttering leaves of late autumn, and the road under his feet was clearly illusory, without substance.

Willow was hardly the scion of an aristocratic clan – his dead father was just a poor scholar who had never passed the civil service examinations. Although his father had been able to write in a good hand and paint flowers, scenery, and the like with real style, he couldn't work with his hands or lift a carrying pole, so how could he support a family, let alone fill his own belly? If it hadn't been for the whole family's reliance on the constant clatter of his mother's loom, Willow would have been hard-pressed to make it through his childhood. His mother's back, bowed by many years of labor, would never straighten. When he was still a little boy, Willow had begun to read poetry and prose under his father's supervision. As the years went by he had inherited his father's disposition. He took to reading off-color books, and although he could write a pretty hand and paint flowers tolerably well, he still neglected the all-important art of the octopartite essay.[1] And so it was that, even as he stepped onto the yellow highway on his way to the civil examination in the capital, he was enveloped by the specter of a father who had languished in poverty after repeatedly failing the examinations.

Willow took leave of the thatched hut shouldering only a gray bundle containing a change of clothes, paper, an inkstone, and a writing brush. Willow traveled penniless. He supped on the wind and slept in the dew, selling his services as a scribe and a painter now and again for some petty change with which to assuage his hunger. Once along the way, he had seen a pair of youths who were also on their way to the examinations in the capital. They were proud scions of aristocratic clans, clad in embroidered tunics, sitting astride

[1] A pedantic form of essay writing on orthodox Confucian themes that was central to success in the imperial civil service examinations in ancient China.

noble mounts, accompanied by a smart-looking valet. Even the valet's outfit had put Willow to shame. He didn't have a valet to escort him along the road – he was accompanied only by the shadow he cast onto the dusty surface of the yellow highway. With every slight swing back and forth of his gray bundle came the lone sound of a writing brush tapping against the inkstone.

After walking all morning, parched and hungry, he happened on a crossroads. Fortunately, there was a stream nearby. The banks of the stream were lined by a profusion of green weeds and weeping willows. Willow walked over to the edge of the stream and looked down at the water, which glittered yellow in the light of the sun, like the highway. It was only under the arching branches of the willow that he found a haven of shady green light. He squatted down, immersed his hands in the water, and for a moment felt at ease. He cupped his hands and carefully washed away the dust that coated his face. Finally, he drank his fill and sat down on the bank. Grass poked through his pants, tickling his legs. A white fish ambled back and forth in the water with a lovely swaying motion. Watching the fish twist back and forth, Willow began to feel gloomy, but whether it was because the fish was all alone or because of the loveliness of its motion, he didn't know.

It wasn't until much later that Willow stood up and made his way back to the yellow highway. Willow felt dizzy and faint as he emerged from the shade of the willow trees. Just at that moment, he caught sight of a cluster of houses surrounded by tall trees in the distance. Behind them lay the indistinct outline of a city wall. He set off at a brisk pace toward the houses.

As he neared the wall, he heard a clamor of voices. Countless porters, bearing merchandise on carrying poles, poured in and out of the city gate. Once inside the gate, he saw that the town was brimming with two- and three-story shops, towers, and pavilions. The houses were packed tightly together, and the people of the town were prosperous. Willow walked through an unending stream of pedestrians and hawkers that filled the main street. The street was lined by innumerable teahouses and wine shops. Fat slabs of lamb hung outside several of the wine shops, and plates stacked with pig's trotters, jellied duck, and fresh fish were neatly arranged atop streetside counters. In front of the teahouses were counters laden with platters of tangerine cakes, flat cakes, lotus-wrapped rice, and fritters.

Willow passed through the marketplace and soon came to a temple. The temple, glittering gold and green, looked as if it had been recently renovated. Standing on the front steps, Willow gazed inside. A noble and ancient cypress in a courtyard, shiny tile floors swept free of dust, columns and rafters gleaming with an oily luster, but not a single monk in sight. A vast space, but clearly quite empty. Willow thought to himself that this might be a good place to spend the night. He took the bundle of belongings from his back, unwrapped it, pulled out his writing brush, paper, and inkstone, and set them down on the stone steps. He copied out a few Song dynasty quatrains – things like "Dawn wind, lingering moonlight, willows on the banks" – and painted a few flowers to sell to passersby. In a short while, the entrance to the temple was thronged with people. Everyone in town seemed to have some money, and with money came a fondness for the touch of elegance that only poetry and painting can provide. After quite a long spell of work, Willow had earned a few strings of cash. When the crowds of onlookers gradually began to disperse, Willow carefully hid his money, packed up his bundle, and slowly retraced his steps into town.

The cashiers at the wine shops and teahouses along the road grinned broadly and, despite Willow's thin cotton robe, warmly called out for his patronage. Willow sat down at a nearby teahouse and ordered a bowl of tea. When he had swallowed all the tea, the emptiness in his gut finally became unbearable, and just as he was considering what he should do, a peasant selling griddle cakes happened to pass by. Willow bought a few griddle cakes, ordered another bowl of tea, and slowly ate his meal.

Two men rode by the teahouse on horseback. One was wearing a dark blue silk gown embroidered with hundreds of little bats and butterflies. The other wore a dark blue silk gown embroidered with innumerable flying birds. They were followed by a trio of women. One was clad in a cloak, another was dressed in a silk dress decorated with a pattern of eight linked circles, and the third was wearing a brocade tunic embroidered with turquoise and golden silk thread. The jewels in their headdresses gleamed, and the pendants hanging from their belts sounded out like chimes as they swayed past. Maidservants followed at the heels of each of the women, waving oversized, scented silk fans to protect them from the light and heat of the sun.

Willow finished up his griddle cakes, walked out of the teahouse, and began to stroll aimlessly through town. It had been several days since he had left home, and in that time he hadn't spoken with another soul. Once the hunger in his stomach had been appeased, he felt a surge of loneliness well up inside his chest. Although the streets were bustling with crowds of people, they all looked like strangers. The clatter of his mother's loom began once again to pursue him.

In the course of his stroll, he happened on a broad, open space, but it was only when he stopped to examine his surroundings that he realized that he was standing by the front gate of a large aristocratic estate. The pavilions and secluded courtyards that lay beyond the gate were terribly impressive. Stone lions, fangs bared and claws brandished, sat to either side of a majestic vermilion gate, which was bolted shut. Peering above the walls, Willow could see birds flying to and fro between the tops of innumerable towering trees. Curving eaves soared among the trees. Willow gazed in silence for a time and then slowly began to make his way down a path that ran along the perimeter of the white-washed palace walls. The path was paved with spotless blue tiles. Leafy branches brushed gently down over the top of the wall. Presently, he caught sight of a side gate. Although this entrance was smaller than the main gate, it too was painted a dignified vermilion and bolted shut. Hearing the muffled sound of laughter from inside the wall, Willow paused for a moment and then continued walking along the path. Just as the wall curved and seemed to disappear, he noticed another gate. This door was open. At that moment, someone emerged from within and hurriedly strode away. Willow waited until the man was no longer in sight and then moved toward the gate, through which he was able to gaze into a small and exquisitely tended garden. He thought to himself that this must be the kind of pleasure garden for aristocratic young ladies that he had read about in books but never actually laid eyes on. Willow hesitated for a moment and then walked into the garden.

Everything inside was as it should be — the place was plentifully supplied with little knolls, running streams, trees, and flowers. Although the hills were made of piled stones, they had been constructed so artfully that they seemed quite natural. A pool lay in the center of the garden. The surface of the water was covered with a profusion of lotus leaves. A serpentine stone bridge zigzagged across the expanse just above them. By the bank of the pool lay a little open-air pavilion, flanked by two lofty maples whose leaves intertwined above its roof. Autumn was still far away, but the maple leaves were almost imperceptibly tinged with red. Inside the pavilion, which was just large enough to seat three or four people, two barrel-shaped porcelain seats were placed in front of a screen. Behind the screen were over a hundred stalks of green bamboo, through which a vermilion railing was just visible. Countless flowers grew behind the railing. Peach, apricot, and pear trees were in bloom, and there were also crabapples, chrysanthemums, and orchids that had yet to flower. The peach flowers were especially lush, with each bloom noisily jockeying for position as the pale pear blossoms in their midst looked on in silence.

Insensibly, Willow passed in front of a wooden tower so intricately carved and brightly decorated that it looked as if it were constructed of brocade. The path under his feet suddenly came to an end, and Willow looked up to see that the latticed window frames of the tower had been thrown open on all four sides. A slight breeze from the opposite side blew through the tower and out the window toward Willow. He was enveloped by wave after wave of sweet fragrance. Sunset was approaching, the sky glowed with dusky hues, and the sound of chanted poetry drifted down from the windows. It was a sound like a zither being plucked or like pearls drizzling drop by drop onto a plate, a sound that was as delicate and drawn out as the murmuring of flowing water. As the fragrant breeze continued to waft down from the window, the dusky glow began to disperse, and the sky grew slowly darker. Rather than trying to distinguish the words of the poem, Willow merely floated within the magical intoxication of its sound.

Night began to fall, and the sky was a stretch of rolling slate gray. Willow stood motionless, eyes trained on the windows, oblivious to his surroundings. A river, as green and narrow as a jade belt, appeared before his eyes, followed in rapid succession by two different scenes. The first was a slender girl walking by the side of the river, and the second was the rising and falling motion of a weeping willow swaying in the evening breeze. The two scenes merged, drifted apart, and finally began to shuttle back and forth until Willow's eyes swam.

The chanting sound slowly grew louder, drew nearer, and a brief moment later a woman as beautiful as jade and as lovely as a flower appeared at the window. The woman's face was flushed pink with delight, and her small, cherry-red lips, from which poetry continued to pour, were pursed in the beginnings of a smile. Her eyes, overflowing with ripples of feeling, played across the garden, as if she longed to divest herself of some secret yearning. After a moment, she caught sight of Willow, cried out in surprise, and, her face quickly coloring with shame, turned and retreated inside. Her eyes had squarely met Willow's, but now she was hidden somewhere deep inside the tower. Dizzied by this encounter with a cloistered young maiden, Willow felt as leaden as a sleeper falling into a dream. Her cry had been like the snap of a broken zither string, bringing the sound of her chanting to a sudden conclusion.

The garden became silent and still, as if everything around him was melting away into nothingness. Only after a long time did Willow come back to his senses. Unsure of whether this encounter had been a mere illusion or something quite real, he looked back up at the window. No one was there. But the breeze still blew, gently enveloping him in fragrance. Willow felt its warmth, and it seemed to him that it must surely have come from the body of the woman whom he had just seen at the window. She must still be somewhere within the tower. Willow seemed to see the breeze moving past the woman's body, catching hold of her warmth and her fragrance, and finally sending it drifting down from the window toward him. He extended his right hand and lightly stroked the warmth in the wind.

At that very moment, a girl who looked like a maid appeared in the window and told him to go away.

Although her eyes were wide with anger, there was nothing particularly threatening in her manner. Willow thought that her fury was perhaps more feigned than otherwise. Utterly unable to tear himself away, his eyes remained fastened to the window. It was the maid who left the window first, discomfited perhaps by the intensity of his gaze.

Night fell around the empty window, and the tower grew blurry and indistinct. Above him, Willow could hear the soft murmur of voices. It seemed like a lady had come into the building, a lady with a low, ringing voice. The maid barked out something sharp and short. But it was only a little later that he heard the maiden's voice. It was as delicate as drops of water, but Willow was drenched in its sweetness. He smiled insensibly, and the smile rippled across his face like a wave before fading unnoticed.

The maid once again appeared at the window. Catching sight of Willow through the gloom, she exclaimed, "What? You still haven't left?"

Her face was obscured by the darkness. Only her dark, glittering eyes revealed her outrage. Willow, who stood as still as a tree rooted in place, seemed not to have heard.

Gradually, the tower fell into complete darkness. Rays of candlelight began to emerge from the open windows, but, rather than descending, the light hovered somewhere above Willow's head. The candlelight also served to cast the maiden's shadow on a column within the apartment that was visible from the outside. To Willow, her huddled, indecisive shadow, flickering and indistinct, was extraordinarily vivid.

Although a few drops of rain had already fallen onto Willow's face, he did not notice the imminent arrival of a summer shower. Soon, the sky opened, and his head and shoulders were pelted with rain. It was only then that he finally became aware of the rain, but despite its arrival he remained obstinately rooted in place.

The maid appeared once more at the window, silently gaped at Willow, and finally shut the window. The young lady's shadow was snuffed out. The candlelight also receded behind the window's oiled paper panels.

The rain slanted violently down, failing to dislodge Willow from his place. His cap was knocked to the ground, and his hair was beaten over to one side of his head. The rainwater slammed into Willow's body, curved, and slid to the ground. Through the noise of the wind and the rain,

Willow could hear the distinct sound of water dripping from his body. But Willow paid the storm no heed. Instead he stared up at the candlelight dancing and leaping behind the window panel, and although he could not see the young lady's shadow, its very absence rendered it all the more vivid in his mind.

For some reason, the window opened once more. The storm had reached its zenith. The maid appeared, turned, left. An instant later she returned with the maiden in tow, and the two women looked out together at Willow. Just as Willow was thrown into a state of happy astonishment, they retreated, leaving the window open behind them. Willow saw the shadows on the column come together and then separate. The two women moved once more to the window, releasing a rope that slid down to the ground, trembling in the wind. Befuddled by the sight of the young lady, Willow ignored the rope. The maid, growing impatient, called out, "Just what are you waiting for?"

The maiden, seeing his incomprehension, chimed in, "If the gentleman would please come up out of the rain . . ."

Her voice, as delicate as tinkling jade, quieted the roar of the wind and rain. Willow at last seemed to experience a flash of comprehension. He took a step toward the rope, only realizing too late that his limbs had grown quite numb and stiff from his long, wet vigil. After a moment or two of clumsy efforts, he grasped hold of the rope and slowly climbed up and into the window. The young maiden had already retreated toward the back of the apartment with the help of her maid. As the maid busily attended to the task of recovering the rope and shutting the window, Willow carefully appraised the young lady. She stood about five feet away from him, her pale, graceful form clad in roseate skirts and a short cape embroidered with shining crescent moons. Before she had even pursed her cherry red lips, Willow could already detect the sweet fragrance of her rouge. The maiden turned bashfully toward him. The maid crossed the room and took up a position at her side. A flustered Willow introduced himself. "My name is Willow."

The maiden returned the gesture. "My name is Hui."

Willow went on to introduce himself to the maid, who responded with the appropriate formalities.

Having finished with introductions, both the maid and the maiden covered their mouths and burst out in peals of laughter. Unsure as to whether they were laughing at his sorry state, Willow joined them with a few chuckles of his own.

The maid said, "You can rest here for a while, but when the rain stops, you have to leave as quickly as you can."

Instead of replying, Willow gazed silently at the maiden, who added:

"Will the gentleman please change clothes as soon as he is able? So as not to catch cold."

With this, the maid and the maiden receded toward an adjacent room. The maiden's red silken sleeves swayed as she moved, revealing to Willow a glimpse of her jade-pale wrists. The motion of her body called to Willow's mind the lovely sway of the white fish he had seen swimming through the stream. The maid reached the curtain to the next room and disappeared under it. The maiden followed her to the door and almost imperceptibly hesitated. As she lifted the curtain, she could not restrain herself from turning her head to steal a glance behind her at Willow. The maiden's eyes were suffused with such undeniable longing that Willow was left nearly beside himself with joy.

It was not until quite a while later that Willow realized that the maiden had left. He felt empty and lost. Looking around the room, he realized that he was in a study. Stacks of books were piled neatly on the shelves, and a zither lay prone on the table. A moment later, he noticed that the room also contained a rosewood canopy bed, the body of which was obscured by a silk curtain embroidered with plum blossoms. Willow felt his heart flutter. Clear spring water began to flow through his entire body. Willow moved toward the curtain, which emitted an aroma not unlike that of a cypress tree. A jade-green quilt reclined on the bed like a sleeping body, and the embroidered flowers flickered in the candlelight. The maiden had departed, but her scent lingered, for, amid the smell of cypress, Willow could still detect a fainter and more elegant fragrance, a fragrance so fleeting that Willow could hardly distinguish whether it was real or illusory.

Willow stood for a moment longer by the bed before lowering the raised curtain, which was as smooth and lustrous to his touch as skin. The bottom of the curtain glided downward until it reached the floor, its edges arrayed in a fan fold.

Willow retreated to the candlelit table and sat down on a ceramic stool. He looked back toward the canopy bed, which was now almost completely hidden behind the curtain. Even so, he could still steal glances through the seams at the jade-green form of the maiden sleeping within. It was as if he had already become her lover. She had retired for the evening. He, absorbed in his studies, was burning the midnight oil.

Willow picked up a collection of lyric poetry that lay open on the table. This was the book from which the maiden had been reciting poetry earlier in the evening. The words danced on the page like raindrops. Immersing himself in fantasy and conjecture, lulled by the sound of falling rain, Willow gradually drifted off into sleep.

From across a hazy expanse, Willow heard the sound of someone's soft calls drift toward him. Startled, he opened his eyes and saw the maiden standing by his side. Her hair fell loose and disordered around her face, on which traces of rouge were still visible. Her image was even lovelier and more moving than before. Willow was unsure as to whether she was real or merely a dreamy apparition until he heard her begin to speak. She said, "The rain has already stopped, and now the gentleman may resume his journey."

What Willow had taken for the sound of falling rain was merely the rustling of leaves in the wind.

The maiden, understanding the reason for his confusion, gently added, "It's only the sound of the leaves."

Willow's position in front of the candle cast the maiden into shadow. Eyes fixed on her dimly lit figure, he sighed deeply, stood, and said, "Today it seems we must part, though we may never meet again."

He moved toward the window.

The maiden did not stir. Willow turned back to see desolate tears glistening in her eyes. Almost despite himself, Willow retreated toward her, taking hold of her jade-white wrist, and clasping it to his chest. The maiden wordlessly lowered her eyes, submitting to Willow's caress. Several moments passed until the maiden broke the silence. "From whence do you come, sir? Where are you going?"

Willow, grasping both of her hands now, told her of his travels. When he had finished, she looked up and began carefully to examine his face. Their clasped hands and gazing eyes bespoke the depth of the sentiments that had arisen between them.

At this point, the candle suddenly went out. Willow responded by pulling the pale, soft, fragrant, warm maiden into an embrace. The maiden cried out softly once before falling silent. She trembled in Willow's arms. Willow was transported. Nothing existed save the melting together of their bodies. In the midst of the endless caresses that ensued, Willow heard the sound of jagged breathing, but could not tell if it was his or that of the maiden. The lonely scholar and the cloistered maiden locked together in an embrace so tight that they were nearly indivisible.

The tolling of the night watchman's bell drifted in through the window. Startled, the maiden hesitantly extricated herself from his embrace. "It's almost dawn. Please, sir, you had really better leave."

Willow, enveloped in darkness, stood quietly in place. After a long pause, he nodded, fumbled for his bundle, and then froze once more.

The maiden repeated, "Please, leave now, before it's too late."

Her voice was incomparably desolate, and, hearing the faint sound of her sobs, Willow insensibly began to cry as well. He groped through the darkness, reached for her, and they fell into yet another close embrace. Willow turned and once more approached the window, but just as he was preparing to slide out, he heard the maiden call, "Wait."

Willow turned and through the darkness saw the maiden's indistinct form move across the room. He heard the "ka-cha" of scissors slicing through something, and an instant later the maiden placed a small, heavy package in his outstretched hands. He rolled the package into his bundle without opening it to see what was inside. Then he climbed out of the window, slid down the rope, and landed on the ground. Turning back to gaze up at the window, he could see only her shadow. She called out, "Please remember this. It doesn't matter to me whether you win honor and glory on the examination rolls. The sooner you leave, the sooner you'll come back."

She closed the window. Willow gazed at the window for a moment, turned, and left. The back gate was still ajar. As Willow left the garden through the chill gloom of dawn, a few lingering drops of rain fell onto his face. He heard the clop of a horse's hoofs, unusually resonant in the silence of the night. The streets were empty, save for a passing watchman carrying a lantern in the distance ahead. Willow soon stepped back onto the yellow highway. Gradually the eastern sky began to fill with sparse dawn light. As Willow continued to walk, the contours of thatched huts lining the route slowly became visible through the gloom, and it was only then that the highway under his feet seemed to take on substance and solidity. By the time the red disk of the sun had risen above the horizon, he was already far from the maiden's brocade tower. He opened his bundle and extracted the package that the maiden had given him. It contained a lacquer-black lock of hair and two slender ingots of silver wrapped in a handkerchief embroidered with mandarin ducks.[2] Willow's heart began to gurgle like a spring. As he tied up the package and repacked his bundle, he seemed once again to hear the maiden's parting words: "The sooner you leave, the sooner you'll come back."

Willow walked down the road as fast as his feet would take him.

2

Having failed the exam, Willow began his journey home several months later. He walked indecisively down the yellow highway, for although he yearned with all his heart to be reunited with the maiden, he could not escape the feeling of shame that had come with failure. He walked in fits and starts, sometimes moving slowly in mincing steps and sometimes taking the road in rapid strides. On his way to the capital spring had been at its zenith, but now the desolate colors of autumn had begun to prevail. Muffled gray skies stretched as far as the eye could see. As he approached the city wall, he was overcome by a wave of tangled emotion. Willow walked over to the bank of a nearby stream. The reflection he saw in the water was clad in cheap cotton, not brocade. He thought to himself that this was how he had looked on his way to the capital. Now, on his return, he was the same. The seasons might change, but he

[2]A conventional symbol of marital bliss.

had not been able to return clad triumphantly in the silks of examination success. How could he face his maiden?

Lost in his thoughts, he made his way to the city gates. A wave of noise and bustle swarmed toward him as scenes of prosperous city life once again arrayed themselves before his eyes.

Willow traversed the noisy market, but he soon drew to a halt. Although he had been away for several months, the town remained just as it had been before, regardless of the change of season. Willow stood immobile, and, as he recalled his meeting with the maiden in the tower, his memories seemed to take on an illusory cast, as if it had all been a wonderful, romantic story and nothing more. But the maiden's words of farewell had been real, substantial. The maiden's words rang out like raindrops in his ears: "It doesn't matter to me whether you win honor and glory on the examination rolls. The sooner you leave, the sooner you'll come back."

Waves of sentiment rolled across Willow's heart. He could hesitate no longer. He walked forward as fast as his feet would take him. As he propelled himself forward, the maiden's window appeared in Willow's mind's eye. She had been waiting too long. Her eyes shone with sadness, brimmed with tears. The reunion would be silent, even dazzling. He would almost certainly scale the tower by means of a rope.

But when Willow arrived at the gate of the aristocratic pavilions and secluded courtyards he had visited once before, he was met with a vista of crumbling buildings littered across a ruinous, empty wasteland. If the maiden's brocade tower was no longer there, how could he find her waiting at the window? Confronted by the ruin of the estate, Willow felt a wave of dizziness pass through him. The pomp and splendor of the estate had deteriorated unimaginably quickly – in his memory the events of several months ago seemed as fresh as yesterday. But now the place was a miserable sight, strewn with rotting wood and broken stones. Even the two stone lions who had stood by the gate had disappeared.

Willow stood for a while in the place where the main gate had once been and then began to walk along the perimeter of the ruins. After a short walk, he sensed that he had reached the place where the side gate had been. This, too, was in ruins. Willow continued to walk and soon reached the spot where the flower garden should have been. Only the garden gate was still standing, half the door propped haphazardly against its frame. Willow walked through the door, stepping gingerly over the rubble, carefully trying to discern where each element of the garden – the serpentine stone bridge, the lotus-covered pool, the open pavilion and the vermilion railing, the stand of green bamboo, the flowering peaches and apricots – had once stood. They had all melted into the air, like tendrils of smoke, like misty clouds. All that remained were the two towering maples that had stood on either side of the pavilion, but even the bark on their trunks looked battered and scarred. The hard frosts of autumn had come, and the trees were now as dazzling red as if they had been varnished with blood. A few leaves drifted down to the ground. The trees were still alive, but it was clear that they were not long for this world.

Finally, Willow came to the place where the brocade tower had once stood. He saw a few stacks of broken tile, a heap of rotting wood, all hemmed in by choking weeds and wildflowers. Where were the glorious peach and apricot blossoms that had once graced the garden? All that remained were little white wildflowers growing out of cracked roof tiles. Willow looked up at the window, only to see the empty sky. He had once scaled a rope through that emptiness. He could see the tower in his mind, the rope itself was almost palpable, and everything that happened played once again through his mind. But when the moment arrived when he had said, "Today it seems we must part, though we may never meet again," his reverie came to an abrupt halt. The tower was gone, the sky was empty. Willow steadied himself, turning these last words over and over in his mind. How could he have known that his words would prove true?

Dusk began to fall. Just as before, Willow stood motionless before turning and leaving the garden. He went out the gate by way of the same path he had followed months before and walked along the edge of the ruins, contemplating for the last time the bygone splendor of the palace.

By the time Willow had walked back to the market, the street lanterns — suspended from the eaves of the wine shops and teahouses — had already been lit. The market was so bright that none of the people in the crowds who still flowed through the area needed to carry their own lanterns. Willow began to ask the townspeople where he might find the maiden. He asked the wine sellers, the tea merchants, the noodle makers, the wonton cooks. No one knew. Just as he was beginning to despair, a servant boy pointed his finger at a man across the street, saying, "He's the one you really should ask."

Willow looked over to see a man sitting on the ground in front of a wine shop counter. His clothes were in tatters, his face grimy, his hair disheveled. The servant boy told Willow that this man had once been the steward of the estate. Willow rushed toward him, only to be met with a vacant stare. The steward stretched out his filthy hand and asked for alms. Willow groped for a few coins from within his bundle and placed them in the steward's palm. The steward brightened immediately, stood, slapped the coins onto the counter, ordered a bowl of wine, and drank it in one gulp. Having finished the wine, he slumped back down to the ground, his back to the counter. Willow asked him what had become of the maiden. The steward listened to the query, shut his eyes, and began to mumble, "Ah, the splendor and glory of the past . . ."

When Willow repeated his question, the steward replied only with this same phrase. And each time Willow renewed his entreaties, the steward opened his eyes, extended his grimy hand, took more coins, exchanged them for watery wine, drank, and finally replied, "Ah, the splendor and glory of the past . . ."

Willow sighed and left, for he knew that further questioning was useless. He walked about ten paces down the street and found himself turning into a smaller alley. There was a lantern hanging in the alley, and under the lantern was a small tea stand. Willow suddenly realized that he was not only parched but also terribly hungry. He sat down on a long bench, ordered a bowl of tea, and slowly drank. A kettle full of rainwater was boiling on a brazier next to the bench. Someone had stuck a few seasonal flowers into a crack in the tabletop. Looking closely at the flowers, Willow discovered that there was a chrysanthemum, a crabapple, and an orchid. Willow could not help remembering that, as he walked into the garden several months earlier, the peach, apricot, and pear trees had all been in bloom. Only the chrysanthemums, crabapples, and orchids had yet to open. Who could have known that they would have blossomed here?

3

Three years later, Willow traveled once again down the yellow highway on his way to the civil service examination in the capital. It was the height of spring, just as before, but this time the landscape had been transformed. There weren't any flourishing stands of peaches and willows. The mulberry and hemp fields were nowhere in sight. Withered trees and yellow, dusty fields stretched as far as the eye could see. The peasants' bamboo fences had all been twisted out of shape, and their dilapidated thatched cottages reeled crazily in the wind. The spring scenery was as desolate as winter. The only people Willow encountered along the way were beggars in tattered tunics.

Despite the harvest's failure, Willow was on his way to the capital to take the civil service examinations. When he left his thatched cottage, he was pursued no longer by the heavy clatter of his mother's cloth loom. His mother had gone to her eternal rest under the Nine Springs. In the days after her death, Willow had managed to support himself only by dint of the two ingots of silver the maiden had given to him three years earlier. If he failed to win a name for himself on the examination rolls this time, the opportunity to bring glory to his ancestors would never present itself again. As he stepped onto the yellow highway, he suddenly turned to look back at his hut, only to see bits of thatch from the roof flying up and shuddering in the wind. Was it a premonition of what the hut might look like if, having failed the exam, he returned home? The thatched cottage, the heavy clatter of his mother's cloth loom – all of these might well disappear without a trace.

Willow walked for several days. He saw neither government couriers nor young aristocratic gentlemen on their way to the examination in the capital. The yellow highway underfoot was worn and uneven, stretching interminably through a season of famine. He had seen a man sitting on the ground, gnawing on a dirt-encrusted root, his face covered with mud. The man's clothes were in tatters, but Willow could tell that he had once been clad in silks. If an aristocrat had sunk so low, the plight of the poor was unimaginable. A rush of feeling surged through Willow's heart.

All along the way, the bark of the trees by the side of the road had been notched and scarred by hungry refugees. Sometimes he saw teeth sticking out of the bark, teeth that had been embedded there when refugees had gnawed too greedily into the bark. Corpses were scattered all along the road. With every passing mile, Willow saw three or four rotting and dismembered bodies. There were men, women, old and young alike, but each corpse had been stripped of its remaining possessions, left naked and exposed to the elements.

All along the way, the fields were yellow and withered. Only once did Willow catch sight of a patch of green weeds. About ten people were crouched above it, buttocks raised high in the air as they grazed, resembling nothing so much as a herd of sheep. Willow hurriedly averted his eyes from this scene, only to be met with the sight of a dying man chewing a clod of dirt across the road. Before the man had even managed to swallow the dirt, he collapsed on the ground, dead. Willow walked past the corpse. His legs felt light, insubstantial. He didn't know whether he was walking down a sunlit highway or a little path through the darkness of the netherworld.

That same day, Willow arrived at a crossroads. Pausing to consider his route, he experienced a sudden twinge of recognition. But everything had changed. There was no trace of the profusion of green weeds and the weeping willows he had seen three years earlier. The weeds had been plucked, in just the same way that the patch of green he'd seen the day before had been grazed clean by hungry refugees. The willow tree, shorn of its leaves, was barely alive. The stream was still there. Willow walked over to the edge of the stream and saw that it was nearly dry. The little water that remained was viscous and cloudy. Willow stood by the bank, recalling this place as it had been three years ago. There had been a white fish ambling in the stream, floating to and fro with a lovely swaying motion. Despite the passage of three years, the image of the maiden gazing out of her window appeared once again in his mind's eye, as clearly as if it had been yesterday. But soon, this image disappeared, to be replaced by a dry stream bed. How could he see a white fish through that muddy, turbid water? Where could the maiden be? Was she still alive, or dead? Willow peered up into an empty sky.

By the time Willow stepped once again onto the yellow highway, he could already see the city wall. The closer he got to the city, the more insistently memories of the past welled up in his heart. The maiden's shadow seemed to flutter by his side, now close, now far away. Images of aristocratic pavilions and secluded courtyards appeared in his mind, followed by a vista of crumbling buildings littered across a barren wasteland. These images began to pile on top of one another, to blur together into a vast jumble.

As he reached the city wall, Willow sensed the air of decay that hung over the town. The entrance to the city was cold and cheerless. The pole-bearing porters who had poured in and out of the city gate were gone. There were no longer any aristocrats wandering idly through the market. Inside the gates, the streets no longer rang out with the clamor of commerce. A few pallid and emaciated stragglers wandered through the market. The town was still brimming with storied buildings and pavilions, but the golden paint that had covered their facades was chipped and peeling, only intimating the miserable poverty within. The travelers and hawkers who had once circulated through the market had been replaced by a few miserable souls clad in grubby cotton robes. Only a few of the innumerable teahouses and wine shops remained. The rest were closed and shuttered, door frames and windowpanes covered with a thick layer of dust. The few places that had stayed open neither hung fat slabs of lamb from the eaves nor displayed tangerine cakes and lotus-wrapped rice outside their doors. The boys who prepared the wine sat by the shops, unable to rouse themselves from their stupor. There were still plates laid out on the counters, but they were piled on top of one another, empty. Griddle cake sellers and noodle vendors no longer hawked their wares.

As Willow walked, he thought back to the prosperity and bustle of the past – all a dream. The world is like mist, spiraling through the air, only to vanish. Insensibly, Willow came to the temple. The glittering gold and green building had been reduced to gloomy decay. The temple steps were as crumbly and uneven as a path through the mountains. The branches of the ancient cypress in the courtyard had been broken off, and its bark was notched and scarred. The lacquer on the columns and rafters was peeling off, revealing rotting wood. Weeds shot up through the cracks in the tiled floor. Willow stood for a moment, took off his bundle, pulled out a couple of ink paintings, and hung them on the temple wall. A few people passed by, but their faces were etched with worry and bitterness. In times like these, who had either the leisure or the inclination to indulge in a touch of elegance? Willow waited for a long time, but the grim scene all around him was convincing enough testimony that no one would buy his work. He packed away the paintings. The fact was that he hadn't sold a single painting during his journey. And for this reason, he had suffered hunger pangs and terrible thirst, for he dared not spend what little remained of the maiden's gift of silver.

Willow left the temple and walked toward the market. Remembering once more the prosperity of the town as it had once been, he was rocked by a wave of feeling, a wave that emanated from the maiden's brocade tower and her aristocratic pavilions and secluded courtyards. He thought of the destitution of the city and the ruin of the brocade tower. No more was the ache he felt in his heart reserved for the maiden alone. He began to sorrow for everything that is transitory, for all that is fleeting and ephemeral.

Lost in these reflections, Willow came to the ruins. Three years had passed, and now even the crumbling remnants of the pavilions had vanished without a trace, supplanted by empty wasteland. He could not even make out where the maiden's brocade tower had once stood. All that remained were patches of weeds, little piles of roof tiles, and hunks of rotting wood scattered sparsely across an empty field. If it had not been for those two maples, sturdy as skeletons, Willow feared that he would not recognize the place at all. The field looked as if it had lain desolate for a century, as if there could never have been any pavilions, any gardens, any stands of bamboo, any trees in blossom, any pleasure gardens for aristocratic young ladies, any brocade towers, or even any maidens called Hui. And it seemed as if Willow himself had never been to this place before, even though he had come three years earlier, only to find crumbling ruins.

Willow stood for a while and then turned to go. As he moved away, he was suddenly aware of a peculiar sensation of freedom. Unaccountably, the solemn burden of recollection had lightened. He left the ruins far behind, his memories of the maiden crumbling away with each step he took, until they were gone, until it was as if he had never been enchanted by their spell.

Instead of returning to the market street, Willow walked down a little alley. As he moved along, he saw cobwebs hanging from the little houses that lined the way. The alley was uninhabited, cold, and cheerless. But this was just to Willow's liking, for the last thing he wanted at this point was to contend with the pedestrians in the main streets.

Having reached the end of the alley, Willow came to a little square, in which there were ten grave mounds that had almost sunk to the level of the ground with years of neglect. A little farther on, Willow saw a little shack, open at the front. There were two men inside who looked like butchers and a few people waiting outside. Before he had realized that this was a market for human flesh, Willow had already drawn close enough to see what was happening inside. The crops had failed this year. The harvest had yielded no grain. Gradually, even tree bark and plant stalks had grown scarce. Soon, markets selling human flesh had begun to appear.

The two men inside the shack were in the process of

sharpening an ax on a whetstone. The people outside, bearing baskets and carrying poles, looked as if they had been waiting for quite a while. Their baskets and carrying poles were all empty. Willow moved closer. He saw three people approaching from the other end of the square. At their head was a man whose tattered clothes barely covered his torso. He was followed by a woman and a child. The woman and the child also wore tattered clothes that exposed much of their bodies. The man went into the shack, and the head butcher stood up to greet him. The man gestured at the woman and the child outside the shack. The proprietor glanced over toward them and held up three fingers. The man did not haggle. Accepting three strings of cash, he promptly went on his way. Willow heard the child cry, "Papa," but the man walked as fast as his feet would take him, without so much as a backward glance, and quickly disappeared.

Willow saw the proprietor come out of the shack with the cashier. He tore off what was left of the woman's rags, leaving her without a stitch of clothing. Her naked stomach was slightly distended, but the rest of her body was strangely, extraordinarily thin. The woman's body trembled for an instant, but she made no move to protest being shorn of her clothes. Naked, she turned to look at the little girl by her side. The two men were tearing off the little girl's clothes. The girl struggled for a moment, but, after looking up at the woman, she stood still. The girl looked like she was somewhere around ten years of age. Although the girl too had been reduced to skin and bones, she was still slightly fleshier than the woman. The crowd outside the shack surged forward and began to negotiate with the proprietor. It soon became evident that most of the customers were interested in the little girl, because many complained that the older woman's flesh was no longer quite so fresh as the girl's. Growing impatient, the proprietor demanded, "Is it for your own family to eat? Or are you selling to someone else?"

Two people replied that their own family would be eating, and the rest said that they planned to resell the meat elsewhere.

The proprietor went on, "If you're selling it to other people, it'll be more convenient to buy in bulk."

The proprietor gestured at the woman.

The negotiations continued until an agreement was reached.

Only then did the woman speak, "She goes first."

The woman's voice was blurry and indistinct.

The proprietor, nodding, took hold of the little girl's arm and led her into the shack.

The woman spoke again, "Do a good job of it. Kill her with the first stroke."

The proprietor said, "That I won't do. The meat wouldn't be as fresh."

Inside the shack, the cashier grabbed hold of the little girl's body, laying her arm out on top of a tree stump. The girl, whose eyes had drifted out of the shack to glance at the woman, did not notice that the proprietor had already picked up his ax. The woman averted her eyes away from those of the little girl.

Willow watched the proprietor's ax blade bear swiftly down, heard the "ka-cha" sound of splitting bone. Blood spattered in all directions, covering the proprietor's face.

The girl's body convulsed in time with the "ka-cha" sound. She turned to see what had happened and, catching sight of her own arm resting on the tree stump, was quietly transfixed. Only after a long pause did she let out a long scream and collapse. Crumpled on the ground, she began to cry in earnest. The sound was ear piercing.

At this point the proprietor picked up a rag to wipe his face, while the cashier took the arm and handed it to someone outside the shop who was carrying a basket. This person placed the arm in the basket, paid, and left.

Suddenly the woman burst into the shed, lifted a knife

from the floor, and quickly thrust it into the little girl's chest. The little girl gasped. Her screams gave way to a lingering sigh. By the time the proprietor had realized what had happened it was already too late. He knocked the woman into the corner of the shed with a punch, picked the little girl off the floor, and rapidly sliced apart her body with the help of the cashier before handing the pieces one by one to the people waiting outside the shed.

A frightened Willow stood dazed for a moment before coming to his senses. The little girl had already been completely dismembered, and the proprietor was leading the woman from the corner of the shack over to the stump. Not daring to watch any more, Willow turned and made his way down an alley. But he was pursued by the dull sound of the proprietor's ax cutting into the woman's flesh, by the woman's lacerating shriek. He shook uncontrollably, and it was only when he had rushed out of the alley and into another part of town that the sounds began to recede behind him. But, try as he might, he was unable to expel the scene he had just witnessed from his mind. It would linger, stubborn, wretched, fluttering across his field of vision. Wherever he might go, the image would implacably follow. Leery of the prospect of spending the night in town, Willow hurried out of the city gates just as dusk began to fall. It was not until he stepped onto the yellow highway that he began to regain his composure. Soon, a harvest moon rose and hung high in the night sky. Walking in the moonlight, Willow was buffeted by wisp after wisp of chill air.

4

The next afternoon, Willow came to a little village composed of no more than twenty shabby thatched cottages. Each cottage had a chimney sticking up out of its roof, but no wood smoke rose and dispersed slowly into the air above the village. The sun shone on the road, revealing a thick coat of dust and ash that roiled off the ground like mist as Willow walked along. There were a few pairs of footprints embedded in the dust, but it was clear that neither horse hooves, dog paws, or any sort of livestock had passed this way in a long while. A little path branched off from the highway toward a small irrigation ditch. The ditch was dry. Only a few yellowed weeds remained. A wooden plank bridge lay atop the ditch. Rather than crossing and continuing down the path, Willow entered a thatched cottage by the side of the road.

The cottage doubled as a tavern. A few plates of white boiled meat were laid out on a counter. There were three people inside the tavern. The proprietor was small and thin, while the two waiters were tall and solidly built. They were wearing cotton robes, but the robes were clean, and Willow couldn't make out any patches on the material. That the wine shop had managed to stay in business in times like these, like a weed sprouting out of a rock, was remarkable. And, while the people in the shop were hardly glowing with good health, they were neither pallid nor emaciated. This was one of the few times along the way that Willow had actually seen people who still looked somewhat like people.

The night before, after he left town, Willow had walked by moonlight until just before dawn, finally rolling himself up like a bedroll in the corner of a broken-down roadside pavilion to sleep. He had risen with the first dim light of dawn and continued his journey. Now, standing at the threshold of the tavern, his body began to tremble, and his eyelids fluttered with fatigue. He hadn't had a bite to eat or a drop to drink for almost two days. Nor had he slept well. This kind of pace would be difficult to maintain. The proprietor beamed and gestured for him to come in. "What is it that you'd like?"

Willow walked into the shop, sat down at a table, and ordered a bowl of tea and a few griddle cakes. The proprietor took his order and, a moment later, brought him the tea and cakes. Willow drained his tea bowl in one swallow and then slowly began to eat the griddle cakes.

At this point, a man who looked like a merchant came into the shop. The merchant, clad in brocades, was quite clearly a man of some distinction. Two servants, bearing carrying poles, followed behind him. The merchant took a seat at a table, and the proprietor furnished him with a cup of good wine, at the same time ladling out a second cupful to set down on the table. The merchant drained his first cup in one draught, extracted a few ingots of silver from his sleeve, and slapped them down on the tabletop saying, "I want some meat."

The waiters rushed over to his table, bearing two plates of white, boiled meat. The merchant glanced at the plates, pushed them toward his two servants, and added, "I want mine fresh."

The proprietor hastened to reply, "Coming right up."

So saying, he and the waiters walked into an adjacent room.

Willow finished his griddle cakes, but, rather than standing up to go, he sat for a while to rest. Spirits refreshed by the nourishment, he turned to appraise the merchant and his retinue. The two servants were seated, but, because their master's meal had yet to be served, they didn't dare touch the food on their own plates. The merchant drained cup after cup of wine, finally crying out impatiently, "What's taking so long?"

The proprietor called back from the other room, "Coming right up. Coming right up."

Willow stood up, threw his bundle on his back, and made his way toward the door. A gut-wrenching, heartrending scream erupted from the other room. The sound was suffused with such unbearable pain that it was as if a sharp sword had penetrated Willow's chest. Willow was left dazed and frightened by this sudden eruption. The scream was long, drawn out, as if an entire life had been expelled in one breath. The sound whistled across the room. Willow seemed to see the sound of the scream as it punched its way through the walls of the other room and into the shop.

The sound died down abruptly, and in the fraction of silence in between, Willow heard the squeak of an ax being wrenched from bone. Images of all that he had witnessed the day before at the meat market reappeared in his mind.

The screams rang out once more, this time in shreds of sound, as if the cries themselves had been chopped apart. Willow thought these sounds were as short as fingers, flying neatly past him, piece by piece. In the midst of these minced cries, Willow heard the sound of the ax bearing down. The sound of the ax and the sound of the screams rose and fell in unison, filling in each other's gaps.

Cold shivers ran down Willow's spine. But the three men sitting at the table seemed not to have heard the screams, for they sat nonchalantly drinking their wine. Every once in a while, the merchant glanced impatiently up at the door.

The sound in the next room began to taper off, and Willow heard a woman moaning. The moans had already lost much of their intensity. They sounded almost calm, so calm that they hardly resembled moans at all, for they were as tranquil as the sound of a zither drifting through the air, as serene as chanted poetry heard from afar. The sound drizzled down like drops of rain. The scene of three years before, when he had stood entranced by the maiden's recitation below the window of the brocade tower, hazily resurfaced in Willow's mind. This image was quickly replaced by an awareness that the sound emerging from the other room was indeed a kind of chant. Without knowing exactly why, Willow suddenly began to suspect that this was the maiden's voice and began to tremble.

Willow instinctively moved toward the door that led to the other room. Just as he reached the door, the proprietor and the two waiters emerged from the room. One of the waiters was holding a blood-spattered ax, and the other was holding someone's leg. The leg was still bleeding. Willow could discern the sound of each drop pooling on the dirt floor. Looking down at the floor, Willow saw that it was spackled with dried blood. A strange stench filled his nose. Clearly, this was not the first person who had been slaughtered here.

Inside the room, Willow saw a woman prone on the floor, her hair in disarray. The leg that had been left intact was held bent slightly to the side. The other leg was gone. Blood and flesh blurred together into an indistinct mass where the leg had been chopped away. Willow went to her side, kneeled down, and delicately brushed a lock of hair away from her face. The woman's almond-shaped eyes were opened very wide, but they were dull and lusterless. Willow carefully probed her face. This, he soon ascertained, was indeed the maiden Hui. The room began to spin around him. How could he have known that, after three years, he would find the maiden here, only after she had become fodder for a merchant's meal? Willow's tears welled up like water from a spring.

The maiden had yet to breathe her last. She continued to moan. The terrible pain was clearly evident from the way in which her face twisted. As her moans began to subside, they became delicate and drawn out, like the purling of flowing water. Although her almond-shaped eyes were opened very wide, she failed to recognize Willow. She saw instead a stranger, a man she entreated with her last moans to finish her off with one stroke of a knife.

Despite Willow's cries, she could not recognize him for who he was. In his helplessness and pain, Willow suddenly thought of the lock of hair the maiden had given him on the occasion of their last parting. He pulled the lock out of his bundle and placed it in her field of vision. After a moment, the maiden's eyes blinked, and her moans came to a sudden halt. Willow watched her eyes grow soft and luminous with tears, as her hands groped toward him unnoticed, stroking the air.

With her last words, the maiden entreated Willow to buy back her leg, so that she could die whole. And she begged Willow to kill her with one stroke of a knife. Finally, she gazed at Willow with great serenity, as if she were now completely content, as if she could ask for no more than to have encountered Willow once more before her death.

Willow stood up, left the room, and went into the kitchen. A servant was in the process of paring the meat from the maiden's leg. The leg had already been hacked to pieces. Willow pushed the servant aside, pulled all of his silver from his bundle, and flung it down on the stove top. This was what was left of the silver the maiden had given him three years ago in the brocade tower. As he gathered up the leg, Willow noticed a sharp knife lying on the kitchen table. The image of the woman at the market stabbing her little girl appeared in his mind. He hesitated for a moment before picking up the knife.

By the time Willow had arrived once again by the maiden's side, she had stopped moaning. Her gaze was tranquil, remote, just as he had imagined it might be as she stood gazing down at him through the window of the tower. Seeing that Willow had brought her leg, she opened her mouth, but no sound emerged. Her voice had already died.

Willow set the leg next to where it had been severed from her body. He watched the maiden's lips curl into a smile. She glanced at the knife in his hand and looked up at him. Willow knew what it was she wanted.

Although the maiden would never moan again, her face had become increasingly distorted by the unbearable pain. Willow lacked the strength to go on gazing at the misery inscribed on her face. He closed his eyes. He groped for her chest, felt the faint pulse of her heart under his trembling fingers. A moment later, he shifted his hand away from her heart and, with his other hand, brandished the knife. The blade bore swiftly down. The body underneath him recoiled violently. As he held her fast, he felt her body gradually relax. When her body stopped moving, Willow began to shake uncontrollably.

After a long pause, Willow opened his eyes. The maiden's eyes had closed, and her face was no longer distorted. Instead, it had become inexpressibly serene.

Willow knelt by the maiden's side, entranced. Countless memories enveloped him like dense mist, descending suddenly, and just as suddenly dispersing into the air. He saw the dazzling spectacle of the pleasure garden, the colorful splendor of the brocade tower. Then, nothingness, a vast empty sky.

Willow picked up the maiden's body and cradled it in arms, oblivious to the way the severed leg lay unsteadily perched over his arm. He walked out of the room and into the tavern, without noticing the elation of the merchant as he gnawed on meat cut from the maiden's leg. He walked out of the wine shop and stepped onto the yellow highway. The fields were enveloped by yellow as far as the eyes could see. It was the height of spring, and not a patch of green could be seen, let alone a field of brilliant flowers.

Willow walked slowly forward, glancing now and again at the maiden's face. She looked content, fulfilled, but Willow's soul had been cut off from his body, accompanied in its wanderings only by a dream.

After traveling a short distance, Willow came to a desolate little stream, flanked by a few withered willow trees. A little water remained in the streambed, and although the water was muddy and turbid, it still flowed, emitting a purling murmur. Willow set the maiden's body down by the bank and sat down.

He began to examine the maiden. She was splattered with dried blood and mud. With the sound of tearing cloth, Willow began to remove her tattered garments. Soon, her body emerged from beneath the cloth, pure and white. Willow carefully wiped away the blood and mud from her body with water from the stream. When he arrived at the severed leg, he was forced once again to shut his eyes, for it was riddled with holes. In his mind's eye, the scenes he had witnessed at the market in town came once again to mind. He placed the leg outside his field of vision.

Opening his eyes, he was dazzled by the place from which the leg had been severed. He could still discern where the ax had cut messily and repeatedly into the flesh, like the stump of a felled tree that has been hastily hacked to the ground. Random strands of skin and flesh hung from the stump in a pulpy mass. Extending his fingers toward this mass, he found it incomparably soft, but his fingers were flustered by the sharp edge of shattered bone that lay within. Willow stared for a long time, until an image of crumbling ruins came vaguely to mind.

He soon came to a stream of dried blood on her chest. Willow carefully wiped away the stain. The skin and flesh that had been displaced by the knife as it had stabbed into the chest had curled out around the puncture, deep red, like a peach flower in bloom. Recalling that it was he himself who had done the stabbing, Willow's body trembled. Three years of longing had culminated in a stroke of a knife. Willow didn't dare believe that such a thing had come to pass.

Having removed all of the blood and dirt, Willow re-examined the body. The maiden was laid out on the ground, her skin as clear as ice, as lustrous as jade. In death, the maiden lived on. And Willow sat by her side, insensible, uncomprehending, desolate. Willow survived, but he was half dead.

Willow removed his only change of clothing from the bundle and dressed the maiden. She looked terribly frail clad in Willow's overly large robe. The sight reduced him to tears.

Willow dug a trench with his bare hands, gathered dry twigs and branches to cover the bottom and line the sides, and lowered the maiden inside. He proceeded to cover her with a layer of twigs. Willow could still glimpse patches of her skin from between the twigs. He covered her with a layer of earth, built a burial mound on top of the grave, and sprinkled it with water from the stream.

Finally he sat down next to the grave, his mind utterly vacant. It was only after the moon rose that Willow came to his senses. He saw the light of the moon gleaming as it shone on top of the burial mound. He heard the murmur of the stream, and he thought perhaps the maiden could hear it too. If she could, this place would not be quite as unbearably lonely for her.

Thus reflecting, Willow stood, stepped onto the broad, moonlit highway, and began to move through the silent colors of the night. As he gradually left the maiden behind, his heart hollowed. With every step he heard the lone sound of the writing brush in his bundle tapping against the inkstone.

5

Several years later, Willow stepped onto the yellow highway for the third time.

He still wore a bundle on his back, but he was not on his way to the examinations in the capital. After he had buried the maiden, he had continued on to the capital, but any desire for worldly success he might once have possessed had by then already disappeared. So it was that he had failed the exam once more. Rather than shame, he had felt a kind of tranquillity as he had stepped onto the highway that brought him home.

When Willow had returned to the stream beside which he had buried the maiden on his way home from the capital, ten or twenty other equally desolate grave mounds had been dug in the same spot, so that Willow had no longer been able to tell which grave belonged to the maiden. Willow stood by the river for a long time, transfixed by the realization that his was not the only heart that had been broken. And this thought was strangely comforting. Willow plucked the weeds growing out of each of the untended mounds and finally covered each grave with a fresh layer of soil. He gazed on his handiwork, and, failing once again to distinguish which of the graves belonged to the maiden, he sighed and left.

Willow traveled home, relying on alms for sustenance along the way. When he arrived, though, he found that the thatched cottage had vanished without a trace. Empty space stood where his house had once been. Even his mother's cloth loom was gone. Willow – having had an inkling that this was to transpire when he had left home several months earlier – was not surprised. He was occupied instead by the question of how to keep body and soul together. He became a beggar, spent his days asking for food and alms. It was only much later, when the times took a turn for the better, that Willow secured a position watching over the graveyard of an aristocratic clan. Willow took up residence in a thatched hut by the graveyard. His duties were light – weeding, piling fresh soil on the mounds – so he had ample time in which to recite poetry and paint pictures. He was poor, but these activities imparted a touch of elegance to his life. Every so often he would start to dwell on the past, and vivid recollections of the dead maiden's face would resurface in his mind for a spell. Each time this happened, Willow's thoughts clouded over until his reveries were finally dispelled with a deep sigh. Several years passed in this manner.

One year, the master of the estate sent the family out to the graveyard to sweep their ancestors' graves and make offerings to their spirits for the Qingming Festival.[3] With a great deal of pomp and ceremony, a dozen handsome young

[3]Literally, the "clear and bright" festival, an April holiday during which Chinese families honor the dead.

men and women, accompanied by their maids, nannies, and servants, poured into the graveyard. In a twinkling of the eye, piles of baubles had been spread before the graves as offerings, fragrant incense burned brightly, and the sound of weeping rose into the air. Standing in their midst, Willow began to cry. He shed tears not for his master's ancestors but rather because it was Qingming and he was unable to fulfill his own filial duty by sweeping his parents' graves. He thought of the maiden's lonely burial mound and was rocked by another wave of feeling, for while his parents could accompany each other on their nether journey to the Nine Springs, the maiden would be miserably alone.

The next morning, Willow left the clan without even saying good-bye. Stopping only to sweep his mother and father's graves, he stepped directly onto the yellow highway and hastened toward the banks of the stream where the maiden lay in eternal repose. Willow traveled for several days through a lovely spring landscape full of happy and colorful scenes. He gazed at stands of peaches and willows flourishing between the mulberry and hemp fields. He saw thatched cottages sitting amid groves of verdant trees and clusters of jade-green bamboo. Water coursed through the irrigation channels. The desolation of the past was nowhere in evidence, and Willow found himself thinking of the prosperity he had seen on the occasion of his first journey down the yellow highway. Images of desolation and prosperity cycled in turns through his mind, shuttling back and forth so that the yellow highway under his feet came to seem real one minute and entirely insubstantial the next. Even as these delightful spring visions leapt before his eyes, the desolation of the past lingered like a shadow cast on the roadside by the bright sun overhead. Willow wondered how long the prosperity could last.

Only after he had encountered several young aristocratic gentlemen en route to the examinations in the capital did Willow suddenly remember that this was an examination year. His own first attempt at examination success was already a vague memory, ten years distant. Contemplating the twists and turns his own life had taken in the interval, Willow sighed. This world, with all its sudden and inexplicable changes, is truly heartless. Each of the aristocrats loped down the road with hearts full of hope and ambition. Willow could not help but sigh for them as well. In a world of infinite, ceaseless change, what good are honor and glory anyway?

Where scarred and withered trunks had once stood, Willow now saw thriving trees with leafy canopies, under which village peasants napped in the shade, with an unconcerned ease that bespoke great prosperity. Tall grass danced in the breeze. Herds of cows and sheep lazily grazed and slept in the open fields. Moving insensibly through this landscape, Willow arrived once more at the little stream by the crossroads.

It was the stream where he had paused on his first journey to the capital. Despite the catastrophe to which they had been subjected, the green weeds by the bank had grown back into a dense, strong clump. The weeping willows that not long before had resembled gutted corpses swayed happily in the breeze. As Willow walked over to the bank, grass stuck through his pants leg, tickling his shins. The stream water was so clear he could see to the bottom. A few green leaves floated on the surface. A white fish ambled back and forth in the water with a lovely swaying motion. All was as it had been ten years before. Willow could not help but be moved. Gazing at the lovely sway of the fish, how could he be expected not to remember the lovely gait of the maiden within the brocade tower? Recalling how this stream had been dry and desolate only a few years before, Willow was even more stirred. The trees, the weeds, even the white fish had somehow been given a new lease on life, but the maiden was left to rest in a lonely grave, never to be resurrected, forever unable to enjoy the return of prosperity to the land.

Willow stood for a long while by the stream before sadly

turning to leave. Regaining the road, he could already make out the city wall in the distance, toward which he hastened with a quickened gait.

As he neared the city gate, he heard a lively clamor of voices issuing from the countless pole bearers busily pouring in and out of the town. Clearly, prosperity had returned to the city as well. Once inside the gate and in the market street, he saw that the town was still brimming with storied buildings and pavilions. The golden paint that covered their facades had been restored to its former luster. Chipped and cracked walls festooned with dusty cobwebs were no longer to be seen. Taverns and teahouses spilled into the street. Green banners beckoned to those thirsty for wine, and tea braziers hailed customers with their smoke and glowing ash. There were noodle sellers, dumpling vendors, letter writers, and fortune-tellers. Fat slabs of lamb lay once again across the taverns' counters, and the tea shop tables were covered with a cornucopia of delectable snacks. Almost all the passersby glowed with good health and buoyant spirits. Several wealthy young ladies, festooned with glowing pearls and glittering gems, strolled the market accompanied by comely maids. A few aristocratic young gentlemen astride noble mounts made their way through the throng of pedestrians. All along the road, serving boys from the taverns warmly beckoned for Willow to come in and enjoy a cup of wine. All was as it had been ten years earlier. Willow, flustered, felt as if he had never passed through the vicissitudes of the past.

Soon Willow came to the temple, now glittering gold and green as before. The temple gate was thrown open, and inside the courtyard the lofty ancient cypress stood tall and straight as a beam. The tiled floors were polished so that not a speck of dust remained, and the courtyard's columns and rafters gleamed with an oily luster. This too was just as it had been ten years before. The decay of the famine years remained only in Willow's own memories of choking weeds and spider webs. Willow opened his bundle, extracted brush, paper, and inkstone, and quickly set a few poems and flower blossoms to paper. Soon enough, a small crowd formed around him, and, while most had come just to admire his handiwork, several were inclined to make a purchase. In a short while, he had sold a few paintings and earned a few strings of cash. Content, Willow packed up his bundle and slowly walked away.

Unthinkingly, Willow came to the place where the pavilions and secluded courtyards of an aristocratic estate had once lain. Nearing the site of the estate, Willow could not help but be startled, for neither the ruins of the mansion nor the vast empty field he had seen on his last journey were anywhere to be found. Instead, what appeared before him were the pavilions and secluded courtyards of an elegant estate. Shocked, Willow began to suspect that what lay before his eyes was simply an illusion. But, after he had gazed for a time and the pavilions had refused to disappear, the estate began to assume an air of solidity. The vermilion gates were shut. Beyond the wall, he saw the soaring eaves of the pavilions within. Birds flew to and fro between the tops of innumerable trees that, although they did not tower above the eaves, were fairly stout. Two fierce stone lions stood guarding either side of the gate. Willow walked over to one lion, extending a hand to assure himself of its reality, and felt the stone cold and hard under his fingers.

Willow slowly walked along a path that traced the perimeter of the palace wall. After a short walk, he reached the side gate. The gate was shut, but he heard the muffled sound of people laughing from within the wall. He paused for a moment and then continued to walk.

Not long after, he reached the other door, which was open, just as it had been ten years earlier, except that this time no one emerged from inside to walk hurriedly away. Willow walked through the door into the pleasure garden. There was an open pavilion by a little pond. There was a tower. There were artificial hills constructed of piled stone. All of it was exquisitely tended. In the center of the garden lay two pools, half obscured by the profusion of lotus leaves that bobbed above the water's surface. A serpentine stone bridge zigzagged between the two pools, on top of which was constructed a little open pavilion. Another pavilion flanked the pool. On either side of the pools stood the two towering maples, which despite the travails of the famine years still looked much the same as before. Four porcelain seats had been placed within the pavilion, backed by a screen. Behind the screen were over a hundred stalks of green bamboo, through which appeared a vermilion railing. Behind the railing grew countless flowers. The peach, apricot, and pear trees were a riot of blossoms, and even the crab-apples, chrysanthemums, and orchids that had previously lain dormant before were in flower.

Willow's forward movement came to a halt. He looked up at the brocade tower. He gazed around the garden once again. All was as it had been on his first journey to the capital. The latticed windows of the tower had been thrown open on all four sides, and a slight breeze blew from the opposite side, through the tower and out the window toward Willow, carrying with it an intoxicating fragrance. Willow, fluttering, sank into a reverie of his encounter with the maiden by the brocade tower. The scene once again unfolded before his eyes, so vividly that he was oblivious to the fact that their meeting was only a memory.

Willow sensed that he would soon hear the sound of a chanted poem drift toward him. And, indeed, the marvelous sound began to float down from the window of the brocade tower, softly dispersing throughout the garden like a fine drizzle. The sound was like pearls raining drop by drop onto a plate, as delicate and drawn out as the murmuring of flowing water. With careful listening, he was able to discern that it was not chanting but the sound of a zither. Even so, the sound of the zither was nearly identical to the maiden's voice. Concentrating all his energies on the music, Willow insensibly began to meld with it. The trials and troubles of ten years' time began to fade, to swirl away like so much dust, and Willow was left standing below the window of the maiden's brocade tower for the very first time. And, though he was aware of the sequence of events that were about to happen, this knowledge failed to distract him, for the past and the present had become one in his mind.

Just as Willow was thinking that it was time for the maid to appear at the window, a girl who looked like a maid appeared at the window, eyes wide with anger, saying, "Go away!"

Willow could not help smiling. Everything was as he had predicted it would be. The maid said her piece and retreated from the window into the tower. Willow knew that she would angrily reappear at the window in a moment.

The sound of the zither continued to waft through the air, and with it came the maiden's chant. The sound moved from elegant melodious peaks to slow, halting indecision. Could it be that the maiden had grown weary from the intensity of her longing?

The maid came once again to the window: "You still haven't left?"

Willow was still smiling. The maid found Willow's strange smile hard to swallow and left the window. Soon, the sound of the zither came to an abrupt halt. Willow heard the sound of people moving within the tower. The heavier sounds would be those of the maid, and the lighter sounds were undoubtedly those of the maiden.

Willow sensed that dusk was approaching. Perhaps he would soon be enveloped by the darkness of night. Then the rain would come, the rain would come with a roar, the window would close, and threads of candlelight would shine through the paper panels of the window. In the midst of the rainstorm, the window would open once again, and both maid and maiden would appear in the window. A rope would sway down to the ground, and Willow would clamber up the rope into the tower. As she retired to the inner apartments of the tower, the maiden would sway with a lovely motion like a white fish. Soon, the maiden would come back to Willow's side, and they would link hands as they stared into each other's eyes, in silent, profound communion. Later, Willow would slide back down to the ground and step onto the highway. Several months later Willow would return, having failed the examination in the capital, only to find a desolate expanse of ruins.

The sudden appearance of the ruins startled Willow out of his reverie. Looking around the bright and sunlit garden, he came to the realization that it had all been a daydream. And at that very moment, he realized that the rainstorm had been a terribly real basin of cold water. His whole body was sopping wet. He looked up at the window. No one was there, but he heard low giggles emerging from within. A moment later the maid appeared once more at the window, yelling, "If you don't leave now, I'm going to have to call someone who'll make you leave!"

Willow, his daydream evaporated like mist into the air, could not help but be overcome by sorrow. The tower was as before, but this was clearly a different sort of maiden. He sighed and turned to leave. Outside the wall, he turned back to gaze at the pavilions of the estate and realized that this, finally, was just not the same mansion as before. He took the lock of hair the maiden had given him on parting many years earlier and carefully examined it. All of the dead maiden's wonderful qualities arrayed themselves in his mind, and Willow began to cry.

6

After Willow left town, he walked for a few more days until he came to the place where he had buried the maiden.

The riverbank was green and luxuriantly covered with plants, among which swayed a constellation of different wildflowers. Willow branches cast countless jade-green shadows on the rippling stream.

As Willow stood by the bank, the water yielded up the reflected image of an aging, careworn face, of hair that was unmistakably growing gray. Lovely scenes can disappear in a twinkling and regain their former beauty just as quickly. But youth, once lost, is gone forever. And the glow of lovely memories, once lost, is also gone forever, as transient as wildflowers in bloom.

Willow looked around at a dozen grave mounds that had been recently covered with fresh earth and swept clean for the Qingming Festival. Little piles of ash – what was left of offerings of incense and spirit money – lay in front of many of the mounds. How was he to tell which of the graves belonged to the maiden? He slowly made his way through the mounds, carefully inspecting each one, but was still unable distinguish the maiden's resting place from the others. Soon, however, he happened on one mound that had gone untended. Through long neglect, the earthen mound was almost level with the ground and had narrowly escaped being completely immersed by weeds and wildflowers. There were no ashes in front of the mound. Catching sight of this mound, Willow was suddenly seized by a strange and unaccountable feeling. This unswept grave must certainly be the maiden's final resting place.

As soon as he had recognized her grave, distant recollections of the maiden's voice and face approached him, slowly rising through the water of the stream. On closer examination of the stream, Willow saw a white fish ambling through the water and disappearing into the depths of the center of the waterway.

Willow knelt down and began to pluck the weeds and wildflowers that threatened to obscure the maiden's grave. When he had finished weeding, he spread earth collected from the side of the road onto the mound. He stopped work only when dusk began to descend. Inspecting his handiwork, he saw that the mound was already considerably taller. He began to sprinkle the top of the grave with water from the stream. With each drop of water, little clouds of dust flew from the earthen mound.

The sky had grown black, and Willow wondered whether he should spend the night outside or continue down the road in search of lodging. He thought for a long time before deciding to stay for the night and leave in the morning. Thinking of how very briefly he had seen the maiden in life, he could not bear to leave her so quickly, even in death. To stay with her for the night, he thought, would perhaps help fulfill something of his obligation to her.

The night was peaceful and quiet. The only sound was the rustling of leaves in the wind, which made a noise like the splashing of raindrops. The stream's murmur sounded like the music of a zither, like a chant. Willow recalled once again the enchantment of the scene by the tower. Sitting by the maiden's grave, Willow seemed to hear faint sounds arising from underneath the ground, like the sound of the maiden moving inside the tower.

Willow did not close his eyes the whole night through. Instead, he sat absorbed in hazy fantasies of reunion with the maiden. It was only when the sky in the east began to lighten that he regained his senses. Although these were but fantasies, he was loath to leave. If he could only pass his days accompanied by these fantasies, life would be lovely indeed.

Soon, the sky was bright with dawn. Willow knew it was time to leave. He gazed around him at the green weeds, at the branches of the weeping willows. He looked at the grave. It glimmered in the morning sun. This was not a bad place for the maiden to rest – only a bit lonely. Lost in thought, Willow stepped back onto the yellow highway.

As he walked along the yellow highway, Willow was oblivious to the lovely spring landscape full of happy and

was like holding a ball of water. She grasped the scissors to cut the umbilical cord, and before she felt any resistance between the blades, she saw the cord snap. Then the man brought her a bowl of noodles. Two eggs floated atop the broth. The midwife was terribly hungry, and the noodles were exceptionally good.

When she had finished eating, the man escorted her out of the house, mumbled something about having to stay and look after the newborn's mother, and went back inside. The midwife retraced her steps through the grove, but the winding path seemed much longer than it had on the way to the little house. As she walked, she happened to run into the fortune-teller's son. He was standing between two of the houses, gaunt as a sapling, gazing into the distance. The midwife approached him and asked what he was doing out so late. He said that he'd just arrived. She sensed a kind of distance in his voice. She asked him what he was looking for. He said he was looking for the place where he was going to stay. Then, with an air of having found whatever it was he was looking for, he turned to his right and strode quickly away. The midwife moved on. When she reached the place where she had tripped and fallen on the way there, she fell again and, without being aware of having righted herself, continued to move along.

2

After she had gotten home, the midwife was overwhelmed by an exhaustion greater than any she had ever felt before. She fell dead asleep as soon as her body hit the bed and didn't wake up until nearly noon the next day. She was roused by the sound of conversation in the courtyard. After a few moments, she climbed out of bed and walked out the door, feeling her legs sway beneath her like soft cotton.

7 was sitting in a rattan chair by his front door. His wife

stood by his side. 7's wife and 4's father were discussing what to do about 4's sleep talking. 7 seemed to be listening to their conversation, but his ashen face betrayed no hint of emotion as he watched his son play, oversized head lolling as he ran back and forth across the courtyard. The midwife stood just outside the door. Suddenly, 4 walked in through the courtyard gate. Her father's conversation with 7's wife came to an abrupt halt. 4 walked toward them, her face grim and colorless. Her brilliantly red book bag trailed behind her. 4 walked by her father, head hanging, and went inside. At about the same time, 3's grandson emerged into the courtyard. He seemed to have heard 4 come in, because he merely stood by the door, watching attentively as 4 unlatched her front door and went inside. The midwife asked 7 if he was feeling any better. Her voice seemed to hover thickly in the air. 7 glanced dully toward her and then lowered his eyes to the ground. His wife said: Nothing's changed. The midwife suggested that he go see the fortune-teller. 7's wife said she had been planning to take him to see the fortune-teller for a while now. She glanced at her husband. 7, however, didn't seem to have heard. His head was dangling so low that it looked like it might snap from his neck. 4's father nodded and said that he really should take his daughter to see the fortune-teller, too. The midwife nodded. Someone asked her who had come to see her so late. She looked up and realized that 3 was also standing in the courtyard. 3's face, she noticed, had recently turned a waxen yellow. Seconds after 3 asked the question, she bent over, let out a series of revolting retching noises, and quickly straightened back up, tears streaming from her eyes.

The midwife told 3: A woman who lives to the west of town was having a baby.

Who was she? 3 asked.

The midwife froze. She simply didn't know. All she could do was describe the man, the woman, and the house. When she was done, 3 was silent for a moment. When she finally spoke, it was to say that she didn't know of any family like that west of town. She asked the midwife: Where exactly did you say it was?

The midwife dutifully tried to recall the route she had taken to get there. She vaguely remembered that she had first caught sight of all those little houses after they had passed through a gap in the old broken-down city wall.

3 was terribly surprised. She told the midwife that there weren't any houses there, just an empty field.

3's reply brought the midwife to a sudden realization of where exactly it was that she had been the night before. At the same time, she noticed that 7's wife was staring at her with startled eyes. 7 sat, head hanging, oblivious to the conversation. 4's father had already gone inside. The way 7 looked made her uneasy. The midwife felt like she shouldn't stand in the courtyard anymore. She wanted to go inside, but at the same time she didn't want to sit quietly in her room, alone with the unsettling memories of all she had been through the night before. She hesitated for a moment, moved toward the gate, and finally walked out of the courtyard.

As she walked down the street, the man who had escorted her the night before appeared in her mind's eye. As she remembered that blurry face, those legs that didn't seem to be there, she began to have an inkling of what she would see when she had passed through the break in the old city wall.

What happened next only confirmed her suspicions. The cypress grove where she had seen countless little houses the night before was full of earthen tombs. She heard herself let out a little sob. It sounded like a frog's croak. She stood for a moment, dazed. Finally, she began to follow the path she had taken the night before, winding back and forth through the tombs until she found herself in the middle of the grove. Most of the tombs had long since been overgrown with weeds, but a few of the newer ones had been swept clean. Suddenly, she stopped short in front of one of the newer tombs. This, she sensed, was where she had been the night before. The area had been swept free of weeds and clutter, and the earth on top of the burial mound was fresh. There was a tangled clump of uprooted hemp and a couple of balls of string lying next to the grave. A wooden plaque was stuck into the earth atop the burial mound. She bent to read a familiar name, a woman's name. The midwife remembered that she had died about a month before, taking an unborn child with her to the grave.

As the midwife left the graveyard, she thought of her encounter with the fortune-teller's son the night before. Almost immediately, she was gripped by a strong desire to see him, so she began to walk toward the fortune-teller's place. As she moved closer and closer to the fortune-teller's place, her recollection of their meeting began to stand out more and more vividly in her mind. She walked past the blind man. A column of noise was ringing out from the schoolyard, and the blind man sat in his usual place, attempting with the utmost care and attention to break the column down into its hundred or so component voices in order to identify which one belonged to 4. The intensity of the blind man's expression made the midwife begin to feel a certain unease, an unease that was only exacerbated when she arrived a moment later at the fortune-teller's door.

The fortune-teller's door was shut, and the building was enveloped in gloom. Two strips of white cloth suspended from the door frame fluttered weakly in the breeze. She knew it was the fortune-teller's son who had died, not the fortune-teller himself.

The fortune-teller came to the door holding a walking stick when she knocked. He told the midwife that he would not be receiving visitors for a few days. Glancing at the fortune-teller's retreating figure, the midwife realized that he looked as frail as a man on the brink of death. Then she remembered the rumors. And she began to wonder. His five sons and daughters had died so that he could continue to live. Now, there was no one left to die in his place. Maybe it was his turn next. And when she thought back to their encounter, she remembered how his voice, gruff, distant, and somehow disjointed, had fallen like little bits of gravel into her ears.

When the midwife got home and began once more to contemplate the events of the night before, an image of the two eggs that had floated atop the soup suddenly came to mind. The image made her feel sick to her stomach. She began to vomit. The heaves were unbearably violent. She felt like someone was digging into her sides. When she was finished, she looked down through teary eyes at a tangle of hemp and two balls of string lying on the ground in front of her.

3

The fortune-teller, who was almost ninety years of age, had fathered five children in all. The first four had died one by one over the course of the past twenty years. Only his fifth and youngest son remained. From the successive deaths of his first four children, the fortune-teller had learned both the secret of longevity and why he himself would be able to live to an unnaturally ripe old age. Each of the first four children's natal coordinates had been in conflict with his own. In the end, however, he had been able to force each of his first four children back into the netherworld. That was because he had discovered that his own life force was stronger than theirs. And, because none of his children had been able to enjoy their proper allotment in this mortal world, the surplus time had accrued to the fortune-teller's own account. For twenty years now, the fortune-teller had never suffered any of the usual signs of decrepitude and age. This happy fact was reconfirmed for him each time he "extracted yin in order to bolster the yang." This ancient practice, itself one of the principal means by which he hoped to prolong his life, involved drinking of the springs of vitality contained within the bodies of young girls. The five fierce roosters he kept in his room, in turn, were his way of fending off the approach of death. For if any little ghosts from the netherworld ever tried to come and settle his account, the roosters would immediately set to howling so fearfully that the ghosts would flee in terror.

The fifteenth of every month was the fortune-teller's day for "extracting yin to bolster yang." On this day, he would leave his house and, in one narrow residential lane or another, find an eleven- or twelve-year-old girl who happened to be playing outside and take her home with him. It was extremely easy to pacify the little girls with something nice to eat or fun to play with. He looked for girls who were especially thin because he found the sight of a fat, naked girl heaped across his bed very disagreeable.

But the fortune-teller's son died quite suddenly on the night of the fifteenth. When he came home around dusk, the fortune-teller had noticed something strange about the expression on his face. Just one hour before, an eleven-year-old girl had left the house.

The little girl had been wonderfully thin. She had lain naked on the bed sucking on a milk candy, her legs splayed carelessly in front of her in a manner that the fortune-teller had found rather enchanting. When she had glanced up at him, her eyes had seemed uncommonly big because she was so thin. When he began to stroke her skin, an almost supernaturally pleasurable sensation had begun to course through him. It was just at this time every month that the blind man would hear a series of ear-splitting cries emanating from the direction of the fortune-teller's building. Now the cries had come once again, but, because of the various obstacles that lay between him and the source of the sound, they arrived low and intermittent to his ears. Despite the distance, the blind man could tell almost immediately that this wasn't the voice for which he spent his days in anticipation.

After the girl had left, the fortune-teller sat down in a rattan chair. He had cooked himself a special soup concocted of yellow rice wine and eggs. Now he sat and slowly drank it. He felt like he had just emerged from a hot bath – drained, but at the same time completely relaxed and at ease. And as he drank the soup, he sensed a warm current circulate through his body and slowly leak out through his pores.

When his son arrived home, the fortune-teller had just closed his eyes in quiet meditation. He only discovered that strange expression in his son's eyes after he had opened his own to look at him. He had seen the same look in the eyes of his other children just before they died.

His son went out after dinner and didn't come back until late at night. By then, the fortune-teller was already in bed. He heard the sound of his son's footsteps coming up the stairs. The footsteps were leaden. He watched his son undress and climb slowly into bed in the moonlight.

The death of his youngest son threatened to destroy all his previous efforts at maintaining his vital essence, for he suspected that the surplus he had sucked from the first four children was already used up. Now he would have to draw on his son's vital energy. Once that was gone, the end would be in sight. He knew that his fifth son could provide him with a few years at most. The boy, after all, had already lived a full fifty-six years. He felt his body begin to wither. The very next day he discovered that the cries of the five roosters had also begun to lose much of their ferocity. He realized that they too were growing old.

4

One night two weeks later, the fortune-teller – who had by now recovered much of his energy – heard an unexpected knock on the door. The knock threw him into a panic. He heard someone calling his name. It sounded like a woman's voice. That in itself was reassuring. Even so, he moved toward the door with the utmost vigilance and silently bent to look under the crack between the door and the floor. He saw two stubby legs dimly illuminated by the street lamps outside the front door. The legs set his mind completely at ease. This was no ghost. He opened the door.

3 appeared in front of him. He was familiar with 3. That she had come in the middle of night led the fortune-teller to believe that she was in some kind of trouble.

As soon as 3 had sat down in a chair across from the fortune-teller, she let out an embarrassed laugh and told him that she was pregnant.

The fortune-teller's face did not betray a trace of surprise at the fact that he was sitting across from a pregnant woman nearly seventy years of age. With a good-natured twinkle in his eyes, he asked who had sown the seed.

3's face flushed with embarrassment. She hesitated for a moment before telling the fortune-teller that it was her grandson.

The fortune-teller seemed nonplussed. 3 protested that she had no choice in the matter. She had to do it with him. She couldn't stand to see him disappointed.

3 had come to ask the fortune-teller whether she should actually go through with it.

The fortune-teller told her to go ahead and have the child.

But 3 was anxious on account of the confusing question of whether the baby would be her child or her great-grandchild.

The fortune-teller told her it didn't matter. He would adopt the child as his own. That way the problem would never even arise at all.

CHAPTER FIVE

I

Although the blind man couldn't have known that the fortune-teller's son had died, he was aware of the fact that he hadn't heard the thin man pass by his place next to the school for nearly a month. Whenever he passed, he felt just the slightest whisper of a breeze, like a current of air wafting under a door. The way he passed was different from the way other people did, and that was how the blind man had come to recognize him. His absence made the blind man feel much lonelier.

It had been a long time since he had heard 4's voice. The same roar of countless voices – boys' and girls', raised in orderly unison or broken into chaotic chunks of sound – still poured out into the area directly adjacent to the school. But try as he might, he was unable to pick out 4's voice from among the general clamor. A few times, as the children walked to and from school, filing past him in groups of two and three, he had heard her laugh. But that had been a long time ago. 4's laughter had made shimmering circles of light burn for a few seconds across the blind man's darkened field of vision. The first time he had ever heard 4's voice, drops of sweet water purled into his ears. The last time he had heard it, her voice had been sad and lonely. And though a long time had passed between the two, the blind man felt that it had passed him by in an instant.

Now 4 was walking toward the blind man with her father at her side. The blind man heard the sound of two people walking past. One set of footsteps was coarse and the other extremely delicate. As 4 passed by him unseen, she saw his withered eye sockets glimmer with moist light. This sight somehow made her feel even more perplexed as to where exactly it was that her father was leading her. Moments after they had passed the blind man, they arrived at the fortune-teller's door.

Later, a few trucks rolled by the blind man's place on the road by the school. The first truck filled his ears with a turbid roar. He heard the sound of people walking and talking on the sidewalk, and a flurry of dust began to settle on his clothes. The voices coming from the street were male.

Their voices made him feel as if he were holding a sharp, heavy rock in his hands. Then a woman called out another woman's name. The second woman began to speak, and her voice was bright with laughter. These voices were glossy and smooth. He thought of cradling his hands around a rice bowl. A few seconds later, he heard 4's voice.

2

4 appeared in the fortune-teller's field of vision just as she stepped into a beam of light slanting down from a skylight. The sunlight frothed across her body as she stared woodenly toward the fortune-teller.

Having listened to 4's father's account of the circumstances, the fortune-teller shut his eyes and began to mumble to himself. His voice, reverberating through the little room, sounded like an old, tattered wall poster rustling in the breeze. 4 watched as a new expression began to steal across the fortune-teller's face. The fortune-teller opened his dull, expressionless eyes. He told 4's father: She talks in her sleep because a ghost has taken possession of her nether regions.

4's father, startled, gazed quietly into the fortune-teller's unfathomable eyes. Finally, he asked if there were any way he might be able to help relieve his daughter of her affliction.

The fortune-teller's face creased with a faint suggestion of a smile. 4's father had the distinct sensation that the smile was a blade slicing toward him. The fortune-teller said: Yes, of course. But I'm not sure whether you'll agree to go ahead with the procedure.

4 tried to listen to the ensuing dialogue between the two men, but all she could hear were sounds that somehow refused to become words. The fortune-teller looked like a skeleton draped with clothes, and the room was terribly humid. She saw five roosters skulking fiercely in the corner.

After the fortune-teller had assured himself that 4's father wouldn't object to the treatment he had proposed, he told him: I'm going to pull the ghost out from inside her nether parts.

4's father was shocked, but, after a moment's consideration, he gave the fortune-teller his silent consent.

This sudden turn of events left 4 helpless. Terrified, she gazed imploringly toward her father. But instead of returning her gaze, he took up a position behind her. She heard him say something, but before she had made out just what it had been, his hands were latched around her body, and she was overwhelmed by a feeling of utter powerlessness.

The fortune-teller bent over and unbuttoned her shirt. Underneath the shirt, he discovered a little sky-blue leather belt. The sight of the belt sent warm currents circulating through the fortune-teller's exhausted body. Underneath the belt was a flat stomach. As the fortune-teller unbuckled 4's belt, his fingers felt a little numb. But then he felt the warmth of 4's body against them. The warmth rolled across his fingers like fog, and his hands began to feel moist. The fortune-teller's hands peeled away several layers of fabric before they finally came in contact with 4's skin. 4's skin, he noticed, was very hot. With a quick downward yank, her body was completely exposed. The fortune-teller saw a ball of cotton trembling beneath him.

4 began to struggle, but all her efforts to escape proved futile. She felt the incomparable shame of having her own body exposed to the view of two grown men.

3

The blind man heard 4's first scream. The scream seemed to have burst through the girl's chest because he could hear what sounded like something tearing mixed up in the sound. The scream was very sharp, but it fell to pieces as soon as it emerged into the air outside the building. The scream itself never made it to the blind man's ears. He heard only a fragment of the sound. The sudden reappearance of her voice threw the blind man into a state of turmoil and confusion. When a second scream came, the blind man was unable to analyze the sound into its various components. The sound was like a flurry of dust settling over the blind man's ears. The sound continued to ring out for several moments, and the blind man was able to home in on its source just as easily as he would have found his way back to the sanatorium across town. As he moved, the blind man tried to sort out just what it was that made the sound so strange, and, without knowing exactly why, he began to feel a sort of terror rising in his chest. In the dark place behind his eyes, he began to picture the scene at the source of the sound. The sound that was coming toward him was neither tranquil nor particularly excited. It was the sound of someone patiently enduring a brutal beating.

The blind man groped his way toward the sound that frightened him. The drops of sound were like a hard rain lashing against his face. As he moved, the sounds grew increasingly loud, until they were less like raindrops than little blades pricking through his skin. Then he felt a hail of bricks. A whole building of sound collapsed against him. And between the bricks, he heard the incomparably gentle sound of breathing reach his ears like a caress. Tears began to trickle down the blind man's face.

By the time the blind man had walked up to the fortune-teller's front door, the screams had already faded into a kind of wail that continued for a very long time, like a wind blowing slowly away into the distance. Then 4's voice disappeared. The blind man stood by the door for a long time until he finally heard the sound of two people's footsteps moving toward the door. One sound was very coarse, and the other was leaden.

4

Two days after 4 got home, 7's wife carried her ailing husband over to the fortune-teller's house. This was their first visit to the fortune-teller's apartment, but the room in which they found themselves didn't seem at all unfamiliar because they had pictured it in their minds so many times before.

As 7 sat down in a chair opposite the fortune-teller, the old man's eerie presence was somehow rather reassuring. For 7, ashen and frail as he was, the fortune-teller's pallid complexion seemed to offer him a peculiar sense of comfort.

Standing between her husband and the fortune-teller, 7's wife was keenly aware of her own good health. But this awareness only served to heighten her sense of distance from each of the two men.

It took only a few seconds for the fortune-teller to determine the cause of 7's illness. He told 7's wife that 7's vital forces were in direct conflict with those of his five-year-old son. It was, he added, entirely a matter of their natal coordinates.

He explained: 7 was born in the Year of the Lamb, while his son was born in the Year of the Tiger. This was quite clearly a case of the tiger devouring the lamb.

There was very little 7 could do to escape his fate. His spirit was already traveling down the road to the netherworld.

His words left 7 and his wife speechless. Instead of gazing expectantly at the fortune-teller as before, 7 bowed his head and looked down at the floor. He felt as if his own frailty were lying prone on the ground beneath his feet. After a long pause, 7's wife asked the fortune-teller whether there was any hope at all for her husband.

The fortune-teller told her that the only way to save him would be to eliminate their son.

She fell silent. The fortune-teller's face began to blur. He looked less like a man than a rock. She heard the sound of her husband's laborious gasps for air and began to feel as if she herself were suffocating.

The fortune-teller added that it wasn't necessary to kill the boy in order to eliminate him. If she would simply deliver the five-year-old boy into someone else's care, severing any and all family ties between them, 7 would be cured without so much as a single drop of medicine.

The fortune-teller's face began to come into focus, but she turned instead to glance at her husband slumped in the chair beside her. Finally, she squinted up into the beams of sunlight pouring down from the skylight.

The fortune-teller told them he was of the opinion that, rather than giving their son up to a complete stranger, they would do better to give the child to him.

If the fortune-teller adopted the child, they could kill two birds with one stone. 7 would regain his health, and the fortune-teller would have a son to see him through to a ripe old age. Although the boy wasn't his own flesh and blood, he would be better than nothing. And, although the boy's natal coordinates were in conflict with his own, the fortune-teller was convinced that his yang energy had recently grown even stronger than ever, so that there was no risk of his falling ill in the same manner as 7 had.

Gesturing at the five roosters striding back and forth across the room, he told 7's wife: If you agree to the plan, then pick one of these roosters to take home with you. As long as the rooster crows every morning, 7's condition will continue to improve.

5

After 4 came home that day, she refused to go outside again. 4's father, standing in the courtyard some days later, felt a chill run through his body. Soon after the truck driver's death, the midwife had disappeared without a trace. Dust drifted down from the eaves, covering her door with a thick layer of grime. 4's father couldn't help but sense an air of dereliction about the place. It had also been several days since 3 had left. Before she had gone, she muttered something about going to visit some relatives in the country. She hadn't bothered to tell them when she would be coming home. Since then, her grandson would come out every so often and sit by his doorstep, staring dejectedly at the front door of 4's house. 7's wife had brought her husband to see the fortune-teller. He didn't ask them what had happened there, and they didn't ask him what had happened to 4. All he knew was that their tow-headed child had been replaced by a doddering old rooster who paced all day across the same ground where the child used to play.

7's health seemed to have taken a turn for the better. Every once in a while he would come out and lean against the door, gazing at the rooster in the yard. The strange turmoil in his eyes as he watched the rooster strut across the courtyard filled 4's father with a kind of startled wonder. Although 7 was on the mend, 4 had the vague impression that both he and his wife had somehow come down with some new disease. He soon discovered a similar phenomenon in his daughter. Although she had stopped talking in her sleep, she seemed to spend her waking hours immersed in a kind of trance. She was constantly mumbling to herself. The mumbling was often accompanied by a strange smile. Her smile, though, was like a withered blossom.

The courtyard just wasn't the same. A deathly silence had grown up around the place, and, in the dust cascading down from the midwife's eaves, he seemed to be able to read an omen of the courtyard's eventual fate. One day, he even began to sense that there was some kind of decay concealed somewhere within the courtyard. After a few days, the smell grew more distinct. After a few more days, he was able to determine exactly where the stench was coming from. It was coming, he realized, from the midwife's locked and shuttered room.

Around the same time, he heard talk that a girl had died. People were saying that she had died under the peach tree by the river. There weren't any signs of a struggle. Her body was unmarked, and her clothes were clean. Rumors as to the cause of her death flurried through the streets. The girl had been a classmate of his daughter's, and he knew the girl's father, 6. 6 liked to go fishing by the river. He remembered she had come over to their house once. She had stood bashfully in the courtyard before being invited in. She had stood there for a long time. She had stood just where he was standing now.

CHAPTER SIX

I

After the midwife had vomited a tangle of hemp and two hemp balls, she felt her body begin to float. By the time she had reached her bed, she felt almost weightless, as if her body was an overcoat that she could throw off with a shrug. And when she lay down on her bed, she felt like a piece of cloth that had been tossed carelessly across the bedspread. Then she saw a river, but the river was solid, and the water didn't flow. A few people floated on the surface, followed by a few rubber tires bobbing in the current. She also saw a street, but its asphalt paving was flowing like a river. A few boats navigated down the street, sails streaming in the wind like broken feathers.

Since his death, the truck driver had often come to visit the midwife as she slept, but he didn't come that night. The light in the midwife's eyes was snuffed out just as the sun set and a pall of cooking smoke rose above the town. Her death blocked the truck driver's only route home.

That night, the truck driver visited 2 instead. 2 dreamed he was standing on the little path that led to his door, the same path that had been blocked by a pool of glimmering water the night of the wedding. 2 saw the truck driver approach. He looked nervous and depressed. His hands were buried deep in his pants pockets. Maybe he's looking for something, 2 thought. The truck driver walked up beside him. His brow was creased, and a sad light glowed in his eyes. He told him that he wanted a wife.

2 discovered that there was a long slender wound on the right side of the truck driver's neck. Blood churned in the wound but didn't bleed.

2 asked: Is it that you don't have enough money for the dowry?

The truck driver shook his head no. 2 watched the blood roll back and forth across the gash in his neck.

The truck driver told him: I just haven't found the right woman.

2 asked the truck driver: And you need my help?

The truck driver nodded: That's exactly it.

From that night on, the truck driver and 2 would inevitably repeat the same conversation sometime before dawn every morning. These spectral appearances effectively put an end to the carefree life 2 had led before the truck driver's death. In his waking hours, he often imagined himself surrounded by a quivering spiderweb. It was only when 2 heard the news of the death of 6's daughter by the river that he began to understand how he might escape from the web that the truck driver had set in place around him.

2

In retrospect, it was clear to 6 that there had been indications of his daughter's imminent death. After the man in the sheepskin jacket had come to the house a few times, 6 began to notice that his daughter had taken to sitting bunched up in the corner like a ball of shadow. But 6 never really took these signs to heart. He simply never realized that his daughter might well have been nursing a secret to which his other six daughters had never had access. It was only later that it occurred to 6 that his daughter may well have been eavesdropping on his conversations with the man in the sheepskin jacket. He remembered one day in particular. He had just seen the man in the sheepskin jacket off at the front door, and when he walked back into the house, he noticed her standing in a daze by the door.

If not for a few unexpected hitches that had come up in the course of their negotiations, the man in the sheepskin jacket would have taken her away right then and there. He told the man in the sheepskin jacket that, of all his seven daughters, she was by far the best. It would be impossible to accept a mere three thousand yuan, as he had for the previous six. He suggested that they raise the buyer's fee by one thousand yuan. After a short round of haggling, the man in the sheepskin jacket quickly conceded the point. But he also proposed that he be allowed to take her away with him that very day in return. He would pay three thousand now and send the rest later. Naturally, 6 had refused to part with his daughter until the entire sum had been paid in full. The man in the sheepskin jacket said he couldn't come up with the money immediately. He had the cash, but he also had to take care of his travel expenses. He would come back in a month or so with the money.

When the appointed date for the man in the sheepskin jacket's return began to draw near, 6's daughter laid herself out under the peach tree by the river. 6 was sitting in a teahouse on the southern edge of the town. Ever since his strange experience by the river, he had given up on fishing and taken to drinking tea instead. A neighbor on his way back from the river told him what had happened. He told 6 he had looked for him everywhere. The teahouse went black, and scattered pieces of the man in the sheepskin jacket began to spin before his eyes. The men sitting at the table next to 6 seemed unperturbed by the news. They told 6 he'd better go to the river and see for himself whether it was true. But 6 wasn't listening. 6 was gazing out the door at a concrete telephone pole. There was a poster plastered to the side of the pole advertising a cure for impotence. 6 couldn't make out the rest, but the pieces of the man in the sheepskin jacket had begun to form a fragmented image in his mind. 6 remembered that the man in the sheepskin jacket was scheduled to arrive in just two days. 6 seemed to see his own pants pocket begin to bulge. With this last image came the deep realization that his insistence on ready cash had been a fatal mistake. He said to himself: This is retribution.

Although he was terrified by the very thought of the river, he decided that he really ought to have a look. As he walked toward the river, he sensed that her decision to die there had not been altogether accidental. As he drew closer, this sensation grew clearer and more distinct. When he saw a clump of people gathered around a peach tree in the distance, he began to picture what the corpse would look like laid out on the banks of the river.

Soon, he had pushed his way through the crowd. A forensics expert was examining the body. She lay prone on the ground, her face obscured by a tangle of hair. Her jacket was unbuttoned, and the sweater underneath shone provocatively red in the sun. He realized for he first time just how slender his daughter's waist had been. He could almost have encircled it with his hands. Then he noticed his daughter's feet. They were childlike feet. Her bare toes were pointed toward the sky.

Someone tapped him on the shoulder, and he turned to see a policeman's bearded face.

The policeman asked: Is she your daughter?

He slowly nodded.

The policeman said: It'll be a few days until we'll be able to determine the cause of your daughter's death.

He wasn't interested. He didn't care whether they told him or not. He wanted to leave. He didn't know what to do with himself, standing there. He turned and started to push past the crowd of onlookers. The policeman grabbed his shoulder: Wait a second. We need to ask you a few things before you go.

By the time 6 had extricated himself from both the police officers and the surrounding crowd, he sensed that several people were following closely at his heels. Instead of stopping to see who they were, he walked toward a lumberyard a short distance from the river. Suddenly, one of his pursuers overtook him. The man gestured toward the peach tree. Then he held up a single finger, as if to say: I'm buying.

6 froze for an instant. Coming to a sudden understanding of just what it was that the man had implied, he whispered: How much are you willing to pay?

The man extended all five fingers of his right hand.

Five thousand? 6 asked.

He shook his head.

Taking this gesture to mean that the man was only offering five hundred, 6 shook his head no. The man looked as if he were ready to bargain, but at that point a second man surreptitiously slid one finger across 6's palm. He was willing to pay a thousand yuan. 6 shook his head. When a third man appeared at his side, 6 quickly tapped two fingers across his palm to indicate that he wouldn't part with her for less than two thousand yuan. The third man hesitated before signaling his willingness to pay fifteen hundred. 6 waved him away and turned to leave.

It was at that point that 2 caught up to the first three men. When 6 once again lifted two fingers in the air, 2 unhesitatingly took them in his hand and squeezed.

6 sat tranquilly down on a pile of wood. 2 glanced at the other men and sat down beside him. Now all they had to do was wait for the gawkers to leave.

3

No one realized that the midwife had died until 2 presided over the funeral of 6's daughter. The news of 6's daughter's death had spread throughout the city, and new rumors explaining her death made the rounds almost every day. Even so, no one seemed to have noticed her funeral. In fact, 2 was the only person who attended the wake. After 2 had brought her ashes home from the crematorium, his next move was a visit to the truck driver's house. He would need the truck driver's urn. That was how 2 discovered that the truck driver's mother had already passed away.

Actually, most of the residents of the courtyard had already begun to suspect as much. The stench wafting through the courtyard had grown stronger and stronger with each passing day. And they hadn't seen the midwife emerge from her house since that day many weeks before when they had seen her come home and shut the door behind her. But, until 2 came to the courtyard, none of them had dared to wonder aloud whether she was dead, despite the increasing difficulty of living under the pall of the stench.

As soon as 2 walked through the gate into the courtyard, he was unnerved by the smell. And as he moved toward the midwife's door, he suddenly noticed that everyone who lived there was standing in the courtyard to watch. By that time, 2 had already come to the conclusion that the stench was emanating from the room he was about to enter. He knocked on the door and heard the sound of his hand against the wood echoing through the silence inside. He gave a little push. The unlocked door fell open with a hair-raising squeal. The stench emerged so powerfully from behind the door that he thought he might faint. He pushed the door completely open and walked into the room. The interior of the house was bathed in gloom. The stench billowed through the air. Tears began to stream down his face. He walked a few steps further into the room and found the midwife's body lying inert on the bed. Her features had already gone blurry, and something shiny and wet was oozing across what remained of her face. 2 looked hurriedly away from the corpse and began to move toward the other room. He found the truck driver's funeral urn sitting atop a card table. As he left the house, eyes streaming, he noticed that the people who had been standing outside watching were drenched with sweat. He told them: She's rotting.

When he got back to his apartment, he carefully laid the truck driver's ashes besides 6's daughter's urn. Then he began to make preparations for the wedding. First, he commissioned four craftsmen to fashion the couple's dowry out of paper – complete with paper models of modern furniture, a paper refrigerator, a paper television set, and several other electrical appliances that might come in handy in the netherworld. The artisans set to their task with a vengeance and within three days had completed the set. Next, he hired a suona player and three three-wheeled bicycle carts. He piled the paper furniture on top of the first two carts. The truck driver and 6's daughter rode on the back of the third cart. 2 and the suona player headed up the procession. The marriage of the truck driver and 6's daughter began with a blast of wedding music from the suona player's horn.

The procession passed through all of the town's major thoroughfares. The paper furniture reeled in the breeze, slanting every which way like the lines of a child's drawing. And everywhere they passed, the streets overflowed with curious onlookers. 2 was satisfied. He had finally done right by the truck driver. In response to the constant hail of questions thrown at him by the people who had come to watch the spectacle, he loudly and repeatedly announced who was getting married as they moved through the streets. Looking up, he saw heads hanging from practically every window of every building lining the street, and in some windows two, three, and even four spectators were visible. Soon, they passed the place where the blind man was sitting. The blind man, listening to the sharp bleats of the suona, knew that a wedding procession was passing by.

The procession wound its way past the broken-down city wall to the graveyard just west of town. A fresh burial mound had already been prepared for their arrival. 2 carefully placed the two urns into the grave. Then he began to fill the hole with earth. Clods of earth and stone hit the urns with a joyful metallic chime. Finally, the craftsmen's handiwork was piled around the burial mound and set alight. Flames galloped across the paper like horses. Black smoke hovered above the fire. A moment later, the flames and smoke began to die down. The blackened paper furniture slumped exhausted over the mound. Suddenly, the wind came up. Black flakes began to flurry above the burial site. Within moments, the furniture had vanished into the air like the smoke.

The truck driver never appeared in 2's dreams again.

4

Not long after the truck driver and 6's daughter's wedding, 4 came out of her room and into the street. She walked down the right lane of the road, oblivious to oncoming traffic, humming a slow, unhurried tune. It wasn't raining that morning. It wasn't sunny either. In the dull gray light, 4 looked as if she were sculpted of ash. The thoughtful cast of her face seemed to suggest that she was remembering something. As 4 glided above the pale gray pavement, she looked very much like a memory.

As 4 walked ahead, her right hand was in the process of carefully and gracefully unbuttoning her jacket. When the jacket had been completely unbuttoned, her body swayed backward like the branch of a tree until the jacket slid down her arms. Finally, she held a corner of the jacket in one hand, letting its tail drag along the pavement. After several more strides, she let go of the corner of the jacket. The jacket crumpled silently to the ground. A moment later, she began to peel off her dark blue sweater and, with fully as much grace and precision as before, let it fall to the pavement. As she continued to walk, 4 tranquilly unbuttoned her white undershirt. A breeze blew, and it billowed around her frame before fluttering to the ground as slowly and gently as a white sheet of paper.

4 stopped next to a wutong tree, reaching out her hand to caress its coarse trunk. She leaned against the tree, humming. She seemed to see clumps of people standing immobile in the distance. She remembered the ink that had splattered on the pavement once when she had shook her fountain pen too hard.

4 unbuckled her belt. Her black pants slid down her pale thighs and collapsed around her ankles. The motion of the pants produced a tickling sensation, and she smiled. Her pink underwear followed her pants down her legs. She carefully pulled her right foot out of the bunched fabric that encircled it. Her right foot was bare. Then she carefully pulled her left foot out from under the fabric. She wasn't wearing a sock on her left foot either. After both bare feet were placed on the coarse, muddy ground, she started to walk.

In the gloomy morning light, 4's naked body was a sickly white. Her skin was so pale and so tender that it looked as if it might be ruffled by the breeze. Her voice, humming as she walked, was as pale and tender as her skin. She saw the blind man. She stopped, smiled in his direction, and continued on her way.

Her voice had been wafting downwind for several minutes before she arrived. The blind man could hardly believe his ears. Something about the song made him doubt whether if it was really her. But, a moment later, her voice streamed into his ears like a draught of sweet water. And then the voice lingered by his side for a moment before it streamed off in another direction. The blind man stood and began to follow the sound.

4 walked all the way to the riverbank before finally coming to a halt. She gazed at the river, losing herself in its vast and hazy flow. She heard a kind of symphonic cadence emerge from within the stream. She moved toward it. The icy cold water rose above her ankles, rose until it had reached her neck. She felt as if she had put on a new suit of clothes. The river rose above her head.

The blind man heard the sound of water leaping into the air. 4's song vanished into the sound of splashing water. He knelt to the ground, hands fumbling at the warm, moist mud beneath him. Finally, he sat down on the banks of the river. He sat by the river for three days. From time to time, he would hear 4's lilting song emerge from the water. On the morning of the fourth day, the blind man stood and moved toward 4's voice. When his feet hit the water, a cold wave engulfed his heart. He sensed that the wave was 4's song. As he gradually immersed himself in 4's song, its cadences grew more distinct. And at the very moment when the blind man himself was swallowed by the river, he heard a cascade of water drops leap into the air. That would have to be the sound of 4 smiling.

The blind man disappeared under the river. The river continued to flow hazily on its way. A few leaves floated by the place where the blind man had been covered by the water. Soon after, a few skiffs bobbed across the surface.

Three days later, on a morning with no sunshine and no rain, the bodies of 4 and the blind man floated to the surface. The peach tree on the riverbank was awash in brilliant pink blooms.

The Past and the Punishments

On a summer night in 1990 in his humid apartment, the stranger opened and read a telegram of unknown origins. Then he sank into deep reverie. The telegram consisted of just two words – "return quickly" – and indicated neither the name nor the address of the sender. The stranger, filing through the mists of several decades of memory, saw an intricate network of roads begin to unfold before him. And of this intricate network, only one road could bring the slightest of smiles to the stranger's lips. Early the next morning, the lacquer-black shadow of the stranger began to slide down that serpentine road like an earthworm.

Clearly, in the intricacy of the network that constituted the stranger's past, one memory, as fine as a strand of hair, had remained extraordinarily clear. March 5, 1965. A simple string of digits, arrayed in a specific and suggestive order, had determined the direction in which the stranger had begun to move. But in reality, at the same time that the stranger had decided on his course, he had also failed to discover that his forward motion was blocked by yet another group of recollections. And because he had been standing at a remove from the bright mirror on his wall, he had been unaware of the ambiguity that had plagued his faint smile in the moments after he had deciphered the telegram. Instead, he had felt only stubborn self-confidence. It was precisely because of this excessive faith in himself that the procedural error that was to occur later on became unavoidable.

Several days later, the stranger arrived at a small town called Mist. It was here that the procedural error became apparent. The error was revealed to him by the punishment expert.

Imagine for a moment the stranger's face and posture as

he walked through Mist. Besieged by several different strata of memories, he had been left virtually incapable of perceiving his immediate surroundings with any sort of clarity or accuracy. When the punishment expert caught sight of the stranger for the first time, his heart cried out like a trumpet. The stranger entered the punishment expert's field of vision like a lost child.

When the stranger walked past a gray, two-story building, the punishment expert blocked his forward movement with an exaggerated grin.

"You've come."

The punishment expert's tone sent a shock through the stranger's body. Although the stranger could hardly credit his own suspicions, it certainly seemed as if this man was hinting at the existence of a certain memory as he stood before him, his white hair gleaming.

The punishment expert continued:

"I've waited for a long time."

This statement did nothing to help the stranger determine what role the man might have played in his past, if any at all. Perhaps he was simply a mote of dust floating across the vast expanse of his memory. The stranger sidestepped past the old man and continued on his way toward March 5, 1965.

Just as the punishment expert had hoped, however, the stranger failed to continue on toward March 5, 1965. Instead, a short and simple dialogue took place between the two men. And because of the punishment expert's warning — which was issued casually and without premeditation — the stranger began to understand his predicament. He discovered that his present course would not lead him to his desired destination. And so he turned in the opposite direction. But the fact of the matter was that March 5, 1965, was receding farther and farther away from him.

This was also the first time the stranger had thought back to the humid night when he had received the mysterious telegram. For days, his mind had circled around the moment in which March 5, 1965, had emerged in his mind. Now his focus shifted. He began to ponder several other dates, other memories that had continued to disturb him even as they lay abandoned at the back of his mind. These memories were January 9, 1958, December 1, 1967, August 7, 1960, and September 20, 1971, respectively. And with this realization, the stranger began to understand why he was unable to move toward March 5, 1965. The telegram's message might have been just as relevant to these four dates as to March 5, 1965. Indeed, it was precisely these memories that had blocked his way to March 5, 1965. And each of these four events represented roads that ran in entirely different directions without ever intersecting with the other. So even if the stranger abandoned his search for March 5, 1965, he would be unable to find either January 9, 1958, or any one of the other three remaining dates.

This realization took place at dusk, when the stranger, thrown into a quandary by his procedural error, began to ponder how to escape his predicament. That was also when he began to devote his attention to the enigma represented by the punishment expert. He began to sense that the old man was a kind of elusive link to his past. This is why he had come to feel that their meeting had been arranged in advance.

As the sky darkened, the punishment expert's intense excitement did not detract from a sense that he was in control of himself and the flow of events around him. The stranger unsuspectingly yielded to some kind of preordination and followed the punishment expert into the gray apartment building.

The living room walls were painted black. Here, the stranger sat down without a word. The punishment expert switched on a little white electric lamp. The stranger began to search his mind for a link between the mysterious telegram and the room that surrounded him. He found something entirely different. He found that the path he had followed on his way to Mist had been crooked.

Almost as soon as the stranger and the punishment expert sat down to talk, a remarkable affinity grew up between them. It was as if they had spent their lives huddled together in deep conversation, as if they were as familiar to each other as the palms of their own hands.

The first topic of conversation, unsurprisingly, was broached by the stranger's host. He said:

"Actually, we always live in the past. The past is forever. The present and the future are just little tricks the past plays on us."

The stranger acknowledged the force of the punishment expert's argument, but it was his own present that remained uppermost in his mind.

"But sometimes you can be cut off from the past. Right now, something is tearing me away from my past."

The stranger, rethinking his failure to approach March 5, 1965, was beginning to wonder if perhaps some other force besides that of the other four dates might be responsible.

But the punishment expert said:

"You're not cut off from your past. On the contrary."

It wasn't simply that the stranger had failed to move in the direction of March 5, 1965. Instead, March 5, 1965, and the other four dates were receding farther and farther into the distance.

The punishment expert continued:

"The fact is that you've always been deeply immersed in your past. You may feel cut off from the past from time to time, but that's merely an illusion. A superficial phenomenon. A phenomenon that, at a deeper level, indicates that you're really that much closer."

"I still can't help thinking that there's some force cutting me off from my past."

The punishment expert smiled helplessly, for he had already realized the difficulty of trying to overcome the stranger with language.

The stranger continued to move along his train of thought – at the very moment that he had left his past far behind, the punishment expert had appeared before him with a strange smile and the cryptic assurance that "I've been waiting for you for a long time."

The stranger concluded:

"You are that force."

The punishment expert was unwilling to accept the substance of the stranger's accusation. Although he obviously found the effort tiresome, he patiently attempted to explain the situation to the stranger once again:

"I haven't cut you off from your past. On the contrary. I have brought you into intimate conjunction with it. In other words, I am your past."

As the punishment expert spat out this last sentence, the tone of his voice made the stranger feel that the conversation might not continue for very much longer. He nonetheless continued:

"I find it hard to explain the fact that you were waiting for me."

"It would help if you could set aside the notion of necessity," the punishment expert continued, "and realize that I was waiting for a coincidence."

"That makes more sense," the stranger agreed.

The punishment expert, content, continued, "I'm very happy we are of one mind concerning this question. I'm sure we both understand just how very dull necessity really is. Necessity plods blindly and inexorably ahead on its accustomed track. But chance is altogether different. Chance is powerful. Wherever coincidences occur, brand new histories are born."

While concurring with the thrust of the punishment expert's theory, the stranger was preoccupied with an entirely different sort of question:

"Why were you waiting for me?"

The punishment expert smiled:

"I knew that question would come up sooner or later. I may as well explain now. I need someone to help me. Someone endowed with the necessary spirit of self-sacrifice. I believe that you are just that sort of person."

"What kind of help?"

"You'll learn everything tomorrow. For now, I'll be happy to discuss my work with you. My calling is to compile a summation of all human wisdom. And the essence of human wisdom is the art of punishment. That is what I'd like to discuss with you."

The punishment expert clearly had an excellent grasp of his field. He was well versed in each and every one of the varied punishments employed by mankind throughout its history. He provided the stranger with a simple and straightforward explanation of each punishment. His accounts of the bodily consequences of each punishment once it had been carried out, moreover, were stirring narratives in and of themselves.

On the conclusion of the punishment expert's lengthy and vivid discourse, the stranger realized with a shock that the punishment expert had neglected to touch on one rather important punishment: death by hanging. A dark, complex, and mercurial reverie had descended on him just as the punishment expert had begun his lecture. He had somehow seemed to have been anticipating the appearance of that particular punishment all along. As the punishment expert spoke, the blurred contours of March 5, 1965, had once again begun to clear. Given the circumstances, the hypothesis that someone intimately connected with the stranger's past had died by hanging on March 5, 1965, began to seem not entirely far-fetched.

In an effort to escape from the dark grip of these recollections, the stranger decided to point out the punishment expert's mistake. In doing so, he hoped to elicit another stirring discourse on this particular punishment and thus escape its grip.

His question only served to throw the punishment expert into a rage. It was not that he had overlooked a punishment, he shouted. He had just been ashamed to mention it at all. The dignity of that particular punishment, he proclaimed, had been trampled on by the indiscriminate and vulgar usage of suicidal miscreants. He bellowed:

"They were unworthy of such a punishment."

The punishment expert's unexpected rage released the stranger from the memories by which he had been besieged a moment before. After taking a long breath, he directed another question to the punishment expert, who sat lividly across the room:

"Have you tried performing any of the punishments yourself?"

The punishment expert's rage was immediately extinguished by this query. Instead of replying, the punishment expert sank into a deep and boundlessly pleasurable reverie. Crows of memory flew across his features. He counted his inventory of punishments like a stack of bills. He told the stranger that, of all the experiments he had carried out, the most moving had involved January 9, 1958, December 1, 1967, August 7, 1960, and September 20, 1971. It was clear that these dates hinted at events that transcended the sterile numbers of which they were composed. There was something of the aroma of blood about them. The punishment expert told the stranger how:

. . . He had drawn and quartered January 9, 1958, tearing it into so many pieces that it had drifted through the air like a flurry of snowflakes. He had castrated December 1, 1967, cutting off its ponderous testicles so that there hadn't been a drop of sunshine on December 1, 1967, while the moonlight that evening had been as dense as overgrown weeds. Nor had August 7, 1960, been able to escape its fate, for he had used a rust-dappled saw blade to cut through its waist. But the most unforgettable had been September 20, 1971. He had dug a trench in the ground, in which he had buried September 20, 1971, so that only its head was still exposed. Owing to the pressure exerted on the body by the surrounding earth, September 20, 1971's blood had surged up into the head. The punishment expert had proceeded to crack open its skull, from which a column of blood had immediately spurted forth. The fountain of September 20, 1971, had been extraordinarily brilliant.

The stranger fell into a silent, boundless despair. Each of the dates of which the punishment expert had spoken concealed a deep well of memory: January 9, 1958, December 1, 1967, August 7, 1960, and September 20, 1971. These were precisely the four events, isolated from the enormity of the stranger's past, that had been pursuing him all along.

The stranger, of course, had long been unaware of their pursuit. The four dates had become four musty breezes wafting toward him. The content that the dates concealed had hollowed, crumbled to dust and nothingness. But their aroma lingered on, and the stranger had the vague impression that if it weren't for these four dates, his strange encounter with the punishment expert would never have transpired.

The punishment expert rose from his chair and walked into his bedroom. As he moved past the white glare of the lamp, he resembled a recollection. The stranger sat motionless in his chair, tortured by a sense that March 5, 1965, was the only memory that he had left. Even March 5, 1965, was far away. It was only later, after he had already fallen asleep, that his features took on the serenity of a memory anchored firmly in the slipstream of the past.

When they resumed their conversation the next morning, there was no doubt that their affinity had grown even stronger. As soon as they had begun to talk, they arrived at the heart of the matter.

The punishment expert had suggested the night before that he needed the stranger's help. Now, he began to explain why:

"Of all my punishments, only two have yet to be tested. One of them is reserved for you."

The stranger, in need of further explanation, was led into another black room. The room was empty save for a table in front of a window. There was a big slab of glass on the table top. The glass glittered in the sunlight pouring in through the window. Leaning against the wall was a freshly sharpened butcher's knife.

Pointing at the glass by the window, the punishment expert said:

"Look how very excited and happy it is."

The stranger walked over to the table, gazing at the chaos of light playing through the glass slab.

Pointing at the butcher's knife leaning against the wall, the punishment expert told the stranger that he would use this knife to slice through his waist and cut him in half. Immediately thereafter, he would place the stranger's torso on the glass. His blood would continue to flow out from the wound until he slowly died.

The punishment expert informed the stranger of just what it was that he would see before he bled to death on the glass. His description of the scene was compelling:

"At that moment, you will feel a tranquillity you have never known before. All sounds will fade, slowly becoming colors that will hover in front of your eyes. You will feel how your blood begins to flow more and more sluggishly, feel how it pools on the glass, how it cascades into the dust below you like millions of strands of hair. And then, finally, you will catch sight of the first dewdrop of the morning of January 9, 1958. You will see this dewdrop gazing at you from the dimness of a green leaf. You will see a bank of brilliant colored clouds glowing in the noonday sun of December 1, 1967. You will see a mountain road. The road will wait patiently for you as the evening mist gathers overhead and night falls on August 7, 1960. You will see two fireflies dancing in the moonlight on the evening of September 20, 1971, shining like a pair of faraway tears."

On the conclusion of the punishment expert's serene narrative, the stranger sank once again into reverie. The dewdrops of January 9, 1958, the brilliant colored clouds of December 1, 1967, the warm dusk on a mountain road of August 7, 1960, the fireflies like dancing tears in the moonlight of September 20, 1971. Each of these memories arrayed itself like an empty canvas before the stranger's roving eyes. The stranger understood the punishment expert's narrative as a promise of things to come. The stranger sensed that the punishment expert had offered him the possibility of reunion with his past. A tranquil smile lit his face, a smile that indisputably signaled his submission to the punishment expert's wondrous designs.

The punishment expert was boundlessly excited by the stranger's expression of consent. His joy, however, was contained – rather than leaping into the air like a grasshopper, the punishment expert merely nodded his head in agreement. Then he asked the stranger to take off his clothes.

"It's not for me. It's just that the punishment demands that you leave the world in the same state that you entered it."

The stranger happily complied – it seemed appropriate. He began to imagine what it would be like to encounter his memories naked. His memories, he mused, were sure to be surprised.

The punishment expert stood by the wall to the left, watching as the stranger stripped off his clothes like a layer of leather, revealing skin battered and scored by the blade of time. He stood next to the glittering slab of glass, his body glowing in the sun's rays. The punishment expert emerged from the shadows by the wall, walked over to the stranger's side, and grasped the gleaming butcher's knife in his hand. The sunlight danced furiously across the blade. He asked the stranger:

"Are you ready?"

The stranger nodded. His eyes were incomparably tranquil. He had the look of a man awaiting the inexorable arrival of unparalleled happiness.

The stranger's tranquillity filled the punishment expert with a sense of confidence and certainty. He reached out a hand to stroke the stranger's waist, only to discover that his hand was trembling. This discovery opened up a world of new and unwelcome possibilities. He didn't know if the trembling in his hands was due to excessive excitement or whether his strength had finally deserted him. The punishment expert's strength had begun to ebb long before. And now as he held the blade his hands began to shake uncontrollably.

The stranger had already turned to gaze out the window in silent expectation of reunion with the past. He tried to imagine the knife slicing his body in two. A pair of wondrous, icy hands miraculously tearing a blank sheet of paper neatly in half. But the punishment expert's gasps forced their way into his consciousness. When the stranger turned to look, the punishment expert, sighing at his own humiliation, directed the stranger's attention to his trembling fingers. At the same time, he explained that it would be impossible for him to sever his body in two with one single stroke of the blade.

The stranger reassured him:

"I don't mind if it takes two."

"But," the punishment expert said, "the punishment only allows for a single stroke."

The stranger told the punishment expert he didn't understand why he insisted on being so fussy.

"Because it would defile the integrity of the punishment," he explained.

"On the contrary," the stranger asserted. "You might actually contribute to the development of the punishment."

"But," the punishment expert quietly explained to the stranger, "if we proceed with the experiment, your own experience of it would be ruined. I would hack your waist to mincemeat. Your stomach, your intestines, and your liver would tumble to the ground like overripe apples. I wouldn't be able to place your torso on the glass. You would just fall over. And all you would see as you approached the end would be heaps of wriggling earthworms and lumpy toad skin. And worse."

The punishment expert delivered his judgment with incontestable authority. There was no longer any doubt that events would begin to move in an entirely different direction. The stranger began to put his clothes back on. He had thought he would never need them again. His pants felt like oil paint as they smeared up his legs. His eyes were hooded and dark with disappointment. Through them, he could see the dark figure of the punishment expert standing by him like a distant memory.

The stranger could no longer avoid the realization: the punishment expert was powerless. The punishment expert could not reunite him with his past. And though the stranger was baffled and angered by the way in which the punishment expert had so beautifully laid his four dates to waste, he was not without a certain compassion for the punishment expert's predicament. The punishment expert suffered because he could no longer muster the strength to carry out his marvelous experiment. His own pain came as a result of being unable to reunite with his past. But they were bound together by their common suffering.

The silence that ensued was as heavy as night. It was only after they returned to the living room that they were finally able to dispel the oppressive quiet that had enveloped them following the failure of the experiment. They had moved to the living room after standing motionless, enveloped by the glitter of the glass that suffused the little room. Having arrived in the living room, however, they were able once more to take up something resembling a conversation.

Soon after they had begun, the punishment expert's voice began to grow hoarse with passion. As they spoke, the punishment expert rapidly recovered his composure, despite the gravity of his defeat. For his final punishment was the best of all. His final punishment was his life's work, his masterpiece, his crowning glory. He told the stranger:

"It is my own creation."

The punishment expert began to tell the stranger another story:

"There is a man. Strictly speaking, a scholar. A true scholar, the kind of scholar that simply doesn't exist any more in the twentieth century. He wakes up one morning and finds several men in gray suits standing around his bed. These men lead him out of his house and push him into a car. The scholar, mystified, repeatedly asks the men where they are taking him. His questions are met with stony silence. He begins to grow uneasy. He stares out of the car window, trying desperately to determine what is going to happen next. He watches as they pass through familiar streets, drive by a familiar stream, and finally move into uncharted territory. Soon, they arrive at a grand public square. The square is big enough for twenty thousand people. In fact, there are already twenty thousand people gathered in the square. From afar, they look like so many ants. When they pull up to the edge of the square, he's pushed through the crowd and onto a platform set up at one end of the square. He gazes down at the crowd. The square looks as if it's choked with weeds. A few soldiers with rifles stand with him on the platform. They aim the muzzles of their rifles directly at his head. The scholar is terrified. But a moment later they lower their guns, having forgotten to load them. The scholar watches bullets glint in the sunlight as, one by one, they are stuffed into the rifles' magazines. Then the rifles are leveled once more at his head. At this point, a man who looks like some kind of judge climbs up onto the platform. This man tells the scholar that he has been sentenced to death. The scholar, unaware of having committed any offense, is dumbfounded. The judge, seeing the shock of his pronouncement ripple across the scholar's face, adds:

'Just look at the blood dripping from your hands.'

"The scholar looks down at his hands but can't find the slightest trace of blood. He extends his hands toward the judge to protest his innocence. But the judge simply moves to the side of the platform without even seeming to notice. The scholar watches as people in the crowd stream up to the edge of the platform to give their testimony. One by one, they relate how he bequeathed his punishments on their loved ones and relatives. At first, the scholar tries to argue with those who have come forward to condemn him. He tries to make them understand that one must sacrifice everything in the name of science. He tells them that their relatives have been sacrificed in the name of science. As the procession of plaintiffs continues to stream toward the platform, however, he finally begins to realize the gravity of his predicament. His predicament is this – in a few moments, a hail of bullets will fly in the direction of his head. His head will shatter like a roof tile. He sinks into a despair that is as vast as the crowd that unceasingly streams toward the platform to air its grievances. The denunciations continue for ten hours. And for ten hours, the soldiers keep their rifles trained on the scholar's head."

The punishment expert paused at this point in his narrative, commenting with an enigmatic air:

"The scholar, of course, is me."

He proceeded to tell the stranger that it had taken him a whole year to perfect each and every detail of the ten hours he would spend on the platform.

"In the ten hours immediately following the scholar's realization that he has been sentenced to death, he falls victim to terrible psychological torment. In those ten hours, his mind becomes a whirlwind of emotions, careening from one spiritual state to another, passing through lifetimes of feeling in mere moments. One moment he is awash in terror and abject cowardice. The next moment floods him with bravery, resolve, and indomitable courage. Seconds later, he feels a stream of urine trickling down his legs. Seconds after he has begun to welcome the prospect of death, he starts to realize just how beautiful it is to be alive. And throughout the turbulent hours, each of these moments is felt just as sharply as a knife piercing his flesh."

It was clear to the stranger that this punishment was almost perfect. When the punishment expert had brought his narrative to a conclusion, he clearly and unmistakably proclaimed to the stranger:

"This punishment is reserved for myself."

He told the stranger that this punishment represented ten years of blood, sweat, and tears. He told the stranger that he couldn't possibly give the product of years of hard toil to someone else. By someone else, he clearly meant the stranger himself.

The stranger smiled. It was a noble smile. It was a smile that successfully hid the doubts he harbored concerning the punishment from view. For he sensed that the punishment was not nearly as perfect or complete as the punishment expert would have liked to think. There seemed to be a flaw that the punishment expert had overlooked.

The punishment expert rose from his seat and told the stranger that he would carry out the experiment that very evening. He hoped that the stranger would appear by his bedside in twelve hours, because by then:

"You'll still be able to see me, but I won't be able to see you any more."

After the punishment expert retired to his bedroom, the stranger sat for a long time in the living room, mulling over the fact that he was really far less confident as to the outcome of the experiment than the punishment expert himself. And later, when he got up to go to his own bedroom, he felt certain that, when he stood by the punishment expert's bedside the following morning, the old man would still be able to see him. He had discovered the flaw that lay beneath the polished surface of the punishment, a flaw so crucial as virtually to ensure the failure of the punishment expert's experiment.

The scene the next morning confirmed the stranger's suspicions. The punishment expert lay atop his bed, face pallid with fatigue, and told the stranger that everything had gone smoothly the night before. But just as he had approached the end, he had awoken. With a tragic sweep of his hand, he threw aside his quilt to show the stranger what had happened:

"I was so scared that I wet the bed."

The bed was sopping wet. The stranger estimated that the punishment expert must have urinated at least ten times over the course of the night. He gazed at the punishment expert panting on the bed. He was satisfied. He didn't want the punishment expert to succeed. For his four dates, his memories, were in this frail old man's hands. The old man's death would spell eternal separation from his own past. And this was precisely why the stranger was unwilling to point out the nature and position of the flaw in the punishment that had led to his failure the night before. Thus, when the punishment expert invited him to come again at the same time the following day, he merely smiled and carefully made his way out of the bedroom.

The scene on the second morning was much like it had been on the first. The punishment expert lay prone on his bed, staring anxiously toward the stranger as he pushed open the door to the bedroom. In order to hide his sense of shame and humiliation, the punishment expert once again pushed aside his quilt to reveal that he had not only wet the bed but also soiled it with a pile of his own shit. But the experiment had progressed in much the same manner as the night before – he had woken up at the last moment. In a voice tinged with sorrow, he said:

"Come back tomorrow. I promise that I'll be dead by tomorrow."

The stranger failed to give these parting words his full attention. He gazed with pity on the punishment expert, feeling as if he should tell him about the flaw. The flaw was simply this: after ten hours, a bullet should appear, a bullet that would shatter the punishment expert's head. The punishment expert had spent ten years perfecting the ten-hour process that would lead to his death but had neglected to include the bullet with which the episode must inevitably culminate. At the same time, however, the stranger was all too aware of the danger of such a revelation. His past would die along with the punishment expert. And he sensed that, as long as he was with the punishment expert, his past was never far away. He left the room without having revealed his secret, secure in the knowledge that the flaw would ensure that his past was not lost.

On the third morning, however, the stranger found an entirely different scene when he pushed open the door to the punishment expert's bedroom. The old man had fulfilled his promise of the day before. The punishment expert was dead. He hadn't died on the bed. Instead, his body hung from a rope about a yard away from the bed.

Confronted by this reality, a withered clump of weeds began to tangle around the stranger's heart. The punishment expert's death would forever preclude the possibility of any kind of connection with the four memories he had once sought. To gaze on the punishment expert now was to see the lynching of his own past. He distantly recalled March 5, 1965. And at the very same moment, he remembered the punishment expert's fury when he had spoken of death by hanging. The punishment expert had finally chosen to take his own life by means of a degraded punishment.

It wasn't until he left the room much later that he discovered a note written on the back of the door:

I have redeemed this punishment.

The punishment expert had clearly been quite lucid and sober as he had written this message, for he had concluded by carefully noting the date:

March 5, 1965.

Many years ago, a mild and unassuming high school history teacher suddenly disappeared, leaving behind his young wife and a three-year-old daughter. From that time on, nothing more was heard of him. Over the course of several years, his wife gradually began to resign herself to her loss. On a hot, dry Sunday afternoon, she married another man. Her daughter also changed her last name to match that of the new husband, for the old name was inextricably tied up with the pain and difficulty of those years. A dozen years had gone by since that day. They lived a tranquil life. The past receded farther and farther behind them, until it almost seemed to have dispersed like so much mist into the air, never to return.

Her husband, of course, was only one of the many who disappeared during the tumultuous years of the Cultural Revolution. When the tumult died down, many of the families whose relatives had been lost began to receive word of their whereabouts, even if it was only to learn that they had died years before. She was the only one who had never heard any news. All she knew was that her husband had disappeared the night he was taken away by the Red Guards. The person who told her was a store clerk who had been among the group of Red Guards who had broken into their home that night. He said, "We didn't hit him. We just took him to his office and told him to write a confession. We didn't even send a guard to watch him. But the next morning, we discovered that he was gone." She remembered that they had come to the apartment the morning after to search for her husband. The clerk had added, "Your husband was always nice to us students, so we didn't torture him."

Not long before, she and her daughter had taken a pile of old newspapers to the recycling station. Standing among the scrap heaps littering the recycling station, she discovered a yellowing sheet of paper dotted with mildew. The writing on the sheet of paper, however, was still legible:

The 5 punishments: branding 墨, nose-cut 劓, leg-cut 剕, castration 宫, dismemberment 大辟.

Former Qin dynasty: roasting in oil, disembowelment, beheading, burning at the stake.
Warring States period: flaying, drawing and fifthing, halving.
Early Liao dynasty: live burial, cannon fodder, cliff hanging.
Jin dynasty: skull crush, death by cudgel, skin peel.

Drawing and Fifthing 車裂: To tie the victim's head and each of his four limbs to five horse-drawn carts and, by driving in different directions, rend him in fifths.
Slow Death 凌遲: To mince the victim's body with knives.
Disembowelment 剖腹: To tear open the abdomen in order to view the victim's heart. . . .

An old man wearing Coke-bottle glasses stood by a scale in the middle of the clutter. The daughter, grown-up and loath to see her mother tire herself out, carried a heavy pile of waste-paper over to the man and set it down on the scale. She wiped the sweat off her face with a handkerchief, as her mother crouched down by another pile of wastepaper behind her. The old man had to bend so close to read the numbers on the scale that she couldn't suppress a grin, but at that moment a sharp cry rang out behind her. When she turned to look, her mother had already slumped unconscious to the ground.

As soon as they took him to his office at the school, they sat him down and told him to write a sincere, honest, and thorough confession. Then they left without even assigning him a guard.

The office was large and lit by two piercingly bright incandescent lamps. The northwest wind whistled over the roof. He sat for a long time at his desk, sat like the building itself, squatting quietly under the bright pale moonlight as the wind whistled around its walls.

He saw that he was washing his feet as his wife sat on the edge of the bed watching over their little daughter. Their daughter had already fallen asleep. The crook of her arm was sticking out from underneath the quilts. His wife hadn't noticed them yet. His wife was staring into space. As always, she wore her hair in two braids. Red silk bows, tied in the shape of butterfly wings, were fastened around the end of each braid. They were just the same as the first time he had ever seen her, the time they had passed each other without a word.

Now he seemed to see those pretty red butterflies floating through the air, towing two shining black braids behind them.

It had been three months since he had first told his wife to stay inside at all times. She had listened intently and done as she was told. He didn't go out very much either. Every time he left the house he saw the women — feather dusters and toilet seats dangling around their necks, half their hair shaved to make a yin-yang pattern on their scalps. He was afraid that they would cut off his wife's braids and ruin the lovely red butterfly bows. That was why he had told her not to leave the house.

He saw snow flurrying through the streets all day long. The snow never fell anywhere else. He saw everyone bend to gather a handful of flakes. He saw them stop to read them. He saw someone slumped beside a postbox. He was dead. The blood was still fresh, still wet. A leaflet drifted through the air and landed on his head, covering half of his face. The people in dunce caps and sandwich boards walked past the postbox. They glanced toward the dead man, but he saw no surprise register on their faces. They looked blank, pitiless, as if they were staring at themselves in the bathroom mirror. He began to recognize a few of his colleagues from school in their midst. He thought maybe it's my turn next.

He saw himself washing his feet. The water in the basin had already grown cold, but he didn't notice. He was thinking maybe it's my turn next. He was wondering how it was that he had taken to crying out at odd times without even knowing why. These cries were always met by a wooden stare from his wife.

He saw them come in. After they came in the room was full of noise, full of voices. His wife was still sitting on the edge of the bed, staring woodenly toward him. His daughter had awoken, and the sound of her sobs seemed terribly far away, as if he were walking down the street, listening from outside a tightly shuttered window. It was then that he realized that the water in the basin was cold. The noise began to settle, and someone holding a piece of paper walked toward him. He didn't know what the paper said. They made him read it aloud. He recognized his own handwriting, remembered something of what he had written. Then they dragged him away, his bare feet clad only in a pair of thongs. The northwest wind blew across the surface of the road, toweling his feet dry.

He shivered when he saw the neat stack of writing paper sitting atop his desk. He gazed at the paper for a moment, fumbled in his pocket for a fountain pen, and discovered that he hadn't brought one. So he stood and looked to see if there was a pen on one of the other teachers' desks. But there were no pens on any of the other teachers' desks. He sat down helplessly and saw two hands imprinted on the desktop. He realized that he hadn't been to the office for over three months. His desk was coated with dust, as were the others. He figured that none of the other teachers had been to the office either.

He saw crowds of people filing through the gate onto campus and knots of people filing out. He saw himself leafing through an old, heavy history book. He had been fascinated by the punishments. Sooner or later, he planned to leave his teaching post and devote himself to their study. In his student days, he had pored through volumes of historical material, taking meticulous notes as he went along. He had also fallen in love for the first time. But the affair did not work out, and his research had come to a premature halt as a result. Just after graduation, he had come across a single page from his notes as he packed to leave. He had intended to throw it away but had somehow forgotten the whole thing in the months that followed. Now he knew that he hadn't thrown it away after all.

He saw that he was washing his feet. He saw himself walking through the teachers college. And he saw himself sitting at his desk. He saw a huge shadow on the wall across from him. The shadow's head was as big as a basketball. He stared at his own shadow. And after he had stared for a long time, he began to think that the shadow was a hole in the wall.

He felt the northwest wind steal into the room and begin to shriek. The wind fastened itself to his clothes and shrieked, slipped into his hair and howled. The sound rubbed against his face, stroked his cheeks, cried out to him. He began to tremble. He began to feel cold. The wind was louder and louder. He turned to look at the door. The door was shut. He turned to look at the windows. The windows were shut.

He discovered that the windows had been washed so spotlessly clean that they were transparent. He didn't understand. How could the windows be so clean if the desk was coated with dust? He noticed that one of the windows was cracked. The sight somehow seemed terribly desolate. He moved toward the cracked pane and its desolation mirrored his own.

But when he reached the sill, he realized with a shock that the broken pane was the only piece of glass left in the frame. All the other panes were empty. He absently extended his hand to caress the broken pane. The edge was coarse and sharp under his fingers. He absently rubbed his fingers against it, feeling something warm seep from the tip of his finger. Bits of glass fell from the window to the floor with his motion, shattering crisply on the floor like a broken heart. Soon, only a small triangle of glass remained.

Suddenly, he saw a pair of leather shoes swaying back and forth just in front of him. He lifted his hand to touch them, recoiled, heard his heart pounding and leaping in his chest. He stood motionless, watching the shoes swing slowly back and forth. Then he discovered the cuffs of a pair of pants. They were fluttering just above the shoes. He slammed open the window frame. There was a corpse hanging from the eaves. He heard someone scream. The sound came from his left. Through the darkness he saw a tree and, under its branches, a shadow. The shadow's feet dangled above the ground. Sharp gasps drifted through the air, reaching his ears as feeble whimpers. He stood for a long time, until he seemed to hear the shadow mumble "it's you" and extend its arms to grab hold of some kind of loop. The shadow's head slipped through the loop. After a second or two of silence, he heard a little stool being kicked over onto the ground followed by a suffocated whisper. He slumped to the floor, hands gripping the window sill.

It was only much later that he gradually became aware of the sound of shouting echoing in the distance. The shouts moved closer, dispersing through the night, surrounding the office. They grew steadily louder as they approached, until they seemed to him like a terrible wave of sound welling in his ears.

He leaped from the floor to listen. The school had erupted into a ghostly chorus of wails and brutish howls. It was as if a pack of wild animals had surrounded the office. The noise excited him. He began to pounce around the room, hands waving in the air, drunk with the hoarse bellows escaping from his own throat. He wanted to escape, to merge with the clamor outside, but he didn't know how. As the shouts rang out louder and louder, his own excitement and anxiety only increased. He continued to leap around the room, bellowing. There was nothing else for him to do. Soon, though, he slumped down onto the seat at his desk, exhausted and agitatedly panting for air.

It was at this very moment that he caught sight of his own shadow. He had suddenly stumbled on a way to escape. There was a hole in the wall. He stood and ran toward the hole, but the realization that the hole had suddenly shrunk to a fraction of its size just a second before stopped him short. Suspiciously eyeing the wall, he retreated to his original position at the desk, hesitated, and charged once more toward the hole. Just as before, the hole began to shrink just as he approached. This time, he held his ground. The hole, he discovered, was precisely the same size as his own body. He stared suspiciously for a few moments. He decided that it hadn't shrunk so much that he couldn't squeeze his way out. He threw himself into the darkness and landed on the floor.

Blown open by a gust of wind, the door began to shimmy against the wall with a series of bone-cracking reports. The wind pounded through the open door and circled the office.

Dazed, he rose and stood for a moment facing the door. He saw a black rectangle cut in the wall, but as he walked stealthily toward it, he was once again assailed by suspicion. This time, the hole stayed the same no matter how close he stood. Instead of catapulting himself into the darkness, he carefully extended a finger toward it. When his finger disappeared into the hole, he extended his arm. He began, slowly and with the utmost caution, to slide through the hole. And when he found himself surrounded by a broad, empty expanse of darkness, he knew that he had escaped.

The shouts that filled the schoolyard were even louder and more stirring than before, and he began to bellow even louder and with even more zeal, leaping off the ground as he ran. And though innumerable shadows – some big, some small, and no two alike – tried to prevent his escape, he managed to evade them all. In a moment, he had reached the street. He paused, trying to determine just where the shouts were coming from, but it seemed as if they pervaded the air, as if they were racing toward him from every possible direction. He stood, at a loss as to where to go. A moment passed. He saw something burning to the southeast, glowing orange like clouds just before dusk. He ran toward the flames, and as he ran the shouts grew louder.

A huge building was aflame. He saw countless people swaying and twisting amid the flames. Countless others tumbled from the top of the building to the ground. He stood on the bridge, bellowing, leaping up and down, laughing at how they tumbled and sliced through the air. Flurries of bodies, one after another, rained down from the building until the structure itself vanished, leaving only a glowing tower of flame in its wake. The tower brought his frenzy to an even higher pitch. Watching from the bridge, he shouted and jumped as if his life depended on it. Soon afterward, he heard a string of explosions. The flames crumpled to the ground but continued to burn across the expanse. He discovered that the flames were flooding toward him across the ground at a breakneck clip. Breathless, he sat on the railing of the bridge, eyes trained on the flames. Gradually, the burning expanse began to break up into isolated piles of flame. The pockets of flame grew smaller and smaller until the fire burned itself out.

When the fire was gone, he slid off the railing and began to walk along the bridge. After a few steps, he turned and walked back to the railing. After a moment, he retraced his steps. He paced back and forth across the bridge for a long time.

It was only much later that the dark sky to the east began to glow. Just before the sun rose, the clouds began to soar into the air, shining red. He saw something burning somewhere in the distance. He began to shout. He ran toward the flames.

When they got home from the recycling station, she started to feel strangely distracted. That night, she heard someone pacing outside the house. There was no moonlight, and the streets were dark and quiet. She heard footsteps approach the house, scraping the ground with an oddly irregular rhythm, as if they were simultaneously slapping the pavement and gliding above the ground. Finally, the footsteps stopped a good distance away from the house without coming any closer. By that time, she had already realized whose footsteps they were.

She heard the footsteps for several nights in a row. The footsteps terrified her. The footsteps made her cry aloud with fright.

Her husband had been taken away on just such a black, moonless night. The Red Guards crashing through the front door, the scrape of her husband's thongs as he left the house for the last time — all of this would always be associated for her with the dark of night. After more than ten years, she still couldn't help being frightened by the dark. With the visit to the recycling station, the darkness she had assiduously tried to bury since that night enveloped her once again.

That day, walking home with her daughter at her side, she had suddenly seen her own shadow lying on the pavement under the sun. The shadow made her cry out. For she now knew that the darkness could pursue her by day as well as by night.

I

The man limped into the small town. It was early spring. One week earlier, a fierce storm had buried the town in spring snow. After a week of sparkling sunshine, however, the snow had almost entirely melted away. A few patches of slush lingered in dark, shady places, but the rest of the town had begun to flower. Soon, the town was enveloped by the sound of dripping water like a harmony plucked from the rays of the sun. The melting sound lightened the hearts of the townspeople. And with each passing night, the stars burned bright in the sky, promising them another brilliant day to come when they awoke the next morning.

Windows that had been shut all winter were thrown open one by one, and in them appeared the expectant faces of young girls above pots of sprouting flowers sitting on the sill. The wind no longer blew cold and bone piercing from the northwest. Instead, the warm, humid breezes of the southeast stroked their faces. They left their rooms, left their bulky overcoats behind them. They walked into the streets, into springtime. If they still wore scarves around their necks, it was because they looked nice, not because they helped ward off the wind. They felt their skin, dry and taut in winter, begin to stretch. Their hands, stuck into pockets or enveloped in gloves, began to sweat. They took their hands out of their pockets, felt the sun moving across their skin, felt the spring breeze sliding flirtatiously between their fingers. And at the same time, the slate-gray willows along the river grew tender with green shoots. All of these changes occurred within a week, and on the streets, bicycle bells sparkled as brightly as sunlight, and the sound of footsteps and conversation rose and fell and murmured like waves.

It was around that same time that the man came to town. His hair tumbled from his head like a waterfall and dangled about his waist. His beard cascaded down to his chest, obscuring most of his face. His eyes were swollen and cloudy. That was how he limped into town. His pants were tattered, and from the knees down, all that remained were some dangling strips of torn cloth. His upper body was naked save for a piece of burlap thrown over his shoulders. His unshod feet were crisscrossed with deep, callused cracks. The cracks were filled with black grit, and the feet were unusually large, so that each footstep rang out like a hand clap against the pavement.

He walked into spring along with the residents of the town. And though they saw him, they paid him little heed, for as soon as he had been noted his image had already been cast aside and forgotten. They were walking wholeheartedly into spring, walking happily through the streets.

The girls stuffed their pretty handbags with makeup and romance novels by Qiong Yao. In the quiet hour before dusk, they sat in front of their mirrors making themselves up for an evening out. And only when they had succeeded in making themselves as pretty as could be did they leave the house in search of the hero of the novel, enveloped in the aroma of their own perfume.

The boy's pockets were full of Marlboros and Good Friends cigarettes. They went out into the streets before it got dark and stayed out late. They too were fond of Qiong Yao's novels. They moved through the streets in search of someone who would remind them of a Qiong Yao heroine.

The girls who hadn't stayed home and the boys who weren't wandering the streets had surged into the movie house, crowded into the worker's club, poured into the night school classrooms. Of those who spent their evening behind a school desk, most came in search not of knowledge but of love, for their eyes were more frequently directed toward the opposite sex than the blackboard.

The old men were still sitting at the teahouse. They had sat there for the whole day, for the last ten years, for the last few decades. And still they kept on sitting. Their time for evening strolls had come and gone, and they were in their own way as content as they had been in the days when they too had promenaded through town.

The old ladies sat at home in front of their color television sets. It mattered very little whether they followed the thread of the drama. To sit in comfort and watch as the various characters floated on and off the screen was happiness enough.

Look behind the open windows. Walk along the main streets until you get to the narrow residential lanes lined by courtyard homes. What will you see? What will you hear? What will you be reminded of when you get there?

The disastrous years of the Cultural Revolution have faded into the mists of time. The political slogans pasted again and again on the walls have all been painted over, obscured from the view of pedestrians strolling through the spring night, invisible to those for whom only the present can be seen. Crowds surge excitedly down the streets. Bicycle bells sound out across the avenues. Cars leave clouds of dust in their wake. A minivan with loudspeakers mounted on its roof drives slowly by, broadcasting information about family planning and contraception. Another minivan moves slowly through the streets warning of the suffering inflicted on the people by traffic accidents. The sidewalks are festooned with billboards. The residents of the town are attracted by the words and the pictures on the signs. They know full well the perils posed by overpopulation. Many among them have mastered the use of several types of contraceptive devices. Now they understand the dangers posed by traffic accidents. They know that even though overpopulation is perilous, the living must do their best to have a good time and avoid being killed in a traffic accident. They note appreciatively that students from the middle school have volunteered to spend their Sunday directing the traffic that pours across the bridge.

It was just around then that the man limped into town.

He saw a person lying somewhere around his feet. The man's foot somehow seemed connected to his own. He tried to kick it away, but the foot recoiled almost before he had even lifted his leg to strike. When he put his foot down, the other foot shifted back to its original position next to his own. Excited, he stealthily lifted his own foot once more, discovering at the same time that the foot on the ground had once again evaded his own. Sensing his opponent's vigilance, he held his foot motionless in the air until he saw that his opponent's foot was also poised motionless in the air. Then he pounced, landing full force on his opponent's torso. He heard a solid thump, but when he looked down, the prone figure below him seemed unhurt, and his foot was still linked to his own. He closed his eyes and began to sprint angrily forward, stomping as hard as he possibly could on the ground. After a moment, he opened his eyes and looked down. The man was still lying on the ground in front of him. He began to feel dejected, to gaze helplessly around. The sun shone on his back, and the coarse burlap bag draped over his shoulders shimmered in the sunlight. He saw a blob of something deep and green somewhere ahead and to the right. A thoughtful smile played sluggishly across his face. He began to creep toward the deep green blob, discovering at the same time that his opponent had shifted into a crouch underfoot. He would have to move even more carefully now. Instead of fleeing, the man was sliding his body along the ground, sliding toward a little pond. And by the time he himself had reached the pond's edge, the man's head slid into the water, followed by his arms, his legs, and finally his whole body. He stood at the edge of the pool watching him float on the surface of the water. He bent to pick up some rocks and began to pelt him, turning away in satisfaction only after the man had shattered into what seemed like a thousand different pieces. Suddenly, he felt a burst of hot sunlight pierce his eyes. His head began to spin. But rather than close his eyes, he looked up through the hot glare and saw a head, streaming with blood, suspended somewhere in the distance above him.

Head held aloft, he began to chase it, but it hid behind a cloud. The cloud began to shimmer like a smoldering cotton ball.

When he looked down, something huge stood in the way of his field of vision. He couldn't see across the fields. He had come to a town.

The thing that had so suddenly blocked his way was like a tomb. He seemed to see drops of sunlight cascade through the air and splatter across its surface. But after a moment, he discovered that the thing in his way wasn't just one thing but a cluster of things divided by countless cracks and sawtooth fissures. The sunlight drifted down between the fissures as silently as dust.

He lost interest in the chase and began to walk down a road enveloped in pallid shadow by the wutong trees lining its flanks, whose densely interlocking branches blocked the intense sunlight overhead. He walked suddenly out of the bright daylight and into what seemed like a dark, gloomy cavern. The road unfolded ahead of him like a carpet of whitened bones. Every few paces, human heads hung suspended from poles on either side of the road. Drained of blood, they too had grown pallid and white. When he began to examine them closely, though, he found that they also looked something like street lamps. He sensed that these heads would begin to churn with gleaming blood at nightfall.

Pedestrians, each as drained and pallid as the heads on the poles, walked by. They all walked in the same monotonous way. He heard a strange noise. Two people approached each other and came to a halt just in front of him. He stopped too. The sound seemed to surround him. But a man with only one leg was limping down the road ahead of him. Compared with the other passersby, there was something terribly interesting, something very vivid, about the way this crippled man moved. He decided to abandon the two people he had seen a moment before and follow the cripple.

Soon, his surroundings grew perceptibly warmer. He was engulfed in a curtain of gold, and the dark gray figures he had seen pass by him on the road just moments before began to gleam. Insensibly, he glanced up once more at the dazzling head. Now he realized that the things in his way were in fact buildings. He recognized them because they were covered with open doors and windows. People filed in and out of the doors. Some of them receded, and some of them approached. He smelled something warm floating from the open window of a butcher's shop. He walked through the warmth, sucking at the air.

He walked to the river. The water was green and yellow in the sun. He saw a thick band of liquid ooze by. Boats bobbed on its surface like corpses. He noticed the willow trees on the banks of the river. Clumps of hair dangled over the water. The hair must have been smothered with fertilizer so that it could grow so unnaturally long and thick. He moved over toward it and held a strand next to a lock of his own hair. Dissatisfied with this initial examination, he tore off a strand from the tree and laid it out on the bank. Then he plucked a strand of his own hair, pulled it straight, and laid it parallel to the willow branch. Once again, he carefully compared the two. What he saw made him feel terribly dejected. He left the willows and walked toward the avenue.

He saw braids swinging in the distance. He saw two red butterflies towing the braids through the air. His chest felt tight and strange, and he moved insensibly toward them.

The fabric shop was thronged with people. Spring had awakened their thirst for color. Chatter, as bright and varied as the bolts of silk on the shelves, echoed across the shop floor. Most of the customers were young women, women whose thirst for color was also a thirst for love. Their mothers surged into the store along with them, seeing in the colorful fabrics the youth of their daughters and memories of their own. Here, mothers and daughters could enjoy themselves on an equal footing.

With a friend at her left side, she walked happily out of the store. Her braids swayed as she walked. She usually didn't wear her hair in braids. She usually let it flow loosely down her back. But the night before, she had stumbled on a beautiful old photograph of her mother. Her mother had looked particularly pretty in braids, and she had decided to try them out on herself. At her first glance in the mirror, she was surprised by just how much the braids had changed her. And when she fastened two red butterfly bows onto her new braids, she was nearly overwhelmed by the transformation. Now, as she delightedly walked out of the store, half of her joy came from the colorful bolts of fabric and the rest from the sheer pleasure of the braids dangling behind her. She pictured to herself the way the red bows would swing back and forth like real butterflies fluttering through the air.

But a madman came walking toward her. She was startled and frightened. And when she saw that he was leering at her, that strings of saliva were dangling from his lips, she gasped and began to run. Her friend shouted and ran after her. They ran for a long time and didn't stop until they had turned the corner onto another street. Finally, they stopped, looked at one another, and burst into laughter. They laughed so hard and so long that they began to rock back and forth with merriment.

Her friend giggled, "I guess even the crazies come out when it gets warm."

She nodded. They clasped hands, said good-bye, and went their separate ways home.

Her street was just ahead, across twenty paces of pavement awash in sunlight and noise. There was a dilapidated clock shop at the corner. The clocks inside the window glittered. An old bespectacled man had sat in the shop for as long as she could remember. She glanced at him as she turned down the sunny little lane toward her house. After another twenty paces, she could see the glass panes of her building sparkling in the sun. The closer she got to her front door, the heavier her steps became.

Her mother, face drained of color, was sitting inside on a chair. She had been that way for three days now, scared of her own shadow, cowering just inside the door. She hadn't gone to work since it had started.

She asked her mother, "Did you hear the footsteps again last night?"

Her mother ignored her. When she finally looked up, her eyes were full of terror.

"No. I hear them right now," she said.

She stood behind her mother for a moment, confused and annoyed, and then walked over to the window. From the window, she could look out on the avenue and see the happiness she'd left behind just a moment before. But all she saw was the back of a man with hair down to his waist and a piece of burlap slung over his shoulders slowly limping down the avenue. She shivered insensibly, felt a wave of nausea, and turned back to face the room. Footsteps began to sound out in the stairwell, footsteps that resounded with all the familiarity of more than ten years of routine intimacy. Her father was back from work. She ran excitedly to open the door for him. The sound became steadily more distinct as she watched the top of her father's gray head move up the stairwell. She greeted him with a happy cry. Her father smiled and lightly patted her head with his fingers. They walked into the house together.

She felt how gently his fingers touched her hair and thought to herself that this was the only father she had. She remembered when she was seven a strange man had come to the house and given her a rubber ball. Her mother had said, "This is your father." He had lived with them from that time on. He was always gentle, always nice, always made her feel good. But, a few days before, her mother had told her, "I hear the sound of your father's footsteps walking toward the house after dark." She was confused, and when her mother explained that she was talking about some other father, she felt frightened. This other father was a stranger. She hated him. She wouldn't let him into her heart because she knew he would take away the only father she had ever had.

She heard her father's footsteps grow heavier as he walked through the door into the house. Her mother looked up at him with frightened eyes. She discovered that her mother's face had grown even paler than before.

2

Dusk was falling, and the sky was dim. A sanitation worker wearing a surgical mask was sweeping a pile of garbage by the sidewalk. The broom hissed over the concrete, stirring up heavy plumes of dust from the pavement to drift in the dim light. There were only a few pedestrians on the street, but cooking steam and the distant sound of chatter had begun to pour from the lit windows of the residential buildings. Watery light streamed from the shop windows onto the street, and the languid shadows of listless shop clerks threw themselves onto the sidewalks. The sanitation worker took a book of matches from his pocket and ignited the trash pile.

He saw a pile of blood begin to burn, illuminating the darkness that surrounded it. He moved toward the burning blood, watching as the crackling mass sent little sprays of blood flying at his face. The drops of blood stung his face like sparks. He realized that he was clasping an iron rod in his hand, so he stuck it into the pile and just as quickly pulled it back. It had taken just a second for the rod to begin to glow red with the heat, so hot that even his hand felt singed. And now those people were stealing toward him, so he began to twirl the rod, to trace glowing red arcs through the air. They continued to advance. They did not run away. They were too scared to run away. He stopped twirling and began to jab at them with the rod. He heard a long and boundless sizzle and saw tendrils of white smoke curl up into the air. He sank the rod into the dark ink, lifted it, and smeared the ink over the wounds he had just inflicted. Seared red welts turned a lush black. They warily stole past him. Elated, the madman bellowed, "塞!"

They had seen the madman as they walked by. They had seen the madman stick his hand into the flames and then rapidly draw it back out because of the heat. They had seen how the madman twirled his arm through the air, how he had pointed and gestured at them. And they had seen him bend down and bury his fingers in a puddle on the sidewalk before drawing it back out of the water and pointing again. Finally, they had heard his incomprehensible shout.

They saw everything. They heard it all. But they were too busy to pay the madman much attention as they walked past.

It often happens that, once everything quiets down after dusk, the movie theater is the first place to begin to liven up after dinner. The little square in front of the movie theater had already been divided up by countless feet into countless little squares, and even more feet were cutting across the pavement as they made their way toward the theater. The show had yet to begin, and those with tickets in their pockets stood smoking cigarettes and chatting with those that didn't. Those that didn't have tickets had banknotes in their hands, which they waved at the people who had just arrived in front of the theater. A sign reading "sold out" hung from the closed ticket window, but even so, a mob had gathered in front of the window just in case it were to open suddenly and a few leftover tickets appear. Shirt buttons, popped from their mooring by the crush, fell to the ground under their feet as they squeezed toward the window. A few people took tickets from their pockets and began to stream into the theater, taking care to say hello to those without tickets as they went by. Fissures began to appear in the crowd. The fissures grew until the only people left were people waving banknotes in their hands and stubbornly refusing to leave despite the fact that the movie had already begun.

He felt the knife twirling in his hands, severing the air around him into fragments. After a spell of twirling, he directed the blade toward their noses. He saw each nose fly up from the knife blade and hover in space. Spurts of blood spouted from the holes where the nostrils had been; flurries of severed noses danced through the air before falling one after another to the ground. Soon, the street was engulfed by the noisy clamor of noses leaping and rolling across the pavement. "剡!" he cried forcefully, limping away.

Just at that moment, someone with a handful of tickets was discovered by the crowd. They swarmed into a circle around him. The sound of the besieged man's shouts retreated farther and farther behind the madman.

Pop music pounded through the café and flowed out through the open door into the street. A few young men followed the song out the door, humming through the Marlboros dangling from their lips. They came to the café every day to drink a cup of Nescafe before strolling through town until well past midnight, talking loudly among themselves, and, every so often, breaking into raucous song. They hoped that everyone on the street would notice them.

Just as they walked out of the café, they caught sight of the madman, who was waving his hands through the air and screaming, "剕!" as he advanced toward them. They burst into laughter, fell in behind the madman, and began to follow him. They pretended to limp like the madman, twirled their hands through the air like him, screamed like him. Whenever a few passersby slowed to look at the spectacle, they screamed even louder. But, after a while, exhausted by their pursuit of the madman, they stopped screaming, lit a fresh round of cigarettes, and let him continue on his way.

The chopping knife sliced toward their legs snapping them off below the knees like cucumbers. Everyone on the street seemed suddenly to have shrunk by at least a foot. Their knees slammed down on the sidewalk with heavy, rhythmic thuds. He saw their knees trample over the severed feet that lay strewn across the ground, pounding them into pieces.

The streets became lush with light. Moonlight splattered across the ground, merging with the lamplight streaming out of the shop windows. Dense patterns of light and shadow blanketed the pavement, like the underside of a leafy wu-tong tree at noon. Countless feet moved across the shadowy filigree, breaking the patterns of light into fragments that came together again only after they had passed. The moist evening breeze carried a cacophony of voices through the air. The windows of the residential buildings were still lit, but now they appeared cold and empty. Only a few people lingered inside, sitting quietly alone or together in pairs. It seemed that the whole town was strolling through the streets, streaming in and out of shops, ambling down the sidewalks.

He realized that everyone around him was naked. The chopping knife flashed toward the lower bodies of each of the men who walked past. All of them had a little tail growing in front. The chopping knife slashed at their tails. Their tails fell to the ground with a ponderous thump, like sandbags. Funny little balls rolled out of the bags after they broke on the pavement. In just a moment's time, they covered the street, careening across the pavement like Ping-Pong balls.

When she walked out of the store, the street made her think of two rivers moving in opposite directions. The few people who swerved into the stores looked like drops of water thrown off to the side by the river's current. In between the streams, she saw the madman. He was limping down the street, twirling his arms, repeatedly bellowing a single word: "官!" But the people moving to either side of him seemed not to have noticed, caught up as they were in the enchantment of the evening. His hoarse screams were buried amid the general clamor of voices as he walked past.

She started to walk slowly home. She walked as slowly as she could. For the past few days, she had taken to going out alone and strolling through the streets. She couldn't bear the silence that had enveloped her home. At home, the sound of a pin hitting the floor was enough to startle.

She reached her front door faster than she would have liked. She stood in front, looking up at the stars. The stars suffused the night sky with glowing light. She looked up at the brightly illuminated windows of the other apartments, heard the soft sound of conversation floating through the night air. She stood for a long time before she began to make her slow and hesitant way up the steps to her own house.

Just as she had pushed open the door, her mother cried out, "Close the door!" Frightened, she quickly shut the door behind her. Her mother, hair in disarray, was sitting by the door.

She stood by her mother for a moment. Her mother said, "I heard him screaming."

She didn't know how to reply, so she simply stood in silence for a moment before walking into the living room. She saw her father sitting blankly by the window. She went to him, calling softly, but he continued to stare out the window, replying only with an absent murmur. It was only when she began to move toward her own room that he turned to her, saying, "From now on, I don't want you to go out unless you really have to." Then he turned back toward the window.

She muttered something in reply, walked into her room,

and sat down on the bed. The house was silent. She gazed at the window. A few strands of moonlight shimmered across the glass like raindrops. In the distance, the moon looked red. She heard the sound of teardrops falling on her shirt.

3

Flying sparks and the sharp sound of metal hammering metal cascaded through the blacksmith's shop. The smelting furnace cast a reddish glow on the bared torsos of the blacksmith and his assistant. Gleaming beads of sweat snaked down their backs like earthworms.

The madman stood at the door. His sudden appearance brought their hammers to a halt, and a piece of red-hot iron lay on the ground where the startled blacksmith had dropped it from his tongs. The madman walked into the shop, his mouth twisted into a strange smile. He knelt down by the smoking piece of iron, which had already begun to blacken and cool. The madman reached for the iron, and a hiss resounded through the shop. He immediately withdrew his hand and began to suck on his fingers. After a moment, he reached for the ingot again. He lifted it and held it against his face. A few tendrils of acrid white smoke began to disperse through the room. The blacksmiths stood, immobilized by fright and by the extraordinary stench that had filled the workshop. They heard him yell, "暑!" as he limped contentedly out of the workshop, down the lane, and to the street corner, where he paused for a moment before turning to his right. A truck drove by, burying him in a torrent of dust. He walked down the middle of the road and sat down. A few people followed him and began to stare. They were quickly joined by a few more curious passersby.

Her mother hadn't gone to work for almost a month. For the past few days, she had sat, silent and immobile, in the front hall. And since her mother cried out in fright whenever she walked in through the door, her father told her not to leave the house at all. She spent every day in her room. Her father still had to go to work, so he left the house early and came home late. He no longer came home at lunch time. She sat alone, wishing that her friends would come to visit. But when they finally did come and knock on the door, she had not dared let them in. Her mother had been so frightened by the sound that her whole body trembled. She didn't want her friends to see her mother like that. She could not help but cry as she listened to their footsteps retreating back down the hall.

Now her mother was afraid even of daylight. Her father had closed all the curtains so that the whole apartment was bathed in darkness. Sitting in her dimly lit room, she felt herself growing distant from the sunlight outside, from the spring, from her youth.

In years past, she had walked through the spring sunshine with her mother and father at her side. And whenever they walked together, arm in arm, they would invariably stop and chat with a few friends of the family. "You still haven't married her off?" they would begin. And her father, with mock seriousness, would reply, "I'm not giving my daughter away to anybody." Her mother, beaming, would add, "How could we give her away? She's the only one we've got."

Many years ago her father had given her a rubber ball, and they had been happy ever since. They had always laughed and smiled when they were together. Father knew how to tell a joke, and mother learned how to be funny from him. She was the only one who had never got the hang of it. She could hardly count the times when their laughter as they walked down the stairs had made the neighbors exclaim, "What is it with you people? Are you always so goddamned happy?" Father would always proudly reply, "I guess that goes without saying," and mother would add with a generous flourish, "We're saving some for you, too." She always wanted to contribute something to the ritual, but she could never think of anything interesting, so she simply stood quietly by their side.

But now the house was dark and silent, even when the three of them were together. There had been a few times when she felt she just had to say something to her father, but the sight of him sitting blankly in the living room forced her back into her room. She shut the door behind her, went to the window, stealthily lifted a corner of the blind, and gazed outside. She watched people move back and forth across the street, watched them stand on the corner and chat endlessly about whatever was on their minds. Whenever she saw any of their acquaintances pass by, she couldn't help but cry.

She had spent several days at the window by now. When she lifted up the blind, she felt as if she were walking once more down those sunlit streets.

She was standing at the window watching the pedestrians through the glass. She discovered that they were moving like ants, swarming across the pavement, clustering around a single black spot. The circle around the spot was growing steadily thicker.

He sat cross-legged on the streeet, hair cascading onto the asphalt like willow branches. The sun had shone on the road for more than a month, slathering it with a layer of golden light, warming the hearts of the passersby. He stretched out his slender arms in front of him. They looked like they were coated with antique black lacquer that had begun to chip and fade. He held a rusty saw, its blade no more than three inches long, in both hands and began to examine it.

She saw a few children shimmy up the trunks of the wutong trees that lined the avenue. A few people stood balanced atop their bikes. She wondered if someone was showing off his shadowboxing to promote herbal tonics.

But if that was the case, why would he stand in the middle of the road rather than on the sidewalk? The circle kept expanding until the entire street was choked by onlookers. A traffic policeman rushed forward to clear the street. But as soon as he hurried to the other side of the circle, those he had shooed away merely rejoined the throng. She watched as the traffic policeman, realizing the futility of this repetitious task, took up position on a spot that had not yet been entirely blocked by the crowd and started to wave newcomers around the sides of the circle. The black spot quickly swelled into an oval.

He shouted, "剌!" as he carefully placed the teeth of the saw against the bottom of his nose. His grimy black lips trembled, almost as if he were smiling. His arms began to rock back and forth, and with each spasmodic motion he shouted "剌" as loudly as he possibly could. The blade worked its way into his flesh, and blood began to seep out from under the skin. His dark lips turned red and shiny as the blood dribbled down from his nose. Within a few seconds, the blade hit cartilage with a soft scraping sound. His shouts died down, and he rocked his head back and forth, emitting low rasps. He looked as if he were happily blowing on a harmonica as the saw ate into his cartilage. But after another few seconds, he began to scream. The numbness of shock had passed, and severe pain had come in its wake. His face began to twist with the pain. He continued to work the saw back and forth, but the pain had become unbearable, and he quickly pulled the saw away from his nose and set it down on his knees. He threw his head back and gasped for air. The blood was flowing freely now, quickly staining his mouth and his chin red. Little streams trickled down from his face, tracing a tangle of intersecting lines across his chest. A few drops landed on his head, slid down strands of hair, and splashed on the pavement like little red sparks. He panted for another few moments before lifting the saw once again to the sun and carefully examining the blade. He extended a long and blood-stained fingernail to the blade and began to pick little bits of cartilage out of the teeth. Saturated in blood, they shimmered red in the sunlight. He went about cleaning the blade with extreme care, moving slowly, methodically, and clumsily. When he was finished, he once again lifted the blade to eye level. Satisfied, he pulled his nose away from his face with one hand while positioning the saw blade under it with the other. But, instead of setting the saw in motion, he merely shouted for a moment and placed the saw back on his knees. Holding his nose between his fingers, he twisted it from side to side until it dangled loose from his face.

She saw that the oval was gradually dissolving as more and more people streamed away from the center to the edges. It began to look like someone had accidentally dropped a bottle of ink on the ground. In the center, there was a solid black mass, surrounded on all four sides by splattered drops of ink. The children slid down the tree trunks like cats. There were fewer and fewer bicycles. The street was beginning to clear, and instead of standing nervously to one side, the traffic policeman was once again moving around the perimeter of the crowd.

He held the saw up to the light for a long time before putting it down. He sat for a few minutes with his hands resting on his knees, as if in repose. Then he began to pick the grime out of the cracks in his feet with the tip of the saw. As soon as he had finished, he proceeded to stuff the grime back in. He slowly and lovingly repeated this process several times. Finally, he set the sawblade on his right knee, looked up around him, let out a great shout, "制!," and started to saw. The skin broke under the teeth, white at first, but gradually growing lustrously red as the blood began to flow from the wound. With a few more strokes, the sawblade hit bone. He stopped sawing and grinned. Then his hands rocked neatly back and forth until a soft scraping once again issued from the saw. Within a few seconds, though, his face twisted into another scream. Beads of sweat rolled from his forehead. He gasped for air. The rocking slowed, and his scream faded to an almost imperceptible low wail. His arms fell limply to his sides. The saw chimed on the pavement. His neck tumbled against his chest. He sat, softly wailing. A moment later, he looked up, grasped hold of the fallen saw, and once again placed it atop his knee, but remained motionless for another moment. Suddenly, as if he had come to a great realization, his lips shuddered into a kind of smile. He removed the saw to his other knee, bellowed "刑" a second time, and began to rock. Seconds later, the blade had cut through his skin and penetrated to the bone. His shouts came to an abrupt halt. He looked up, laughed for a long time, gazed at his leg, and finally produced a throaty rasp. Still rasping, his arms began to rock back and forth. His head bobbed back and forth and, with it, his body. His rasp and the rhythmic sandpapery scrape of the saw sounded together like a pair of cloth sandals swishing through a weedy thicket. A strangely appealing smile lit up the madman's features. Seen from behind, he might have been polishing a pair of nice leather shoes. Suddenly, the saw blade snapped in two with a sharp metallic chime. The broken pieces of the blade fell to the pavement. His body flopped back and forward as if it had lost its balance. The pain came in waves, and with each wave, his body shivered like a leaf in the wind. He waited a few minutes for the shivers to subside. Then he picked up the two halves of the broken blade, held them up to the light, and appraised each one in turn, as if he were trying to ascertain which was the longer of the two. This process was repeated, one blade after the other, again and again, until he had finally cast one half of the blade to the side. He continued to saw at his right leg with the one that remained. But as soon as he had managed to make a gentle sawing motion across the bone, he screamed once more in pain. Picking up the piece that he had discarded, he once again compared the blades in the light. He dropped the second half back to the ground and tried the other one. But after only a few strokes, he began once again to compare one blade with the other.

She saw that there were fewer and fewer people clustered together, as if the drops of ink were shooting away, one by one, from the black mass in the center of the spill. The crowd had trickled away until all that remained was a narrow ring. Traffic was moving freely, and the traffic policeman had long since gone on his way.

He compared the two blades for a long time. Finally, he tossed them both aside, inspected each of his legs, and returned to his original cross-legged position. He examined his knees. Then he squinted up at the sun. His blood-red lips began to quiver. He stretched his legs in front of him, fumbled at his waist, and slowly pulled down his pants. When he saw his tail, his lips curled into a sluggish grin. He appraised it the same way he had examined the broken sawblade. He grasped hold of it with his hand and jerked it up and down. His head began to rock back and forth. He reached behind his back and fumbled for a rock. He splayed his legs out in front of him and lifted the rock above his head. He glared up at the rock for a moment, finally nodding his head with evident satisfaction. Bellowing "害!" at the top of his lungs, he pounded the rock against the tail as hard as he possibly could. Then he began to roar.

Within a few seconds, the circle disintegrated. She watched as the spectators scattered like a flock of magpies frightened into sudden flight. In the distance, she could see something bloody sitting on the pavement.

4

Just before dawn, she was startled awake by her mother's scream. She heard her mother putting on her clothes as her father murmured something soft and indistinct. Her father would be telling her to stay in bed. She heard the bedroom door open. She heard her mother take up her customary position by the door. The chair emitted a few low, hollow squeaks. She imagined watching her mother sit down in the chair. She heard her father's heavy, helpless sigh. She could no longer sleep. The moon glimmered weakly through her window curtains. She lay under her quilt listening to her father get out of bed. As her father paced across the floorboards, she felt tiny tremors shaking her bed. Her father slumped back down on the bed, which squealed under his weight like a crying baby. After that the house was so quiet that she could hear herself breathing.

The window curtains changed from pale silver to red. The sun was rising. She climbed out of bed, pulled on her clothes. She heard her father get up from bed, walk to the kitchen. The sounds he made were barely perceptible. He had grown accustomed to the silence. She too had taken to moving silently through the house. As she dressed, she watched the color of the curtains brighten until fiery shafts of light filtered through the cloth and onto her bed.

By the time she appeared in the living room, her father was just leaving the kitchen. Mother sat motionlessly in her chair. She couldn't repress a wave of sadness when she saw her tangled, unkempt hair. She hadn't really looked at her mother for a long time. And now she had discovered that her mother had grown suddenly and unrecognizably old. Unthinkingly, she reached out her hand to touch her shoulder. Her mother started, looked up at her with terrified eyes, and said, "I saw him last night. He was standing next to the bed. He was covered with blood." She too began to shiver as she remembered what she had seen the day before outside her window.

Father walked over and gently squeezed her mother's shoulders. Mother stood up and slowly walked toward the table. They sat and ate a little in silence.

It was time for Father to go to work. He moved toward

the front door, and she returned to her bedroom. Her father hesitated by the door, turned, and followed her back inside. She had just begun to lift the curtain to look outside when she heard him whisper, "Why don't you come out and take a walk?" She turned, looked at her father, and then followed him out the front door.

But when they had descended the stairs into the light and he asked her if she was going to go see any of her friends, she could only shake her head in response. She felt lost outside the dim apartment. She felt like going back inside. She had grown accustomed to seeing the world through a square of glass that looked out on the street. But she followed her father out of the lane and into the street, stopping at the corner for fear that someone would come to visit. They would come up the stairs and pound on the door. Her mother would be so scared. She decided to stand guard at the intersection. Her father turned right. It was rush hour and swarms of bicycles moved down the street to the accompaniment of chiming bells. She watched her father disappear unexpectedly into a shop down the block. When he emerged, he walked back and stuffed a handful of candy into her hand. She watched until her father had disappeared once more and then looked down at the candy. She put one piece in her mouth and stuffed the rest into her pocket. She heard herself chewing, but no taste came. She watched a young man maneuver his bicycle at breakneck pace down the street until he was swallowed up by the swarming rush-hour traffic.

A friend from school sauntered up, saying, "Where have you been?"

She stared blankly back, then shook her head.

"Then why don't you ever answer the door? Why are the curtains always closed?"

She rubbed her hands together.

"What's wrong with you?"

"Nothing," she said, her eyes searching the street for the bicyclist.

"You look pale."

"I do?" She looked at her friend.

"Are you sick?"

"No."

"You don't seem very happy."

"I'm fine." She braced herself, forced a smile. "What are you doing today?"

"The commodity fair. Today's the first day." Her friend took hold of her arm. "Let's go."

Her friend's footsteps rang out excitedly beside her. She thought to herself, "Forget about all of that."

The spring commodity fair was on another street. The fair made people forget about everything else, let them live in the excitement of the moment. Winter was over. Spring had already arrived. They needed to change their lifestyle. They crowded together to browse, crowded together to explore. As they strolled between the makeshift stands that had been erected on either side of the street, they picked out new clothes, chose which household items to purchase, selected the kind of life that was to come. A megaphone hung from the roof of each of the concession stands, and each megaphone was blaring music and pitching products at ear-splitting volume. They were buffeted by a chaos of sound at every step. Despite the deafening noise, the dizziness, and the fatigue, they squeezed and pushed their way through the fair, shouting excitedly to each other as they went along. What with having to shout to be heard, the crowd itself was even noisier and more chaotic than the megaphones. Suddenly, one of the megaphones began to blare out a solemn piece of funerary music, thereby winning the battle for their attention. The crowd, laughing and elated, began to stream toward the stand, for rather than taking the music as an ugly prank, they found it amusing. And together they surged into the humor of the moment.

They had already given up trying to control where they went. There were so many people pushing behind them that the only option left was to keep moving forward. There was no retreat. She clasped her friend's shopping bags in her arms. Her friend bought enough for both of them to carry, but her eyes continued to shuttle hungrily between the various concession stands. She herself hadn't bought a thing. She had merely squeezed through the crowds, gazing all the while at the products on display. That was enough. Buried in the happiness of the crowds and the noise, she could forget all the things she had decided to forget. It was as if she were experiencing once again the way her family used to be. Hadn't her family been something like the fair?

They were driven forward until they were pushed beyond the perimeter of the crowd. The force at their backs suddenly disappeared. She stood there like a boat washed ashore by strong waves. The waves quickly receded, leaving her stranded. She gazed blankly back at the crowds, feeling hollow.

She heard her friend say, "I loved that skirt. Too bad it's too crowded to get back to it."

She too had seen the skirt, but she hadn't liked it as much as her friend had. She hadn't really liked any of the clothes on display. She very much wanted to squeeze back into the crowds, but not for the skirt.

"Let's try to squeeze back through," she said.

Instead of replying, her companion nudged her with her hand. She looked over to where her companion had pointed to see the madman.

He was standing a few feet away, spattered with dry blood, his hands twirling through the air. He was screaming something at the top of his lungs. He seemed just as happy and excited as everyone else who had come to the fair.

The boundless crowds of people swarmed toward him, and with a flash of his knife, their heads flew into the sky. Thousands of skulls collided in the air with an incomparably thunderous crash. The crash began to crack into smaller shards of sound until the shards came together once again in a bone-crunching sonic wave. The shattered skulls swirled through the air like broken tiles and began to fall. Blood rained down like sunlight. And at that very moment, a shining hacksaw materialized in his hands. It was soaring through their waists. Headless torsos stumbled across the ground, rolling fat brush strokes of blood across the pavement. The disembodied legs began to walk like automatons along the twisting and intersecting paths they made on the pavement. Every so often, two pairs of legs would collide and tumble helplessly to the ground. A steaming cauldron of hot oil appeared. Those bodies that were still untouched rained into the cauldron. The oil began to sizzle. One after another, bodies popped out of the liquid like flying fish and fell to the side. The sky now emptied of heads, which fell to the ground, carpeting the pavement and burying severed torsos and legs beneath them. And bodies continued to fry and pop from the cauldron. He reached toward the people who continued to walk toward him and started to peel off their skin. It was like peeling posters off a wall, producing a marvelous tearing sound, as if he were shearing through bolts of silk. After they had been peeled, the subcutaneous fat began to bulge and dribble away from the muscle below. He stuck his hand through the muscle and began to pluck out the ribs. Their bodies slumped. Then he pulled at the chest muscles until he could see the lungs still heaving for air. He carefully tore open the left lung to watch as the heart continued to expand and contract with each beat. Two braids swung somewhere in the distance. Two lovely red butterflies towed the braids through the air.

She saw the madman staring at her once more, saliva dripping unceasingly from the corner of his mouth. She heard her friend cry out in surprise. She felt her friend grab hold of her wrist, and her legs began to pump up and down. She knew her friend was running beside her, pulling her away.

5

The spring snow had long since been forgotten. Peach flowers were slowly beginning to bloom. The willows by the river and the wutong trees on the sidewalk were a deep green. And the sun, of course, was sparkling even more brightly than before. Although spring had yet to run its course, they had begun to carry out all the familiar rituals with which they welcomed the arrival of summer. The girls embroidered their dreams with skirts from the fair, imagined the way the silky fabric would flutter around their legs as they walked the summer streets. The boys fumbled through their closets looking for swimsuits and, having found them beneath piles of summer clothes, imagined the way the water would sparkle in the summer sun. They kept the swimsuits on their dressers for a few days. Finally, they tossed them back into the closet. Summer, after all, was still a long way off.

The madman was sitting cross-legged on the street. The sun was splattering across the pavement, and a breeze blew overhead. Dust rose through the air and drifted away like a fine mist. The asphalt was sticky with sunlight. People streamed down the sidewalk, dragging their slanted shadows behind them. Their shadows, in turn, glided happily over the pavement, oblivious to the heat. A few of the shadows slipped under the madman's buttocks. He was single-mindedly assessing the blade of a kitchen cleaver.

The cleaver had been picked out of a trash heap, and its blade was rusty and pitted with holes.

He turned the knife over and over in his hands until a sluggish grin of contentment lit his face and saliva dribbled down his chin. The wound on his face had begun to ooze, his face was swollen, and his nose was hugely distended. Pus dribbled down with his saliva. An extraordinarily strange odor streamed from his body, relentlessly filling the air around him. Pedestrians, smelling this strange stench, felt as though they were moving through a dark place as they navigated past the madman, a place from which they escaped as soon as they moved past him and into the distance.

He set the cleaver on the ground and carefully examined it. He flipped the cleaver over and methodically appraised the other side before flipping it back to its original position. He stretched out his legs in front of him and gnawed at his lips, his face contorting into a series of grimaces. After a few moments had gone by, he extended his long fingernails toward the sun, as if he were trying to disinfect them. He reached down and began – extremely carefully, extremely methodically – to peel off the dried blood that coated his legs like a thin layer of cellophane. He pulled the week-old film away from his skin, bit by bit. As soon as he had peeled one piece, he placed it carefully to his side and patiently set to work on the next patch. When he had finished, he once again began to inspect his legs. Having determined that the blood had all been removed, he raised a handful of the dark red film to eye level. He looked through it at the sun. He saw a dark red square of blood. After he gazed at the reddish square for a moment, he moved the little pile to one side. Then he began to pick up the pieces one by one and gaze excitedly through them at the sun. Another few moments of rapturous examination passed before he collected all the pieces together into another pile and sat on it.

He picked up the cleaver and lifted it to eye level. He saw a black rectangle surrounded by light. He held the cleaver over his lap, testing the blade with his fingers. He brandished the cleaver in the air above his thigh and screamed, "凌遲!" The cleaver pierced his thigh, and he cried out in pain. He looked down to watch the blood begin to seep from the wound. He inserted his fingernail into the wound and, discovering that it was shallow, discontentedly lifted the knife to the sun to examine the blade. After having run his finger along the edge, he smeared it with some of the blood that was dribbling from his thigh. Finally, he began to furiously grind the blade against the pavement. The friction produced a sharp squealing sound. His body rocked until sparks began to fly from the asphalt. The blade, hot with friction, fell from his hands. He bent to examine his handiwork, tested the blade with his finger. Dissatisfied, he set to his task with almost maniacal energy, grinding until beads of sweat began to roll down his torso. A moment later, he dropped the cleaver and teetered forward, panting and exhausted. Having caught his breath, he lifted the cleaver, inspected the blade, running his finger slowly along the edge. This time, he was satisfied.

He brandished the cleaver high above his head, shouted, and brought the knife down onto his other thigh. This movement was immediately followed by a single sharp moan. A second later, he broke into wails as his body began to flutter like a leaf in the wind. His hands fell limp to his sides, shuddering uncontrollably. The cleaver, still embedded in his leg, trembled with the motion of his leg. He trembled until the cleaver jumped from the wound and hit the ground with a dull chime. The blood welled from the wound and dripped to the ground like rainwater falling from the eaves of a house. After a long time, he groped for the cleaver by his side. The knife began to tremble. He hesitated, steadied the handle with both hands, and reinserted it into the wound. Wailing, he slowly cut a piece of flesh from his leg. His body shook violently, and the wails grew louder. These were no longer short and sharp exclamations but protracted, almost bestial howls.

The pedestrians were terrified by the sound of his howls. The street was empty, but the sidewalks were packed with onlookers. They listened to his grisly howls through a haze of fear. A few brave souls walked toward the madman to get a closer look, only to return to the sidewalk white with fear. A few people tried to move back from the edge of the sidewalk, and those who had just arrived kept well away from the middle of the street.

The sound of his howls began to grow softer, but, for some reason, this was all the more frightening. They drifted to their ears from afar like ghostly wails, piercing and dark. They stood packed together, but each of the spectators felt themselves alone, hurrying through the dark of night, pursued by the sound of howls implacably ringing out somewhere behind them. They felt as if an enormously heavy weight was bearing down on their hearts. They felt their breath come in slow, grudging heaves.

"Someone should get a rope. Someone has to tie him up." A muffled voice broke out from the crowd. It was only then that the spectators began to talk, but the sound of their voices failed to rise above a suffocated whisper. Everyone agreed. A few young men moved quickly away, returning a moment later with a length of rope in hand. But no one would move any closer, and the man who had made the suggestion was gone. The wails were even softer now, mere gasps whistling weakly across the pavement. They could bear it no longer, but they did not leave. They sensed that if the madman wasn't captured now, his howls would keep ringing in their ears, no matter how hard they tried to escape. They suggested that the traffic policeman take care of the problem. It was his job, after all. But he refused to do it by himself. After several minutes of whispered negotiations, four young men offered to accompany him. They armed themselves with sticks to fend off the madman's cleaver and began to advance.

He had stopped wailing. He was no longer in pain. His body was burning, parched. White foam bubbled from his lips as he continued to hack desultorily at his leg. Although he seemed to be gasping for his life, he approached the task with as much earnestness and care as before. But, within moments, his hands fell limp to his sides. The cleaver clattered to the pavement. He sat dead still for a long time, sighed, and fumbled for the cleaver.

Five men approached, rope in hand. One of them slapped the knife out of his hand with a wooden baton. The others immediately set to winding the rope around his limbs. He didn't struggle. He simply gazed laboriously up at them.

He saw five executioners approach, somehow managing to walk across the heaps of severed heads, scraps of flesh, scattered bones, and blood underfoot as if they were on level ground. Behind them, he saw a blood-soaked mob. They had hacked off chunks of their own flesh until their bones lay exposed to the open air. They surged forward, following the lead of the executioners. Each of the five executioners was leading a horse-drawn cart with a rope. The horses' hooves rose and fell without a sound. The wheels of the horse carts rolled noiselessly over the heaps of flesh and bone. As they drew closer and closer, he realized why it was that they had come. He didn't try to escape. He merely gazed quietly in their direction. They were standing just in front of him. The mob of bloody skeletons at their back formed a large circle around him. One of the executioners clasped his neck, while each of the remaining four took hold of one of his limbs. His body rose from the ground, hung suspended in the air. He looked up at the blood-red sky. Pieces of dried blood drifted in front of the sun. He felt a length of coarse rope being fastened around his neck. More rope was wound around his arms and legs. The five carts were arrayed around him, pointing in five different directions. Each of the five executioners climbed atop their carts. His body dangled from the ropes between the carts. He saw each of the five executioners raise their black leather whips above their heads. The whips danced, snake-like, through the air, suspending themselves for a moment in mid-flight before cracking down onto the horses' flanks. Five horse-drawn carts galloped in five different directions. He saw his head, his arms, and his legs separate from his torso. His torso fell with a thud into the heaps already littering the road. His head and limbs hovered behind the carts until the executioners reined in their horses and they fell to the ground. The five executioners, followed by the mob of bloody skeletons, led their horses into the distance. Soon they were all gone. He began to look for his head, for his limbs, for his torso. But he couldn't find them. They were lost among the severed heads, limbs, and torsos that covered the ground.

As twilight deepened, pedestrians were as few and far between as falling leaves. Most of the town was gathered around dinner tables laden with steaming dishes of food. Light streamed out of the apartment windows, brushing past the incandescent rays of the street lamps before merging with the moonlight. The entire town was dappled with slanting skeins of light.

They gathered joyfully around the table to see off the day. There was no reason to hurry, no feeling of being pressed for time. The approach of dusk was delightful. The day was fading behind them, but this was the most marvelous part of the day because it heralded the liberty and leisure of the night to come.

They cheerfully ate and talked. The dinner conversation was relaxed and happy. Everything made them laugh. After a while they started to talk about the crazy things they had seen, the crazy rumors they had heard going around town.

Some of them had seen the madman. Some of them had only heard about him.

They said they couldn't believe he had cut apart his own body with a cleaver. They registered their surprise. Finally, they burst into laughter. They talked about the madman, the one who had sawed through his own nose and sliced his own legs a few days back. They gasped and swore and, having run out of exclamations, were reduced to sighs. Their sighs had more to do with sheer amazement than pity. As they talked, the terror began to fade. It was something unusual. They always discussed anything unusual that had happened around town. And when the first topic got stale, they would always move on to something else. That was what they did at the dinner table. That was how they passed the time until they were done.

They walked over to the window, stepped out on the balcony. They looked at the moon, felt the evening breeze blowing warm and sweet on their faces. They said to one another, "Let's go out for a walk," and strolled out of the house and into the streets. They knew that a walk after dinner was good for your health. The older people didn't feel like taking a walk. They sat by the television and began to watch other people lead different lives that somehow reminded them of their own, while their children had already begun to roam the streets outside.

The parents weren't really sure when the kids had gone out, but they vaguely remembered seeing them around the dinner table.

When the young people began to fill the streets, the night grew thick with lively voices. They streamed under the street lamps, disturbing the tranquillity that had reigned moments before. Although they streamed into the movie theater, into the worker's club, toward friends, and toward love, the streets stayed busy. The crowds still poured in and out of the shops like waves, into one place and out of another. They walked for the sake of walking, hurried into the stores just so they could continue moving. Their parents walked for a few minutes to stretch their legs and went home. But the young people continued to walk deep into the night because they needed to walk, because walking was what made them young.

But evening lasts only so long, and, almost before it had started, the deep of night had arrived. The evening was almost over; they had already said their good-byes. They walked alone toward their respective homes. But they weren't lonely. They had enjoyed the evening to the fullest. There were many more nights to come. They happily made their way home, and the streets once again grew tranquil and still.

The shops were dark, and the windows of the apartment buildings no longer shone. Now there was only the gleam of the street lamps, the light of the moon. They had fallen into slumber. The town went to sleep along with them. But the few remaining hours until dawn would pass quickly, and the morning sun would rise once more.

The madman was still sitting in the middle of the road. The rope was so tight he hadn't moved a muscle since the afternoon. He sat, in a stupor, until the sun was about to rise. The sky to the east shone red. He opened his eyes and saw the red light. He heard the sound of howls echoing in the distance. The howls moved closer, growing louder as they approached, like a pack of wild beasts sprinting toward him. He began to rally, to grow excited. He saw something huge, burning red in the distance. Now he knew where the howls were coming from. He saw countless bodies falling through the flames. He leaped up from the ground and began to run toward the flames.

It seemed that he had just come to from a deep sleep. His chest gradually filled with a strange new feeling. His eyes struggled open. It was dawn. He saw a street, lined by wutong trees, immobile as a stage set.

It seemed that he had been in a kind of stupor for a very long time. Now he was awake. The swirling mists in his head seemed to drift off into the air. And, when they were gone, his mind was an empty room. But, peering through a little window, he began to be able to see something, and at the same time, something new began to come into the room.

But now he had no sensation of himself. He wanted to move, but his body wouldn't move. He tried to shake his head, but his head wouldn't react. At the same time, his mind was getting clearer and clearer. But the clearer his mind became, the less he could feel his body. He had the distinct sensation that he was losing his body, or maybe just trying to find it. He started to wonder if you can lose your body. He was startled to find that it was gone.

He started to remember. There were so many things to remember. They were tangled together in a heap. He struggled to put them in some kind of order. He remembered that he was in his office. Two bright incandescent lamps, the northwest wind whistling over the roof. Dust coated the desktop, but the windows were clean. He remembered walking down the street in thongs, a crowd of people at his back. He remembered them breaking through the door. He was washing his feet; his wife was sitting on the edge of the bed. His daughter was asleep.

Now he was wide awake. He realized that it had happened last night. The morning clouds had begun to rise; the sun was on its way. He was certain it had happened last night. He had left his house last night. He was taken away last night. His wife had watched numbly as they took him away. His daughter had started to cry. Why did his daughter have to cry?

But he knew that he wasn't in the office anymore because, instead of spotless windows and dust-caked desks, he saw a street lined with wutong trees. He didn't understand how he could have gotten here. He desperately tried to straighten his mind, but he still couldn't understand what he was doing here. He decided not to think about it. He felt that he really ought to go home. Maybe his wife and daughter were still asleep. His daughter's head would be cradled in his wife's arm. His wife's head would be resting on his shoulder. But somehow he was here instead. He wanted to go home. He wanted to stand up. But his body wouldn't react. He didn't know where he could have lost his body. He couldn't go home without a body. His heart would break if he didn't go home. Now he seemed to recognize the street. If he walked down the street for a few minutes and turned at the next corner, he would be able to see the windows of his apartment just up ahead. He was certain he was quite close to home. But he didn't have a body, so he couldn't go home.

He seemed to see himself walking across campus carrying an armful of heavy books. He saw his wife, hair in braids, walking in his direction. They didn't know each other yet. They passed by each other without a word. He had glanced back to see a pair of pretty red butterflies. It seemed that the street was covered with snowflakes. He saw people pick the snowflakes off the ground and begin to read them. He saw a dead man slumped against the postbox by the side of the road. The blood was still fresh, still wet. A leaflet drifted through the air and settled on his head, obscuring half of his face.

The sun had risen, and hazy light slid silently down from between the clouds. The street began to stir with life. He watched people come in from the wings, appear on stage, talk with one another, strike poses. He was not among them. Something separated him from them. They were who they were, and he was who he was. He felt himself stand up and move toward the edge of the stage. But he remained in place, and instead of moving toward him, the stage simply retreated further into the distance.

She woke as the sun rose. She heard the sound of bowls clanging in the kitchen. Her father was already making breakfast. And her mother was probably sitting in her usual place by the door with the same look on her face. She didn't know how much longer this could go on or how it might end. She really didn't want to think about it. Instead, she watched as the sparkling morning light began to slide through the curtains. She wanted to open them, to let the sun shine through the clean glass panes onto her bed, onto her body. She climbed out of bed and slowly began to comb her hair by the mirror. The face in the mirror was pale and lifeless. She wondered how she would make it through another day. She walked out into the living room. With a shock, she discovered that the room was suffused with light. The curtains had been thrown open. The sun swarmed through the open windows. Her mother's chair sat empty, one wooden leg bathed in sunlight.

"But where is she?" she thought. Her chest tightened with dread. She ran toward the kitchen. Her father wasn't in the kitchen. Her mother turned and smiled gently toward her. Her hair was neatly combed, and her face, though haggard and pale, had regained its familiar composure. Sensing her shock, her mother explained, "Just after the sun came out I heard him walking away." Her mother's voice sounded so tired, but she couldn't help smiling in relief. Her mother began to busy herself with breakfast, and she gazed for a moment at her back. Suddenly, she remembered something important and turned back toward the living room. Her father was already standing just behind her. Her father's face was as bright as the sun. She realized that her father already knew. Her father patted her gently on the head. His hair was white. She knew why his hair was white.

After breakfast, her mother picked up the shopping basket, asking, "What do you think you'd like to eat?"

She quietly added, "It's been a long time since I cooked you a good meal."

Father looked at her, and she looked at him. Father was at a loss, as was she. Her mother waited for a moment before repeating with a smile, "Come on. What do you want to eat?"

She tried to think of what she might want to eat, but nothing came to mind. She glanced once again toward her father.

He turned towards her. "What do you feel like eating?"

"What do *you* feel like?" she returned.

"I'll have anything"

"I'll have anything too," she said. She thought that seemed like the right thing to say.

"All right then. I'll buy anything."

The three of them chuckled. She said, "I want to come with you." Her mother nodded. The three of them went out together.

They walked arm in arm. Things were back to normal. They stopped to chat with some friends, who began to chat and joke with them just as they always did. She walked joyfully between them.

When they got to the corner, her father turned right on his way to work. She and her mother stood and watched as her father strolled easily and confidently down the block. After a few seconds, her father glanced back, and, discovering that they were still looking his way, he started to swagger down the sidewalk. She and her mother burst into happy laughter.

But as she laughed, something occurred to her. Fearing that he would be too far away to hear, she began to shout his name. He stopped and turned. She shouted again, "Buy me a rubber ball."

Father froze, nodded, and walked away. She began to cry. Mother pretended not to notice. They began to walk forward without a word.

They saw a crowd of people gathered around in a circle. They stood at the edge of the circle to get a glimpse of whatever it was everyone else was looking at. They saw the madman. The madman was bound with rope. The madman was dead. His body, which seemed to have been varnished a deep red, was slumped against a postbox. Two sanitation workers were muttering to themselves as they picked up the body and deposited it on top of a bicycle cart. Another, grumbling under his breath, a pail of water in one hand and a broom in the other, approached the postbox. He upended the pail, carelessly swept the broom across the bloodstains on the sidewalk, and left. The cart slid away from the curb and down the street. The crowd began to break up. Mother and daughter continued on their way. Watching the madman's body being borne away by the cart, she felt a sudden surge of relief. As they walked, she began to tell her mother that she had seen the madman twice before and how she had been so scared she had run away. Her mother couldn't help chuckling as she listened to her story. The sunlight was splattering across the pavement, and as they walked down the street, they were walking through the sunlight too.

6

That was how spring ended and summer took its place. No one saw it coming. They had been waiting for it since early spring, but no one heard its footsteps walking into town. They knew that they had left their jackets at home. But no one saw it coming. Until the very end, they imagined that it was still spring. Each day was as lovely as the next, and the season seemed to extend before them indefinitely. It was only when they began to walk the streets in shorts and skirts that they realized that summer had long since arrived. They began to hear the cicadas hum and the ice cream carts chime. They began to think it was nicer to sit in the shade than to stand in the sun. And they grew even fonder of nighttime than before. The night breeze blew as cool as water drawn from a well. When night fell, they poured from their apartments into the street. Some of them pushed chairs onto the balcony or set them outside the front door. Some people dragged bamboo cots into the lanes when it was time to sleep. Still more fled to the vast fields outside of town to stroll along the earthen embankments that curved above the rice paddies, savoring the moonlight, the croak of frogs, and the gleaming tracery of fireflies dancing through the air.

She always left the house after sundown, meeting her friend in the lane outside the house just as the evening mist had begun to rise. Her friend was wearing a skirt that was every bit as pretty as her own. They walked onto the avenue shoulder to shoulder. She could feel her skirt brushing against her friend's skirt and her friend's brushing against hers. The street was awash in skirts. Skirts drifted out of open doors and narrow residential lanes into the street. Skirts merged, separated, and swayed through the streets as if performing some kind of intricate dance.

It was then that a madman came hopping toward them like a flea. The madman was clean and well groomed. He gazed toward them, crying, "Sister, sister, sister . . ."

They tried to remember who he was. People used to say he had gone crazy during the Cultural Revolution. His wife had left him long ago. His daughter was in their class. People said that when he cried, "Sister," it meant that he was looking for his wife.

"I haven't seen that one in a while. I thought he was dead," her friend said. A second later she tugged gently on her hand and nodded toward a woman and a girl walking together. "That's them," her friend whispered, "that's his wife and daughter." But she already knew who they were.

She watched the woman and her daughter walk past the madman as if they had never met. The madman kept on hopping down the sidewalk, calling all the while for his "sister." The mother and her daughter kept on walking down the street. They didn't look back. They moved forward with ease and grace.

Blood and Plum Blossoms

Fifteen years before, Ruan Jinwu, the greatest swordsman of his generation, had died at the hands of two warriors of the Black Way. That day, Ruan Jinwu's five-year-old son, Ruan Haikuo, saw bloody leaves flutter across the sky.

Ruan Jinwu's wife had long since lost her former beauty. White hair grew from her head in weedy clumps. And just as surely as the fifteen hard years since her husband's death had stolen her beauty, they had also effaced the memory of the dashing figure her husband had cut in the world of swordsmen in the days when he had wandered the land with his incomparable Plum Blossom Sword in hand. The sword itself, however, had not been forgotten, and among the heroes who now roamed the rivers and lakes of China in search of duels and high adventure, stories of its magical properties continued to circulate.

For once its blade had been slathered with the blood of a foe, one gentle wave of the hand would suffice to send the blood flurrying from the blade like red snow, leaving a single stain in the shape of an exquisite plum blossom embossed on the blade for all eternity. The sword had been passed down through several generations of swordsmen. By the time it fell into Ruan Jinwu's grasp, seventy-nine plum blossoms were arrayed across the blade. Ruan Jinwu had stalked the land for twenty years, and in that time a score of blossoms had been etched on the steel. And so impeccable was Ruan Jinwu's swordsmanship that, once the Plum Blossom blade left its scabbard, the blood of his opponent was sure to be spilled.

It was for this reason that the riddle of Ruan Jinwu's death had tormented his wife throughout the long years since she had first discovered his death. He had died on a dark, quiet night. She had fallen into deep slumber just as her husband had been silently and mysteriously dispatched in a weedy field in front of their cottage lit only by the gleam of a full moon. In the days and weeks after his death, she had obsessively cataloged each of her husband's enemies in her mind, in search of one who perhaps could have been capable of the murder, but all her efforts had proved futile.

In the last year before her husband's death, there had been several bright mornings when, having pushed open the front door, she had seen a corpse gleaming in the sun in front of their cottage. Her husband, she knew, had slipped out of bed to fight a life-or-death duel in the dead of night. And each time she had seen a corpse, she had been chilled by a premonitory vision of her husband's lifeless body shining amid the weeds. One serene morning, she woke to find that her premonition had been fulfilled. Ruan Jinwu's corpse lay across the weeds in a heap, limbs splayed helplessly out around him. The black handles of two daggers sprouted from where his eyes had once been. A few withered leaves that had fluttered down from a nearby tree hovered across the ground next to the body. She watched as her son, Ruan Haikuo, began to gather the leaves into his outstretched hands.

In the years that followed, the boy grew as slowly and painstakingly as the roots of an old tree. By the time he had turned twenty, he began to take on something of his dead father's good looks and elegant bearing. It was clear, however, that Ruan Haikuo had inherited none of his father's prodigious skills with a sword, much to his mother's dismay. When this frail young man stood before his mother inside the cottage, she almost could not bear the sight of his slender frame. This clearly was no swordsman. But despite her reservations, her patience had been tried beyond endurance by years of brooding expectation. The time had come to cast Ruan Haikuo out of the house and onto the open road.

And so it was that, on that bright morning, she began to speak once again of that momentous morning fifteen years before, of how she had seen her husband's body lying lifeless in the weeds:

"I couldn't even see his eyes."

After fifteen years of speculation, she told her son, she had failed to determine who had killed his father:

"But there are two men who may be able to help."

The men she spoke of had sung and sparred with Ruan Jinwu twenty years earlier at the foot of Mount Hua. Indeed, of all the swordsmen Ruan Jinwu had encountered throughout his long career, they had been the only two he had never managed to best in swordplay. One or the other, she continued, would certainly know exactly on whom he was destined to take his revenge for the death of his father.

"The first man is called Master Blue Cloud, and the second is called White Rain."

Both Master Blue Cloud and White Rain had long ago retired from the strife and discord of the world of swordsmen. They lived as hermits, passing their days deeply absorbed in meditation. Despite their reclusion, or perhaps because of it, these two men alone held the keys that would unlock the secrets of the most intractable mysteries that still troubled the world of swordsmen.

Ruan Haikuo sat motionless, transfixed by the sound of his mother's voice. He knew all that was to transpire. He saw ash-gray roads stretching before him. He saw rivers so green they looked black. His mother's shadow fluttered just outside the perimeter of these visions of the trials that lay before him. A moment later, his father's fabled Plum Blossom Sword lay across his outstretched palms like a branch floating on the surface of a river. He took the sword from his mother's icy fingers.

His mother told him the weapon was etched with ninety-nine plum blossoms. She told him that the blood of his father's murderer would make a new flower bloom on the blade.

Ruan Haikuo hung the sword at his back and strode out of the cottage. In the distance, the red morning sun was rising through an extraordinarily empty expanse of blue. Walking underneath the sky, he felt like a lonely gray magpie in flight.

When he reached the road, he could not help but gaze back at the cottage. A color like that of the sun had begun to engulf its thatched roof. Flame danced in the morning breeze. In the sky behind the cottage, harsh morning light was burning redly through a bank of clouds. Ruan Haikuo stopped in his tracks, fearing for a moment that the clouds had somehow descended on the cottage and begun to burn. He heard the sound of cracking beams. He saw sparks whirl through the air like fountain spray. A heap of flame tumbled to the ground, flooding across the field in front of the cottage like water.

As Ruan Haikuo turned and began to walk away, his legs fluttered in the morning breeze. The road ahead unscrolled before him like a mirage. He was all too aware of the warning conveyed to him by his mother's self-immolation. In the months and years to come, there would be no home to which he could return.

It was thus that, without so much as an inkling of the skills required of a swordsman, Ruan Haikuo shouldered the celebrated Plum Blossom Sword in order to find and take his revenge on the men who had killed his father.

2

In the seemingly endless journey that followed, the names Ruan Haikuo's mother had entrusted to him in the moments before her death came to seem as empty as echoes in a mountain gorge. She had told him that he was to find them but had given no indication as to where they might be found. This was why Ruan Haikuo's progress across lakes and rivers, through mountains and forests, and past tiny villages and bustling towns quickly took on an aimless and illusory cast. For Ruan Haikuo, however, it was just this sort of aimless rambling, with its constant promise of boundless horizons to come, that provided him with the inspiration to continue his journey.

On that first morning, he had followed the road by the cottage for nearly ten miles before coming to a river. By the time he had crossed the little wooden bridge that spanned the water, though, he had already forgotten which direction he had planned to take. And, from that day on, he abandoned any attempt to navigate his way across the land. Instead, he simply meandered across the earth's surface, moving in whatever direction his feet happened to take him. He passed through countless towns, but all of them were made of the same kinds of buildings, shaded by the same trees, and packed with the same sorts of people walking through the same kinds of streets. With each new town, Ruan Haikuo felt merely as if he had walked through another memory.

One day, after more than a year on the open road, Ruan Haikuo came to a crossroads at dusk. This, of course, was not the first crossroads he had come to in the course of his journey. Nor was it to be the last. Each crossroads would either lead him closer to or take him farther away from Master Blue Cloud and White Rain. Throughout his journey, Ruan Haikuo had given the decisions presented by these junctures no more thought than if he were simply walking down a straight and uninterrupted road.

This particular crossroads gradually drew toward him through the dimness of dusk. He saw wave after wave of mountains rolling into the distance ahead. Narrow rays of red sunlight shot down through the gaps between the mountain peaks. A second road ran perpendicular to the mountain range across an expanse of muddy earth, its rough, pitted surface thrown into relief by the reddish glow of dusk. He decided to walk straight toward the mountains before he had even reached the crossroads. It was precisely because of scores of random decisions over the course of the past year that he had arrived at this particular spot in the first place.

Sometime after he had come to this decision, however, he suddenly became aware of the fact that he was moving further and further away from the mountains. Instead of continuing past the crossroads as he had originally intended, he had unwittingly turned down the road that led across a desolate expanse of mud. The sun had already fallen below the horizon, and the sky was black as ash. When he turned to look behind him, he could barely make out the crossroads from which he had come. He continued to walk, thinking all the while of the moment he had turned at the crossroads. But try as he might, he was unable to remember it. It was as if it had never actually happened at all, for there was only empty space where the memory should have been.

Despite the darkness, he was forced to continue his forward motion, for the landscape he had unwittingly begun to cross was not and seemingly never had been inhabited. It was only much later that he caught sight of a low, thatched hut in the distance. Soon, he saw candlelight emerge from within the cottage and flutter across the night, igniting afternoon sun in his heart. And as he approached the house, he sensed wave after wave of bright floral and vegetable aromas rolling toward him like mist dispersing underneath the morning sun.

He walked to the door and stood for a moment, listening. The cottage was silent. Looking back at the boundless and desolate landscape through which he had come, he raised his hand to knock.

The door immediately emitted a squeal of surprise, and an incomparably lovely woman stood before him, her appearance there so sudden that it seemed as if she had been waiting quietly by the door for him to come.

She seemed to know at a glance exactly why it was he had come and, without any further questioning, invited him to spend the night.

Flustered, Ruan Haikuo silently followed her into the cottage and sat down at a table in the center of the room. In the soft gleam emitted by a single candle, he began to appraise the woman who stood before him. It seemed as if her face were caked with several layers of powder and rouge, rouge that gave the alluring smile pasted across her face a strange and hallucinatory cast. But a moment later, he discovered that the woman had disappeared, although he was unable to recall having seen her leave the room. In a short while, though, he heard the sound of her climbing into bed emerge from an adjacent room. Her bed creaked like branches swaying in the wind.

She asked him, "Where are you going?"

Although she was separated from him only by a thin wall, her voice seemed to have traveled across a vast distance in order to reach his ears. Suddenly reminded of how his home had collapsed in flames as his mother sat inside it and of the cold breeze that had whipped through his legs as he had begun his journey, he said:

"I am looking for Master Blue Cloud and White Rain."

At this, he heard the woman sit up in bed with a start and say, "If you should find Master Blue Cloud, please ask him where I might be able to find a man named Liu Tian. Tell him that it is the Lady of the Rouge who requests his guidance."

Ruan Haikuo agreed to do as she asked. She settled back under her quilt. After a moment, however, she added, "You will remember, won't you?"

"I will," Ruan Haikuo replied.

With this assurance, she slept. Ruan Haikuo, however, sat until the candle had burned down to the quick. Soon, dawn began to break. Ruan Haikuo slipped out of the cottage into the morning light, seeing for the first time that the cottage was surrounded by strange blooms and exotic plants, all of which were sending waves of strange and unfamiliar fragrance wafting through the moist morning air. Regaining the road, Ruan Haikuo looked back in the direction he had come, only to see an incomparably desolate plain stretching toward the horizon. Wheeling in the opposite direction, he saw a jade green river wreathed by billows of dawn mist. Ruan Haikuo began to walk toward the river.

Several weeks later, when Ruan Haikuo tried to recall his strange encounter with the Lady of the Rouge, the memory had already come to seem like an illusion. For even though Ruan Haikuo was a direct descendant of a celebrated swordsman, he had never lived or traveled in the company of his father's brothers-in-arms. This was how he came to be ignorant of a warrior as singularly notorious as the Lady of the Rouge. Known throughout the land as the most powerful potentate of poison under heaven, her entire body was powdered with a poisonous essence concocted from the noxious blooms that she cultivated around her cottage. So deadly was her rouge that a single puff could kill a man in a matter of seconds from several yards away. This was why the Lady of the Rouge had refrained from speaking to him until she had moved into another room.

3

In the weeks after Ruan Haikuo took his leave of the Lady of the Rouge, he continued to roam across the land, drifting this way and that like a leaf floating helplessly across the surface of a pool. But as he wandered, he gradually began to draw closer and closer to the Black Needle Knight, without knowing how, why, or indeed that he was even doing so at all. The Black Needle Knight was a figure whose name was almost as widely celebrated among swordsmen and fighters as the Lady of the Rouge herself. After more than twenty years of valiant adventure and martial intrigue, the Knight had become known as a master of a secret weapon. When the Knight took aim, he never missed, even in the dark of night. His secret weapon was a strand of hair plucked from his own head, for once a hair left his scalp it would stiffen into a lethal black needle. Propelled into the dark of night, the black needle was completely invisible to its target and thus could not be deflected. After many years in the world of swordsmen, bald patches were beginning to appear on the Black Needle Knight's scalp.

Several months after his meeting with the Lady of the Rouge, Ruan Haikuo's incessant motion finally brought him to a lively and noisy market street in a large town. Dusk was falling just as he arrived on the outskirts of the town. Here, the road forked. If he had arrived earlier, Ruan Haikuo may well have followed the road that led away from the town. The impending darkness, though, forced him toward it. After a night's rest at an inn, he would resume his original route the next morning.

The long months of travel had exhausted him, and as he strolled through the bustle of the market, he felt his frame flap in the breeze like an empty tunic. He drifted off to sleep as soon as he had found an inn, slumbering through the boisterous snatches of song and quiet murmurs coming from the balcony of the brothel across from his room. Just before the first light of dawn, he started awake like a window being blown open by a strong breeze. The moon was still shining through the window lattices onto his bed. He sat up in bed until he heard the clop of horses' hooves outside.

With the thunder of the hooves came an image of the road he had left the evening before. The road, disappearing into a distant horizon, brought him to his feet. He left the inn.

As it happened, Ruan Haikuo never actually returned to the road he had left the night before. Instead, a small path by the side of a stream beckoned to him through the mist and moonlight. He followed the sparkling water of the stream until sunlight broke through the mist. It was only then that he realized that he had somehow walked in an altogether different direction than he had planned. A peaceful little village lay a little further along the path. Ruan Haikuo walked toward the village. He saw an old mossy well and an elm tree by the village gate. There was a man sitting under the elm tree.

As Ruan Haikuo approached, the man under the elm fixed his eyes on him without seeming to be looking at anything in particular. Ruan Haikuo walked straight over to the well. Another Ruan Haikuo looked up at him from within the tranquil water within. Ruan Haikuo picked up a bucket that was tied to a stone by the well and cast it down onto his face. The water alighted like a bird frightened by an arrow. As he pulled the rope back out of the well, his face rose inside the bucket. Ruan Haikuo took a few swallows of extraordinarily cold, clear water. Then he heard the voice of the man under the elm tree: "You've been traveling for quite a long time."

Ruan Haikuo turned to look at the man. The man gazed silently back at him, as if he hadn't spoken to him at all. When Ruan Haikuo shifted his eyes back toward the well, the voice continued, "Where are you going?"

Ruan Haikuo turned toward the man. Both the tree and the man underneath its canopy shimmered red in the light of the morning sun.

"I'm going in search of Master Blue Cloud and White Rain."

The man stood and walked toward the well. He was tremendously tall. More striking still were the patches of coarse black hair that grew from the crown of his head. Arriving by Ruan Haikuo's side, this strangely authoritative figure said, "When you have found Master Blue Cloud, tell him that the Black Needle Knight asks where he might be able to find a man called Li Dong."

Ruan Haikuo nodded and said, "I understand."

Ruan Haikuo walked back down the little path by which he had come to the village. He walked hesitantly through the moist morning air, the words of the Lady of the Rouge echoing once again through his mind. Her request and that of the Black Needle Knight were like two leaves that had collided above his head, and the noise of their collision reverberated along the path.

4

Six months later, on the bank of a river choked with floating leaves, Ruan Haikuo found White Rain. Somehow, he had veered away from the highway he had been following at that point in his journey and aimlessly made his way toward the river. A ferryboat bobbed across the water on its way toward the opposite bank. A fine mist rose from the water's surface.

An old man, clad in a white robe and grasping a long sword in his hand, approached him through the dense stand of withered trees that covered the banks. Despite the fact that the old man walked with quickness and vigor, his progress across the leafy bank was strangely noiseless. The old man's long hair and flowing white beard floated toward him in the breeze.

The ferryboat had reached the opposite bank. Three travelers clambered onto the deck, and the ferry began to float back toward them.

White Rain, standing a few feet behind him as he waited

for the ferry, could not help but notice that Ruan Haikuo wore the Plum Blossom Sword slung behind his back. The obsidian luster of the hilt, framed by the rippling surface of the river, immediately evoked in him a cavalcade of memories. As the ferryboat began to approach the bank, White Rain began to recall the heroic figure Ruan Jinwu had cut some twenty years earlier at the foot of Mount Hua.

As soon as the boat had landed, Ruan Haikuo stepped on deck. The boat lurched to one side with his weight and began to rock back and forth. As soon as White Rain had boarded behind him, however, the boat immediately became as steady underfoot as a boulder. Soon, they began to ferry toward the middle of the river.

Although buffeted by waves that sent foam and water spraying in all directions, Ruan Haikuo soon realized that the boat was no less calm than the shore. At the same time, all his efforts to recall what it had felt like to stand by the bank a moment before were in vain. Ruan Haikuo stared back at the bank receding behind him, oblivious to the fact that White Rain's attention was fixed on his sword. It was easy enough to see in Ruan Haikuo something of what Ruan Jinwu had looked like twenty years before. Ruan Haikuo ultimately could not measure up to his father – his features exhibited none of the splendid martial spirit and brash pride that had suffused those of Ruan Jinwu. Ruan Haikuo looked almost pathetically frail as he stared bewilderedly back at the bank of the river.

When they were halfway across the river, White Rain greeted Ruan Haikuo:

"Isn't that the Plum Blossom Sword on your back?"

Ruan Haikuo, turning to look at the old man behind him, replied, "Yes, it is the Plum Blossom Sword."

White Rain continued, "Did your father give it to you?"

An image of his mother handing him the sword suddenly seemed to float up from amid the mist rising from the water's surface. He nodded.

White Rain, gazing at the water skimming past the prow, continued, "And who might you be looking for?"

Ruan Haikuo said: "I'm looking for Master Blue Cloud."

In thus responding, Ruan Haikuo unwittingly disobeyed his mother's instructions. He had neglected to mention White Rain's name. Indeed, over the six months since his encounter with the Black Needle Knight, he had nearly forgotten White Rain, simply because both the Knight and the Lady of the Rouge had asked only after Master Blue Cloud.

White Rain, falling silent, shifted his gaze toward the approaching riverbank. The ferry landed, and White Rain and Ruan Haikuo began to walk in opposite directions along a road that ran parallel to the river.

As any swordsman would have known, White Rain and Master Blue Cloud, for years the best of friends and closest of allies, had parted ways five years earlier as sworn enemies.

5

During the next six months of difficult and fruitless travel, Ruan Haikuo's chance encounter with White Rain was never far from his mind. Of course, Ruan Haikuo could not have possibly known that the curious old man he had seen by the river was actually White Rain. For some reason, though, he found the nonchalance with which the old man ambled away hard to forget. As Ruan moved off in the opposite direction, he happened to look back in the old man's direction, catching sight of the old man's white mane dwarfed by the vastness of the dark blue sky and the green fields that surrounded him.

Months later, weakened by the travails and constant hunger of the road, Ruan Haikuo fell ill in a small town perched in the mountains just north of the Yangzi River. He was walking along a path that meandered by the riverbank. A few yards ahead, a wooden bridge lay suspended above the rapids. Despite his weakness, he began to cross the bridge, but just as he had reached halfway across, he collapsed. He watched the water swirl underneath the bridge as he lay crumpled on the walkway. It was hours later, as dusk began to fall, before he felt strong enough to stand and slowly make his way through the gathering darkness to a small town he had passed on his way to the bridge.

Lying weakly on a bamboo mat at the town inn, he listened to the sound of falling rain splattering outside the room. He lay ill for three days. The rain fell for three days. The roar of the river grew louder and louder, and yet ever more distant to his ears, as if its constant burbling were the sound of his own restless footsteps continuing, even as he lay ill, to wander across the countryside.

On the morning of the fourth day, the rain suddenly came to a halt. At the same time, the affliction that had racked his frame began to disperse. Ruan Haikuo stood and left the inn, only to find that the rain had swollen the river so high that the bridge had been washed downstream. He stood for a long while by the place where the bridge had been, gazing across the river at a road that ran toward a distant mountain range. Finally, he began to walk along the river's edge in search of another bridge.

After nearly half a day, he had come across several roads that led south across the river, but each one had stopped at the river's edge, only to continue on the opposite side. Just as he had begun to despair of ever finding a way across the river, he caught sight of an ancient, decaying temple surrounded on all sides by lofty trees. Carefully threading through clumps of dense foliage and boulders, Ruan Haikuo made his way into what was left of the structure.

The walls of the temple were riddled with holes, filling the dank prayer hall with innumerable columns of viscous light. Suddenly, a bell-like voice rang in his ears:

"And who is Ruan Jinwu to you?"

The voice hummed through the hall. Ruan Haikuo searched the room for its source, but his gaze was met only by the chaotic tapestry of light and dust woven by the sunlight slanting through the walls.

"He's my father," he replied.

The voice modulated into a laugh as mellifluous as flowing river water:

"That is the Plum Blossom Sword that you carry on your back, is it not?"

"Yes, it's the Plum Blossom Sword."

The voice continued to drone:

"Ruan Jinwu came to the foot of Mount Hua twenty years ago, with his Plum Blossom Sword in hand . . ."

The voice came to a halt and continued only after a lengthy pause:

"Exactly how long has it been since you began your journey?"

Ruan Haikuo, at a loss, did not reply.

The voice asked:

"Well then, why did you leave home at all?"

Ruan Haikuo said, "I go in search of Master Blue Cloud."

At this, the voice erupted into a chuckle that resembled nothing so much as the wind rustling through the trees:

"I am Master Blue Cloud."

The messages with which the Lady of the Rouge and the Black Needle Knight had entrusted him leaped quickly to mind. Ruan Haikuo said, "The Lady of the Rouge needs to know where she might find a man named Liu Tian."

Master Blue Cloud mumbled to himself for a moment.

"Liu Tian traveled to Yunnan seven years ago. As we speak, however, he has already left Yunnan to journey to the swordsmanship tournament that is held once every ten years at Mount Hua."

After repeating this information to himself, Ruan Haikuo continued, "Where is Li Dong? The Black Needle Knight asks that you help find him."

"Seven years ago, Li Dong went to Guangxi. By now, he too is on his way to Mount Hua."

It was only at this point that he remembered the mission with which he had been entrusted by his mother in the moments before her death. But just as he steeled himself to ask Master Blue Cloud who had killed his father, the Master intoned:

"I answer only two questions at a time."

Ruan Haikuo heard a current of air whistle past him, rustle through the trees outside the temple, and disappear. Master Blue Cloud was gone. He stood for a long time in the dank silence of the temple before turning to leave.

On the heels of this encounter, Ruan Haikuo continued along the river's edge, recalling once again a name that seemed to have vanished from his memory in the months after his encounter with the Black Needle Knight. After several hours of walking, he came to a road that led away from the river. Rather than continuing to look for a bridge, he turned and walked down the road in search of White Rain.

6

Ruan Haikuo's search for White Rain further prolonged his aimless journey. Master Blue Cloud disappeared from his mind like a wisp of smoke into the air. He had fulfilled the tasks entrusted to him by the Black Needle Knight and the Lady of the Rouge. In the months of peregrination that followed, he was often aware of their presence, a presence as fleeting as moonlight appearing behind night clouds. Although it was true that he might accidentally encounter them at some point in the future, he had long ago forgotten where exactly they lived, and this alone made them seem as distant and illusory as White Rain himself.

Without his knowledge, however, Ruan Haikuo's slow and meandering progress across the countryside had already begun to carry him closer and closer to the Black Needle Knight. And one day, he unwittingly approached the gate of the village in which the Black Needle Knight resided.

He arrived at dusk, but the village looked much the same as the morning of his first visit. The Black Needle Knight sat under the elm tree, framed by the red glow of the sunset at his back. And it was only when he saw the Knight under the tree that Ruan Haikuo realized exactly where he was. He walked once again to the well, picked up the bucket, lowered it into the well, hauled it up, and drank several mouthfuls of cold, fresh water. The water reminded him of the darkness that was falling all about him. He turned to look at the Black Needle Knight. The Black Needle Knight was looking at him. Ruan Haikuo said, "I found Master Blue Cloud."

He saw a look of puzzlement play across the Black Needle Knight's face. It was clear that he had forgotten Ruan Haikuo just as completely as Ruan himself had forgotten where he could find the Knight. Ruan Haikuo continued, "Li Dong has already left Guangxi. He's making his way toward Mount Hua."

A look of sudden realization rolled across the Black Needle Knight's face. He lifted his eyes heavenward and erupted in a bout of raucous laughter. Elm leaves fluttered to the ground with the force of his guffaws. Before another moment could pass, the Knight stood and strode toward a nearby cottage. He emerged in a moment with a bundle of belongings slung over his back, pausing only to address Ruan Haikuo. "You can stay in my house."

With these words, he hurried away from the village.

Ruan Haikuo watched as the Knight moved off into the gathering darkness. A moment later, he walked toward the Black Needle Knight's cottage.

Throughout the days that followed his stay at the Black Needle Knight's cottage, Ruan Haikuo could not help but sense that he was gradually drawing nearer and nearer to the Lady of the Rouge. One day soon after, he found himself moving down an empty road surrounded on all sides by a wasteland of mud. The route by which he had arrived, however, had been equally as fortuitous as that which had led him to a second encounter with the Black Needle Knight.

It was noon. The road that he had trod in the darkness of night now appeared before him bathed with brilliant light. Even the lovely midday sunshine, though, could not conceal the utter desolation of the land the road ribboned across. It was this desolation, finally, that brought Ruan Haikuo to a halting realization of the fact that he had unwittingly stumbled on the Lady of the Rouge.

Moments later, he sensed innumerable tendrils of fragrance float toward him on the breeze. In the distance, he caught sight of a cottage. As he drew closer, he saw a plot of exotic blooms and strange plants shining so brilliantly in the sun that he was almost overcome by a strange, feverish sensation in his limbs.

The Lady of the Rouge stood amid the flowers. Hemmed in by blossoms of every imaginable shape and hue, she seemed even more beautiful than she had the first time he had come. She seemed to be gazing at a river flowing toward her as she waited for Ruan Haikuo's arrival.

Soon, her face lit with a strange smile that brought Ruan Haikuo's motion to an abrupt halt. He said, "Liu Tian has already left Yunnan. At this very moment, he is traveling down the road that leads to Mount Hua."

The Lady laughed brightly, threaded her way out of the garden, and walked into the cottage, trailing a shadow that slid across the ground like a stream of water.

Ruan Haikuo waited for a moment, but when the Lady failed to emerge from the house, he turned and left.

8

Ruan Haikuo's search for White Rain continued for another three years. One afternoon, fatigued by his seemingly endless peregrinations, he decided to rest in a little roadside pavilion.

While Ruan Haikuo slept, a bearded man clad in flowing white robes drifted past the pavilion, stopping when he caught sight of the Plum Blossom Sword at Ruan Haikuo's side. This, he determined after gazing at Ruan Haikuo's unassuming form, was the son of Ruan Jinwu whom he had encountered several years before. He knelt down at Ruan Haikuo's side to pick up the Plum Blossom Sword.

With this movement, Ruan Haikuo woke with a start. This was how his second meeting with White Rain occurred.

White Rain, sword in hand, smiled.

"Did you ever manage to find Master Blue Cloud?"

This question sparked memories of a man that had lain dormant for the duration of the three years that he had spent looking for White Rain.

Ruan Haikuo said, "I'm looking for White Rain."

"And you've found him. I am White Rain."

Ruan Haikuo hesitated, mumbling softly to himself as he averted his eyes from the man who stood before him, haunted by the growing certainty that these marvelous years of peregrination were about to come to an end. He would be forced to find and take his vengeance on the man who had killed his father fifteen years before. And that, of course, was tantamount to going in search of his own funeral.

After a moment, he asked, "I want to know who killed my father."

White Rain listened, smiled, and said:

"Your father was murdered by two men. One of them was named Liu Tian. The other was called Li Dong. Three years ago they both met their end on the road to Mount Hua at the hands of the Lady of the Rouge and the Black Needle Knight."

Ruan Haikuo's heart was thrown into turmoil. He watched as White Rain held the Plum Blossom Sword to eye level and slowly extracted it from its sheath. Illuminated by the brilliant sun outside the pavilion, he saw ninety-nine spots of rust dappling the blade.

The Death of a Landlord

I

Many years ago, a landlord clad in a black silk robe, with white hair and silvered whiskers, emerged from the courtyard of his brick house, palms clasped together behind his back, and began to stroll slowly through the fields of his own estate. When the peasants working in the fields saw him approach, they all respectfully set down their hoes and called out their greetings:

"Old Master."

When he went into town, the townspeople called him "sir." This distinguished gentleman would always walk earnestly out from his walled home as the sun set in the western sky, his long, white beard fluttering in the breeze. An almost ritualized solemnity was dimly apparent in his bearing as he walked toward the night soil vat by the village gate. This self-satisfied old member of the landed gentry moved stiffly to the edge of the vat, lifted up a corner of his robe with his right hand, turned calmly around, and squatted over the vat. Finally, he undid the stays of his trousers, revealing a pair of wrinkled buttocks and thighs criss-crossed by prominent bluish veins, and began to shit.

There was, of course, a chamber pot by his bed, but he preferred to relieve himself outdoors in this animal manner. Perhaps he found the view of the sun setting behind the mountains or the gentle caress of the early evening breeze amenable or even uplifting. The landlord, well past his prime, still maintained the habits of his youth. Unlike many of the peasants who simply sat on the edge of the vat, he squatted above it. But as he had grown older, his bowel movements had become more difficult as well. Every day as dusk approached, the villagers would hear the sound of the landlord's moans, for when all was said and done, things just didn't come out as easily now as they had when he was young. What was more, his legs, perched on the edges of the vat, would tremble uncontrollably.

The landlord's three-year-old granddaughter, wearing a black jacket embroidered with red flowers, her hair pulled up into two sheep's-horn braids, made an angry face. She hopped over to the vat, curiously inspecting the trembling of her grandfather's legs, and asked:

"Granddad, why are you moving?"

The landlord smiled and said: "It's the wind."

At that moment, the landlord's squinted eyes caught sight of a white shadow moving along the little cart track in the distance. The last rays of the sun shone toward him in gleaming swaths, and his eyes filled with dancing speckles of color. The landlord blinked, asking his granddaughter:

"Is that your dad over there?"

The granddaughter carefully examined the horizon, but her gaze was also obstructed by innumerable spots of light, and all she could detect was a tiny shadow, now appearing, now disappearing, glittering in the sun's rays like flying spittle.

The granddaughter burst into giggles, saying:

"He's dancing back and forth."

The man walking toward them was the landlord's son. This young gentleman, clad in white silk, had been away from home for quite a few days. By now, the landlord was able to distinguish exactly who he was, and he thought to himself: "Little bastard's coming home for more money."

The landlord's daughter-in-law emerged from the house in the distance carrying a chamber pot by her waist, swaying as she approached. Although she was weighted down by her burden, her unhurried swaying motion made the landlord smile with delight. His granddaughter had already left his side and was now standing indecisively among the paddies as she wavered between deciding to run toward her father or her mother.

A great roar came down from the sky. The landlord raised his eyes to look and saw an airplane flying just under the cloud cover to the north. The landlord squinted as it flew closer and closer, but he was still unable to find what he was looking for. He turned to a peasant woman standing nearby, who was also gazing skyward, scythe in hand. "Is it a white sun against the blue sky?"

The woman shook herself. "It's a red sun."

A Japanese plane. Just as the landlord swore to himself, he saw two gray bombs fall from the airplane toward the ground. The landlord slid backward and fell inside the vat. The resounding splash of runny night soil and the detonation were simultaneous. The explosive cries of a multitude of bees buzzed inside the landlord's ears, and wave after wave of dust stirred by the detonation settled slowly over his head. The landlord's eyes were shut tight, and his head steadily buzzed. Even so, he could feel the night soil rippling around him. Feeling an itching sensation crawl across his face, he opened his eyes, lifted his right arm out of the night soil, and saw a few white maggots clinging to his hand. He disposed of them with a flick of his wrist and then began to attend to the maggots on his face, which seemed to melt underneath his fingertips as soon as he touched them. The odor inside the vat was quite strong, so the landlord opened his mouth wide in an effort not to breathe through his nose. This was an improvement, and he might have felt relatively comfortable had it not been for the buzzing in his ears. There seemed to be a lot of yelling and screaming coming from somewhere very far away, like a multitude of torches glittering through the darkness. The landlord raised his head to see the last patches of light before dusk fell. The sky was a deep, deep blue.

The landlord stayed inside the vat until the sky grew black. The buzzing in his ears gradually receded. He heard the sound of approaching footsteps and knew that his son had arrived. No one else's footsteps could possibly sound so listless. The young master walked to the side of the vat, gazed around in every direction, and finally caught sight of his father sitting inside it. He tilted his head toward him, saying, "Dad. We're all waiting for you to start dinner."

The landlord looked up at the sky and asked, "Are the Japanese gone?"

"They left a long time ago. Get out of there."

The young master turned on his heel, muttering to himself:

"It's not a bathtub, after all."

The landlord stretched his right hand toward his son. "Give me a hand."

The young master hesitated as he looked at his father's hand, for even through the gloom, he could see countless white maggots crawling on his skin. The young master knelt, picked a few pumpkin leaves, and gave them to his father: "Wipe your hand first."

The landlord took the fresh leaves. They were covered with fine hairs that stung his hand, like wiping his skin with coarse wool. The scent of the green juice that dribbled out from the broken leaves lingered in his nostrils. When he was done, he once more stretched his hand out to his son. His son looked, bent down to pick a few more leaves, and finally wrapped them around his own hand before he grasped hold of his father's hand and helped him out of the vat.

The landlord, dripping with night soil, shook himself as he gazed at his son walking back to the house in the new moonlight:

"The little bastard."

2

Wang Xianghuo, the scion of the wealthy landlord Wang Ziqing (of Anchang Gate just outside town), was sitting in the Kaishun Tavern. The tavern was empty save for an old man huddled drowsily in the corner, clasping an erhu[1] to his chest. Three small dishes, a pot of wine, and a wine warmer sat on the table in front of him. His hands were clasped together inside the sleeves of his embroidered robe, and he wore a melon-shaped skullcap on his head. He seemed to be dozing, but his narrowed eyes were actually fixed on the tavern window.

The scene outside was gray and gloomy. Rain caromed across the sodden road like boiling water, and the big, round drops falling from the eaves of the houses on both sides shimmered through the air. The window faced the town's West Gate, and in the portal set into the city wall stood four rifle-bearing Japanese soldiers, who searched each person leaving town. A mother and her daughter emerged from within the gate, carrying an oilcloth umbrella that looked as bright as a plot of shiny yellow rape blossoms through the curtain of rain. The woman's hand was clasped around her daughter's shoulder. The yellow blossoms suddenly collapsed. The pair walked through the gate and presented themselves before the soldiers. One of the Japanese soldiers playfully mussed the little girl's hair while the other rubbed and pinched at her mother's body. From the tavern, he looked as if he were plucking feathers from a boiled chicken. The rain slanted and swirled in the air so that he was unable to see the woman's discomfort as she bore the insult of the soldier's roaming hands.

Wang Xianghuo lifted his eyes toward a view he had looked on many times before. Beyond the city wall, he could see a seemingly endless stretch of water. The rain seemed to have abated somewhat – there were gaps in the curtain of rain, and like a window in the process of being washed, the scene outside gradually cleared. He could even see the tops of bamboo enclosures – placed there in order to trap fish – protruding from the water. A little boat propelled itself over

[1]A two-stringed Chinese violin.

one of these barriers and floated across the steaming surface of the lake like a fallen leaf. There were three tiny figures on the deck. The one standing at the prow seemed to be probing the river bottom with a bamboo pole. Then he watched as one of them dove into the cold, wintry water, looking for a catch, and resurfaced a moment later. First, his arms made a kind of violent throwing movement toward the cabin, and then he suddenly appeared standing up on the deck. Because of the distance, the figure's movement from the water onto the deck looked to Wang Xianghuo like a kind of somersault, as if the diver had tumbled back onto the boat by the sheer force of the choppy surface of the lake.

A commotion of voices came through the window from within the city walls, sounding as if someone's house had caught fire. Two Japanese soldiers, holding a man who looked like a merchant, advanced to the center of the road and then came to a halt. The man was standing directly across from the window, arms held firmly to his sides by the soldiers. A third soldier leveled his bayonet at the man's back and began to scream a string of unintelligible phrases. There was no expression on the man's face – perhaps he did not realize that the screams signified his death. Wang Xianghuo watched his body flutter twice, as if he had been shoved forward, and then the tip of the bayonet protruded from his chest. The man's eyes opened so wide it looked as if they might fly from their sockets. The soldier lifted a leg and let fly with a vicious kick, taking advantage of the forward momentum of the man's tumble toward the ground to extract the bayonet from his torso. Blood sprayed from the wound, soiling the soldier's face. His two companions erupted into another string of shouts and laughter. The bloodied Japanese soldier appeared unconcerned, though, simply raising an arm in salute, shouting something, and marching elatedly back through the city gate.

The sound of thick cotton soles advanced up the tavern stairs. This was the proprietor's fifty-year-old wife, clad in a coarse cotton robe and absently rubbing a bit of stove ash across her face as if it were rouge. As he watched her ponderous approach, Wang Xianghuo thought to himself, "At least the Japanese might spare someone like her."

The woman said, "Young Master Wang, you'd better hurry on home."

She slumped down opposite him, pulled a pink handkerchief from her sleeve, and began to sob. "That scared me to death."

Wang Xianghuo noticed that it was only after she had wiped her eyes that a few teardrops began to spill from her eyes. Her distress was brilliantly performed, betrayed only by the excessive delicacy with which she wielded the handkerchief.

The dozing old man in the corner began to cough, rose to his feet, and peered toward the two figures by the window. He appeared to be on the verge of speech, but, noticing that his movements hadn't been noticed, his mouth simply folded into a yawn.

Wang Xianghuo said, "The rain's stopped."

The woman stopped sobbing, carefully wiped her eyes, and replaced the handkerchief in her sleeve. Gazing at the Japanese soldiers below, she said:

"They've ruined a perfectly good business, that's for sure."

Wang Xianghuo left the Kaishun Tavern and began to walk slowly along the sodden road. The dead man's body lay on the pavement, separated from his hat by several feet. The hat had begun to fill up with rainwater. Wang Xianghuo could not see any blood – perhaps it had been washed clean by the rain. His back was a dark red mess. Bits of cotton padding had leaked out from his jacket, only to be flattened by the rain. Wang Xianghuo walked around the corpse and moved toward the city gate.

Now there were only two soldiers standing in the portal observing his approach. Wang Xianghuo halted in front of them, removed his skullcap, held it to his chest, and made a low bow toward each of the soldiers. He watched as their faces broke into happy smiles and one of them waved him past through the gate with his index finger. He walked between them and out of town, without even having been subjected to a search.

The road was almost unbearably slippery, muddy, and pitted, having soaked in rainwater for several days running. Wang Xianghuo had to walk down the strip of weeds that ran along the side of the road so that his feet wouldn't sink into the mud. The weeds, battered flat and pliant by the rain, stretched before him in a tangled mat. Black clouds rolled in the sky overhead. Walking with hands in his sleeves and his head tucked in against the chill of the early winter breeze, Wang Xianghuo looked very much like the barren black elms that stood silhouetted against the gloom in the fields around him.

A troop of Japanese soldiers had gathered in front of a Daoist nunnery that lay just ahead. They had detained a dozen or so passersby and made them stand, single file, in a drainage ditch by the side of the road. The cold water came up above their knees, and it was already impossible to tell whether they trembled for fear or simply because of the chill. Nor had the nuns been able to escape a similar fate. They knelt in a row in front of the nunnery as two elated soldiers desecrated them with mud. As the soldiers plastered their bald pates with the mire, it slid over their faces, rolled down their necks, and slipped inside their robes. The other Japanese soldiers hovered behind them, howling and rocking, seemingly drunk with laughter. As Wang Xianghuo approached, one of the soldiers was trying to sculpt a fringe for one of the nuns, but the mud, refusing to stay put, repeatedly slipped off her forehead and onto her face. Finally, one of the soldiers plucked a weed from the ground and, with a bit of mud as adhesive, pasted it to her forehead.

The brigade was on its way to Songhuang. When they

had finished with the prank, a Japanese who looked like the commanding officer and a Chinese who seemed to be his translator moved toward the detainees in the irrigation ditch, inspected them one by one, and exchanged a few phrases. Soon, it became clear that they were looking to recruit a guide to lead them to Songhuang. When Wang Xianghuo walked forward and presented himself, it appeared to him that the pallor of the sky had swallowed their laughter whole. Their empty, gaping mouths reminded him of the big porcelain jars piled up in the family courtyard. He took off his hat and bowed deeply to the Japanese soldier. He watched as the commanding officer smilingly strode forward and tapped him several times on the shoulder with his baton, before turning to his translator and spewing out something that sounded like a duck quacking, an impression that was only heightened by the flapping of the officer's thick lips.

The translator took a step toward him:

"You. Take us to Songhuang."

3

Winter had come early that year. It was only November when the landlord's family had begun to use the charcoal brazier to heat the house. Wang Ziqing sat snugly in a great, fleece-upholstered armchair, hands extended over the brazier, staring vacantly into space. The patter of rain and the popping of dry kindling within the brazier merged together, and tiny bright sparks flew periodically from the vent into the darkened room.

The sound of his hired hand Sun Xi chopping wood carried into the room from outdoors. The cold snap had come far too suddenly – even the coal briquettes had yet to be prepared. His only option had been to have Sun Xi prepare some makeshift coals in the stove.

The three women of the landlord's family — his wife, daughter-in-law, and granddaughter — were also clustered around the brazier, bundled up in thick cotton padded robes, their feet resting on bronze foot warmers full of stove embers, which sent up currents of warm air through little vents on the covers. Even so, their bodies were huddled against the cold, as if they were sitting in the teeth of a chill, whistling wind.

The landlord's granddaughter was distracted from the cold by a drum-shaped rattle. No matter how she twirled it in her hands, she still could not induce the little beads at the end of the tassels to strike the head of the drum. When she tried to twirl a bit harder, the rattle slipped from her hands and fell to the ground. Still sitting, she stuck her head out over the edge of her chair and gazed longingly down at the rattle, her legs kicking back and forth in front of her. Realizing that she was simply too far above the floor to collect it, she reached out a hand and began to slap at her mother as if she were trying to kill a mosquito.

A basin of water cascaded down on the embers inside the stove with a gurgling hiss, rousing Wang Ziqing's spirits. He shifted his buttocks in the chair, and a sense of ease spread through his limbs.

Sun Xi appeared, bearing a dustpan full of steaming coals. His cotton padded jacket was open in front, revealing the sturdy flesh within. Sweating profusely, he threaded through the family, their clothes bundled thick as armor, and placed the pan in a convenient spot from which Wang Ziqing would be able to pick up the coals with a pair of pincers and feed them to the brazier.

Wang Ziqing said, "Take a quick break, Sun Xi."

Sun Xi wiped the sweat from his brow, straightened, and replied, "Yes, master."

The landlord's wife, fingering a Buddhist rosary, lifting her left leg, and pushing her foot warmer forward with her right, addressed Sun Xi:

"It's not as hot as it was before. Put in some more coals for me."

Sun Xi immediately bent and raised the foot warmer to his chest, saying:

"Yes, mistress."

The landlord's daughter-in-law also wanted new coals. She too shifted her legs, but without uttering a word, because she knew that to have her coals changed at the same time as those of her mother-in-law would be vaguely inappropriate.

Having sat for quite some time, Wang Ziqing's joints began to ache. He stood and slowly made his way to the window, feeling slightly oppressed by the constant, heavy patter of the rain on the roof. The trees outside were barren, and streams of water coiled down their trunks. Wang Ziqing's eyes followed the streaming water down to the clumped weeds underneath, all of which had been battered flat by the rain. The earth next to the weeds was swollen with moisture. Wang Ziqing heard a drum sound, followed by his granddaughter's giggles. She had finally hit the mark. Her crisp laughter brought a faint smile to Wang Ziqing's face.

The news that the Japanese had occupied the town had reached them the day before. Wang Ziqing thought to himself, "That little bastard should have been back by now."

4

"The commandant says," the translator told Wang Xianghuo, "that you'll get a big reward if you take us to Songhuang."

The translator turned toward the officer, and they exchanged another string of gibberish. Wang Xianghuo shifted his head to one side and saw the Japanese soldiers sticking little white wildflowers into the barrels of their rifles. One machine gun had a circlet of the flowers wrapped around the barrel. The flowers fluttered slightly under the dense smoke-dark clouds overhead, and the prospect of the broad, barren fields stretching into the distance before him made Wang Xianghuo quietly expel a long breath.

The translator's white-gloved hands pulled Wang Xianghuo's face back toward him. "The commandant's asking you whether you can guarantee that you'll get us to Songhuang."

The translator's accent was northern, and his mouth tended to twist to the right when he spoke. His nose was very large but very flat, and it looked to Wang Xianghuo like a big head of garlic.

"What are you, a motherfucking mute?"

Wang Xianghuo's mouth was slammed by a hand, and his head lolled back and forth. Then he spoke:

"I can speak."

"Motherfucker."

The translator gave Wang Xianghuo another hard slap, turned, and angrily let out a stream of quacking sounds toward the officer. Wang Xianghuo replaced his skullcap, put his hands in his sleeves, and stood watching them. The officer took a step forward, screamed for a while in Japanese, stepped back, and finally waved for a couple of soldiers. The translator barked:

"Take your fucking hands out of your sleeves."

Wang Xianghuo ignored him, turning instead to observe the approach of the two soldiers and wondering just what it was they were going to do. One of the soldiers pointed a rifle barrel in his direction. The flower in the barrel trembled and looked as if it might fall. Suddenly, Wang Xianghuo's left side received a tremendous jolt, his legs went limp underneath him, and he fell to his knees. So did the flower, whose petals were still white against the mud. But the blossom was soon obscured under the other soldier's boot.

Wang Xianghuo looked up to see a piece of iron wire in

the soldier's hand. It was about as thick as a rice seedling, and both ends had been sharpened to a point. The other soldier was short, compact, and looked very strong. He quickly pulled Wang Xianghuo's hands from out of his sleeves, stood behind him, and positioned his hands atop one another. The soldier with the wire chuckled and drove the point of the wire into his hand.

The intense pain made Wang Xianghuo's head slump toward his right shoulder. There was a terrible clarity to the pain, for when the wire encountered the resistance of his bone, he seemed to hear a kind of clicking sound. Finally, the wire curved around the bone, passed through his right hand, and pierced the left. Wang Xianghuo heard the sound of his own teeth begin to chatter.

Just as the wire had penetrated through both palms, the soldier grinned and began to jerk the wire up and down. Wang Xianghuo let out a low moan. Through slitted eyes, he saw that the wire was coated with blood, as if it had been dipped in a can of paint. Gradually, the blood darkened until it was no longer distinguishable from the mud on the ground. The Japanese soldier stopped jerking the wire and began to twist it around his hands. After a moment, the soldier walked away, and he heard a whistling clamor in the distance that might have been the sound of the other soldiers cheering. He felt his whole body shake uncontrollably, and his palms felt hotter and hotter, as if they were on fire. His vision dimmed, and he shut his eyes.

But the translator was screaming at him, a foot was kicking him, not hard enough for him to fall, but hard enough so that his body rocked from side to side. He swayed back and forth, like a little fishing boat bobbing on the steaming surface of a lake.

He opened his eyes, trying to focus on the translator's face. His hair had been grabbed hold of by a hand that belonged to that face:

"Stand the fuck up!"

His body curved, stood. Now he could see everything clearly. The sodden fields appeared behind the soldiers, the Japanese officer was yelling something in his direction, and he gazed toward the translator, who said:

"Move."

When the wind blew onto the rolling boil in his hands, he felt a sharp, icy pain. Wang Xianghuo glanced down at his hands. They were spattered with little drops of blood, and the wire seemed to be twisted in a tight coil around them. He caught the edge of his sleeve between his teeth and pulled until his palms were covered. He felt much better, almost as if nothing had happened, as if his hands were clasped under his sleeves just as before. Two of the nuns still knelt on the ground, their mud-splattered faces like mottled walls through which shone two glittering pairs of eyes, gazing at him. He looked pityingly back at them. The people in the drainage trench still stood shivering in place. The weeds on the embankment behind lay splayed over by the rain, roots exposed to the air.

5

The landlord's hired hand Sun Xi arrived in Li Bridge one afternoon, still clad in a battered old cotton jacket open to the waist. A length of rope hung from his belt as he moved forward, face coated with dust.

He had heard in a village he had passed through the day before that the soldiers who had taken Wang Xianghuo were going to Songhuang. Just as he got to Li Bridge, the strap on his right sandal broke. He took off both sandals and tied them to his waist, continuing into the small market town with his bare feet slapping against the earth.

There was a crowd gathered in a circle in the center of town, laughing boisterously and filling the air with grunting catcalls. He had been able to hear the commotion all the way from the fields on the outskirts of town. Now he also heard the sound of animals squealing from within the clamor. The earthen wall around the town sparkled in the sunlight, and though the ground was still moist and pliant under his bare feet, it was not nearly as muddy as before. If it weren't for the pebbles that bit into his feet, it would be almost like treading on rice chaff.

Sun Xi stood for a moment, gazing toward a knot of women in embroidered jackets standing under the eaves and wondering whom he should ask about the young master's whereabouts. He moved to a point directly between the women and the crowd. Noting with a sense of embarrassment the sidelong glances cast toward him by the clump of women, he soon continued on to the periphery of the crowd.

A wiry man was forcing a ram to mount a sow. The sow let out a constant stream of howls as the ram, bleating and unfazed, mounted her back. But as soon as the wiry man removed his hands, the ram slid back down to the ground. The sow turned to butt the ram with its head, and the ram counterattacked with his hoof. The wiry man proceeded to curse them both:

"Oh-ho! You wanna start a fight just as soon as it gets between your legs! Motherfucker!"

Another man suggested:

"Turn the pig on its back with its legs up in the air like a woman with a man."

The crowd roared its approval. The wiry man grinned:

"All right, all right. But you people are all talk and no action. Give me a hand."

Four men wearing jackets just as tattered as Sun Xi's own stepped forward and rolled the sow, exposing its glistening starch-white belly to the sun. Perhaps the sow was overly conscious of its predicament – its thick trotters sliced back and forth in the air amid a chorus of enraged squeals. The four men simply knelt to the ground and held down its legs, as they might a woman's. The wiry man gathered up the ram and prepared to loose it atop the sow, but now it was the ram's turn to flail his legs in stubborn protest. The wiry man spat out a gob of phlegm and began to curse:

"A nice fat bitch for you, and you don't even fuckin' want any. Worse than a motherfucker!"

Another four men stepped forward and took hold of the ram's legs, pressing it down atop the sow. Both creatures let out cries of despair: a loud squeal and a low bleat. The crowd's laughter erupted like a gale, subsiding only after several moments of merriment. Sun Xi pushed his way to the middle of the circle and saw the two animals' faces pressed tightly, unwillingly, and rather amusingly together.

Someone said:

"Maybe it's a sheep, not a ram."

The wiry man nodded, motioned for the ram to be rolled back to the ground, reached under its belly, and took its reproductive organs in hand:

"Take a good look, kid. This isn't a titty, is it?"

Now Sun Xi began to speak:

"He can't find it."

"What are you saying?"

"I mean the ram can't find the sow's thing."

The wiry man slapped the side of his own head, as if he'd just seen the light:

"Ah-hah. You really get right to the point, don't you."

Sun Xi's face reddened, but he continued excitedly:

"You have to show him, then it'll work."

"And how do you go about showing him?"

"All animals pretty much smell the same down there. If you put his nose by her thing for a whiff, he'll know where to put it."

The wiry man clapped his hands:

"You may look like an idiot, kid, but you're a real scholar. Where you from?"

"Outside Anchang Gate." Sun Xi said. "Master Wang Ziqing's place. Have any of you seen our young master?"

"Your young master?" The wiry man shook his head.

"We heard the Japanese were taking him to Songhuang."

Someone told Sun Xi:

"Go ask that old lady over there. We all ran away when the Japanese came through. She was the only one left. She can even tell you about how the Japanese did her till she was sore."

Amid another wave of laughter, Sun Xi looked in the direction in which the man had gestured to see a woman in her sixties sitting in the sun with her back to an earthen wall. Sun Xi walked slowly toward her. She surreptitiously glanced up at him as he approached, hands in her sleeves. Sun Xi forced himself to smile broadly in her direction, but this produced no change in her attitude. Under a canopy of unkempt hair lay a wrinkled, wooden face. The closer Sun Xi got to her, the more uncomfortable he felt. Fortunately, the woman was the first to speak, but only after a long moment of cold inspection:

"What are they up to over there?"

The woman's eyes pointed in the direction of the crowd.

"Ugh," Sun Xi said. "They're mating a ram and a sow."

The old lady's mouth twisted with disdain:

"A bunch of stupid bastards."

Sun Xi hurriedly nodded his agreement. Then he asked:

"They say that you saw the Japanese troops?"

"Japanese troops?" The old lady scornfully continued, "They're even worse bastards than them."

6

The rain hovered across the misty, ashen sky, plastering his neck and dripping into his robe. The robe grew heavier and heavier, but his body trembled with fever. His skin felt like it was coated with chili powder, and his joints ached.

The rain seemed almost to have come to its end. Wang Xianghuo saw a patch of pale white sky to the west. The rain no longer slid past his eyebrows and onto his face. The Japanese soldiers' boots gurgled across the mud like frogs, leaving frothy white bubbles in their wake.

The translator said, "Hey! What's that place up ahead?"

Wang Xianghuo squinted toward the market up ahead. Li Bridge stood silhouetted against the gray sky like a tomb. Under the rolling black clouds, the town gradually drew near.

"Hey."

The translator pounded a few times on his head. He swayed, then said:

"We're at Li Bridge now."

He heard another stream of Japanese that sounded like popping water bubbles. The Japanese soldiers came to a halt as their commanding officer extracted a map from out of his leather pack. Several of the soldiers stood around the officer, shielding the map from the rain with their overcoats. Dripping wet, they watched for a signal from the officer and, when it came, arranged themselves despite their exhaustion into a ramrod straight column and began to jog spiritedly toward Li Bridge.

The drizzle-enveloped town greeted them with deep silence. Not even a magpie was visible in the moist winter air. A scattering of footprints and one slender tire track were visible in the mud, indicating that it had not been very long since the residents of the town had fled.

The Japanese troops soon found a relatively large building, which Wang Xianghuo recognized as the private residence of a local silk manufacturing family, the Ma's. They, too, had fled only a short while earlier — a charcoal brazier was still burning faintly in the living room. The Japanese officer looked around the room, gave a cry of satisfaction, removed his coat, and sat back in an armchair with his leather boots propped up on the brazier. Wang Xianghuo, detecting a strange odor, noticed that little curls of steam were emerging from the officer's rain-soaked boots. The officer babbled something or another to a few soldiers, slamming the heel of his boot on the brazier for emphasis. The soldiers left the room. The rest of the soldiers still stood at attention. The officer waved his hands and said something else. The soldiers grinned, took off their coats, and sat in a circle around the brazier. From his position behind the officer, the translator turned toward Wang Xianghuo, saying, "You can sit too."

Wang Xianghuo chose a distant corner of the room and sat down on the floor, surrounded by the raucous babble of the soldiers. As he sat, he smelled something rotten hovering around him. He had endured the pain in his hands for so long that it seemed like it had always been there, that it was indeed an essential part of his hands, and now he did not even notice. He saw that his sleeves were glossy with fluid. This sight threw him into a quandary, for no matter how hard he tried, he could not recall exactly why his sleeves were so wet and sticky.

The Japanese soldiers who had left now returned, bringing with them a woman in her sixties. The officer leapt up from his armchair, inspected the woman, and exploded into anger. His hoarse yells seemed to signify the incompetence of his inferiors. One of the Japanese soldiers stretched himself to his full height and croaked for a while. The officer's anger cooled. He looked the woman over once more before waving his arm at the translator, who hastened toward her:

"The commandant wants to know if you have any daughters or granddaughters?"

The old lady glanced at Wang Xianghuo sitting in the corner and then shook her head:

"All I have is a son."

"Then there isn't one woman in the whole town?"

"Who says there isn't?" the woman replied, seemingly upset. "Do I look like a man?"

"You don't fucking count."

The translator wheeled toward the officer and spoke. The officer creased his brows in an effort not to look at the woman's wrinkled and furrowed face. He waved for a pair of soldiers, who dragged the old lady over to a mah-jongg table and held her down on the tabletop. The old lady began to howl in protest – not because she knew what was going to happen to her, but because it hurt.

Wang Xianghuo watched a Japanese soldier cut her belt with a bayonet while another peeled off her pants. The legs that were revealed were skinny and covered with varicose veins, while her fleshy stomach and buttocks protruded like drums. Her body reminded Wang Xianghuo of a prone insect.

Now, the old lady knew just what was coming. When the officer stretched out his hand and began to finger her vagina, a curse rolled out from deep in her throat:

"You're shameless!"

She looked over at Wang Xianghuo and screamed:

"I'm already sixty-three years old! They'll even do a sixty-three-year-old?"

Realizing that she was quite helpless, the old lady shelved her anger and simply lay prone without putting up any resistance. Instead, she gazed toward Wang Xianghuo and continued, "You're the young master of the Wang family outside of Anchang Gate, aren't you?"

Wang Xianghuo looked back at her but remained silent.

"You look like him to me."

The Japanese officer was clearly disappointed by the looseness of the woman's vagina. He croaked loudly for a moment, brandishing his whip at her crotch.

Wang Xianghuo saw her body convulse as she howled in pain, "Aiyo! Aiyo!" The whip crackled through the air as it bore down on her, and the hard snapping noise of its impact confirmed just how painful each blow had been. Despite the suddenness of this assault, the old lady forced her head up off the table and screamed:

"I'm sixty-three years old!"

The translator responded with a slap that sent her head slamming back down on the table:

"Don't you know your place, bitch? The commandant's doing you a favor. He's helping you recover your youth."

The elderly woman could only express her grief with a series of low sobs. Only after she had been whipped swollen and red did the officer throw down his crop. He tested the area with his finger. Gratified by its degree of elasticity, he proceeded to unbuckle his belt, push his pants down to his thighs, and take two steps forward. The old woman began to cry and scream once more at this point, so a soldier hurriedly draped her ugly, wrinkled face with a Japanese flag.

7

When a breathless Sun Xi had run home to report on Wang Xianghuo's whereabouts, an inauspicious augury of things to come — as real as the sunlight bouncing off his bald and shiny pate — had been revealed to Wang Ziqing. He tossed Sun Xi a string of cash from the top of the stone steps in front of the house and said:

"Go take another look."

Sun Xi picked up the cash, bowed, and replied:

"Yes, master."

As he watched Sun Xi sprint away, Wang Ziqing muttered to himself, "The little bastard."

After guiding a brigade of Japanese troops to a place called Bamboo Grove, the landlord's son had veered away from the route to Songhuang and begun to move in an entirely different direction. Wang Xianghuo was leading the brigade toward Orphan Hill. And according to Sun Xi's report, after the brigade had passed through Bamboo Grove, the locals tore down the bridge behind them. Sun Xi also told Wang Ziqing:

"It was the young master who ordered them to do it."

Wang Ziqing's whole body convulsed, and a gray pallor like that of withered flower blossoms suddenly filled the clear sky above him. He stood in a daze, thinking, "The little bastard's looking to die."

After Sun Xi was gone, the landlord stood on the steps, gazing at the crest of the ridge in the distance. Perhaps because of the distance, the ridge looked as light and insubstantial as a bank of clouds. The rainstorm was over, but the clear winter air was still moist.

After a while, the landlord went inside. He was greeted by the sobs of his wife and daughter-in-law. He sat in his chair, watching the two huddled, sobbing women as they dabbed their eyes with the corners of silk handkerchiefs. Although their cheeks shone with tears, they insisted on using only a corner of the silk, letting the rest of the fabric dangle down over their chests. The landlord shook his head. From their jagged, wailing sobs, one would think that they were already mourning his death. His wife said:

"Old master, you have to do something!"

His daughter-in-law immediately began to cry even louder to express her agreement. The landlord creased his brows and remained silent. His wife continued:

"What the hell is he doing, bringing them over to Orphan Hill? And having them tear down the bridge, too. How's he going to get back when the Japanese find out?"

The older lady clearly had very little grasp of the gravity of her son's predicament, and her distress was not without its blind spots. Her daughter-in-law found her stepfather's silence unbearable:

"Papa, you have to do something!"

The landlord sighed and said, "That's not the issue. It doesn't matter whether we can save him or whether the Japanese decide to kill him or let him live. What matters is that he's looking to die."

The landlord paused for a moment, then burst out in a curse:

"The little bastard."

The two women immediately began to wail even louder, and their cries were so piercing that the landlord felt as if he were being thrashed by the sound. He closed his eyes, thinking: Just let them cry. It's awful to be with women at a time like this. He blocked out the noise as best he could.

After a few minutes, the landlord felt a hand cover his face, a muddy hand. He opened his eyes to see his granddaughter staring back at him, her body caked with mud. It was clear that, flustered and upset by the two women's lamentations, the girl had come to her grandfather because of his relatively tranquil air. When the landlord opened his eyes, his granddaughter burst into giggles:

"I thought you were dead."

His granddaughter's shining face made the landlord smile. She gazed over toward the crying women and asked:

"What are they doing?"

The landlord said, "They're crying."

A palanquin carried by four porters entered the Wang family courtyard. The landlord's old friend, Old Master Ma, who owned a silk factory in town, stepped down from the carriage, bowed slightly at the door, and said:

"When I heard about your young master, I hurried right over."

The landlord smiled in greeting and urged his friend to come in.

When they heard the guest arrive, the two women immediately stopped sobbing and, with red and swollen eyes, smiled toward Old Master Ma. As soon as Ma had taken his seat, he leaned over toward the landlord and asked, "What's happened to the young master?"

"Uhh . . ." the landlord shook his head, "the Japanese

wanted him to guide them to Songhuang, but he brought them to Orphan Hill instead, and then he ordered people to tear down the bridge behind them."

Old Master Ma, astonished, exclaimed:

"That's stupid, very stupid. Or doesn't he want to go on living?"

With this, the two women burst once again into tears. The landlord's wife weepingly entreated:

"What can we do?"

Old Master Ma sat awkwardly, rubbing his hands together and gazing at Wang Ziqing. With a dismissive wave of his hand, the landlord said, "It's nothing. Doesn't matter. It's not important."

Then the landlord sighed and went on:

"If you want trouble for a day, invite someone over to visit. If you want enough trouble for a year, build a house."

He continued, "And if you want troubles that'll last you a lifetime, get married and have kids."

8

Bamboo Grove was a promontory surrounded on three sides by water. There were two long wood-plank bridges to either side of the promontory that continued across the water from where the land road dead-ended by the shore. The bridge to the east went to Songhuang, and the bridge to the south crossed over to Orphan Hill. Just as the weather had begun to improve, Wang Xianghuo led the Japanese troops into Bamboo Grove.

He was accompanied along the way by the stench of his hands. In the sunlight, it was clear that his sleeves had grown increasingly greasy. His rain-soaked robes had now begun to smell of mildew. His legs felt as if they were stuffed with cotton, and he walked forward with halting steps. But he had finally caught sight of the wide waters of the lake. Its dark blue waves were a sparkling expanse of shade underneath the hot sun. He inhaled deeply – the transparent water was as clean and spotless as the interior of a temple. The tops of the bamboo fishing fences sticking above the water resembled water fowl sitting and observing the motion of the waves.

The landlord's son slowly lifted his arms, grasped onto his robe with his teeth, and slid back the slick edges of his sleeves. He saw his maimed hands. The coiled wire seemed to have grown much thicker, and it was coated with white pus. His swollen palms looked like soy-pickled pig's trotters, not hands. Wang Xianghuo let out a soft moan and lifted his head in an effort to escape the stench. That was when he noticed that he had already arrived at Bamboo Grove.

The translator yelled from behind:

"Will you fucking stop!"

Wang Xianghuo wheeled around, discovering at the same time that the Japanese troops had fallen out of formation. Except for a pair of rifle-bearing sentries, the soldiers had all taken off their coats and begun to wring them out in the water. The officer, accompanied by the translator, approached a group of men standing by an earthen wall.

Perhaps the people of Bamboo Grove hadn't had time to flee. The town appeared to Wang Xianghuo to be as densely populated as ever. He caught sight of several children's heads popping up one by one above another earthen wall to peek at the Japanese troops. An old man also appeared in the distance, moving hesitantly toward him. He continued to watch the officer move toward the group of men, all of whom lowered their heads and bent their waists in a bow. The Japanese officer responded by tapping their shoulders with his crop in a gesture of goodwill and then began to speak with them through the translator.

The hesitant man walked slowly up to Wang Xianghuo and timidly called out to him:

"Young master."

Wang Xianghuo carefully looked him over. This was Zhang Qi, a man who had worked as a hired hand for his family until the year before, when he had been dismissed. Wang Xianghuo smiled and asked:

"You're still in good health, I hope?"

"Fine, fine," the old man said, "except all my teeth are gone."

Wang Xianghuo continued, "Where are you working nowadays?"

The old man smiled sheepishly and replied in an embarrassed tone:

"Nowhere. Who would hire someone like me anymore?"

Wang Xianghuo smiled again.

When the old man saw that Wang Xianghuo's hands were bound with wire, his eyes clouded over, and he asked with a flutter in his voice:

"What crime did you commit in one of your past lives to deserve this, young master?"

Wang Xianghuo glanced at the Japanese troops in the distance and replied:

"They want me to take them to Songhuang."

As the old man rubbed away his tears, Wang Xianghuo said:

"Listen, Zhang Qi, it's been a few days since I took a crap. Can you undo my pants for me?"

The old man immediately took two steps forward, lifted up Wang Xianghuo's robe, unbuckled his belt, and pulled his pants down around his thighs:

"There you go."

Wang Xianghuo squatted with his back to the earthen wall. The old man joyfully remarked:

"Young master, this is just like old times. I never thought that I would have the chance to be of service to you again."

The old man began to sob. Wang Xianghuo shut his eyes,

grunted, exhaled, and grunted again. Finally, he opened his eyes, telling the old man:

"I'm done."

He lifted his buttocks up, and Zhang Qi used a discarded piece of tile to scrape away any remaining shit before helping him with his pants. Wang Xianghuo stood and saw that two women had been brought before the Japanese officer. Seven or eight soldiers milled around them, looking on. Wang Xianghuo told the old man:

"I'm not taking them to Songhuang. I'm taking them to Orphan Hill instead. Zhang Qi, listen. Go tell the people along the way that they're to tear down the bridge as soon as I pass by."

The old man nodded, "Yes, young master. I understand."

The translator was yelling and cursing for him in the distance. He glanced at Zhang Qi and began to walk back toward the troops. Zhang Qi called after him, "Young master, when you get home, remember me to the old master."

Wang Xianghuo smiled bitterly, thinking, "I'll never see my dad again." He turned and nodded, adding, "Don't forget about the bridges."

Zhang Qi bowed and replied, "I'll remember, young master."

9

Sun Xi arrived in Bamboo Grove the day after the Japanese troops had come through town. The sun was lovely and bright, and it was clear that the winter wind had also lost some of its bite. A few people were gathered in front of a small grocery shop, lingering in the sun to chat. The proprietor of the shop, a man in his forties, stood behind the counter. There was a tattered corpse lying across the street.

From the look of the body, it appeared to have been an old man. The proprietor said:

"He died right before the Japanese came."

Another man added:

"That's right. He was already dead before they got here. I saw it myself. One of the Japanese soldiers went over and kicked the body. He didn't even flinch."

Sun Xi walked toward the group, glanced at each one of them, and squatted down next to the wall. The proprietor gestured toward the lake and said:

"Those fishermen are always pretty free with their money when they're just getting started in the business."

Then he pointed at the dead old man, continuing:

"When he was a young man, he'd always come here to buy his liquor. My dad was still alive then. He'd just reach into his pocket, take out a big handful of coins, and slam them on the table. He had style . . ."

Sun Xi saw a little boat on the lake. There were three men on deck. One man stood at the stern rowing, and another stood forward, probing the water with a bamboo pole. With the coming of winter, the fish had concealed themselves in the deep pools pitting the bottom of the lake. The man bearing the pole had clearly just come on such a pool, so he motioned to the oarsman to stop the boat. A naked man in the middle of the deck rose, drank a few swallows of white grain spirits, and dove into the water. Someone said:

"This season the price of fish is going almost as high as ginseng."

"But that kind of fishing will do you in after a while, brother," the proprietor replied.

Someone else added, "When you're young and strong, it's just fine. But once you start putting on years, you're sunk."

Now the barber who was giving the proprietor's wife a trim off to one side of the shop also spoke up:

"Being young is no guarantee. Sometimes people dive

into those pools and never come back out again. The deeper it gets, the more giant clams you run into. You feel around for fish, but sometimes your hand'll end up inside a shell. And if it shuts, you're a goner."

The proprietor nodded sadly. Everybody gazed back over at the fishermen, wondering if they would get caught by a clam. The boat bobbed on the water, and the man with the submerged bamboo pole seemed to be looking back toward them. The other man had to keep the oars in constant motion just to hold the boat in place. The diver finally resurfaced and threw a handful of fish onto the deck, their white, scaly bellies sparkling in the sun. Then he grabbed hold of the deck rail and pulled himself back on board.

The group gathered around the shop shifted their attention back to the dead fisherman. The old man was lying beneath a wall, face up, right leg splayed open so that his crotch looked unnaturally wide. He had been wearing only a single cotton jacket, and even that was in tatters.

"Must have frozen to death," someone commented.

Having finished washing the proprietor's wife's hair, the barber tossed a basinful of water onto the ground:

"Whatever you do, you have to do it with skill. If you're planting crops, do it with skill. If you cut hair, do it with skill. Having a skill is like having a full rice bowl. Even when you get old, you'll never go hungry."

He took a comb out of his front pocket and began to brush out his customer's hair vigorously with one hand, while at the same time squeezing drops of water from the ends of her hair and onto the ground with the other. His hands worked quickly, the one moving in perfect coordination with the other. At the same time, he still managed to gesture toward the dead old man and say:

"The reason he came to this is that he didn't have any skill."

The proprietor seemed slightly displeased by this remark. He looked up and slowly began to present his own view:

"Now that's not necessarily so. Seems to me that the only people who make really good money are the ones who don't have any skills at all. Look at factory owners, government officials, people like that. They're the ones making big money."

The barber put the comb back in his pocket, exchanging it for a long silver earwax scoop. He replied:

"You need skills to be a big boss too. Like you have to know when to order materials, how much to buy, how much to produce. Knowing the market is a real skill."

The proprietor smiled and nodded:

"You're right there."

Sun Xi fixed his gaze on the proprietor's wife, who sat lazily ensconced in a comfortable chair, her eyes shut as the sunlight played across her body and her high, prominent breasts. The barber was cleaning her ears with the silver spoon with one hand and stroking her face with the other. She seemed to be asleep. Someone said, "Well, she sure as hell doesn't have any special skill."

Sun Xi saw a woman emerge from a little house across the way. Her face was smeared with makeup, and her hips swayed as she walked toward a barren tree, leaned against the trunk, and glanced over at the shop. The loiterers began to giggle, and someone said:

"What do you mean she doesn't have a skill? Her skill is inside her panties!"

The barber, turning to look, chuckled:

"Her skill is knowing how to please a man, and it isn't easy. It all depends on whether they know how to lie there. If they just lie flat, it's no fun. They have to know how to bend, how to curve their body around you."

The boat bumped against the embankment, and the diver leaped ashore, running toward the shop clad only in a dripping pair of shorts, dark legs twitching with the motion. His face and chest were the color of old bronze. Having reached the shop, he extracted a handful of coins from his pocket and slammed them down on the counter:

"A bottle of white grain spirits."

The proprietor got the bottle for him and grabbed four coins from the pile of change. The rest of the money rapidly found its way back into the diver's pocket. The diver sprinted back toward the lake and jumped onto the boat. It swayed with the impact. The diver found his footing as the boat began to steady. With the aid of the bamboo pole, the boat pushed away from the shore. As it slowly drifted into the lake, the diver once again stood on the deck gulping spirits from the bottle.

When the boat had disappeared into the distance, the group began once again to discuss the dead fisherman. The proprietor went on:

"When he was young, he was one of the best in the business. But after he got a bit older, it was all over for him. Now there's no one left who's willing to take care of the body."

"No one'll even touch his clothes," someone added.

The barber was still cleaning the woman's ears, and Sun Xi watched as he periodically reached over to surreptitiously fondle her breasts. The woman, feigning sleep, looked as if she wanted to smile. The sight made the blood rush to Sun Xi's head, and what with the added stimulus of the enticing woman standing across the way, Sun Xi could hardly sit still. He stroked the string of cash the old master had given him as a reward, stood, and crossed the road. The woman glanced at him from the corner of her eye, sizing him up:

"And what do you think you're doing?"

Sun Xi chuckled:

"The northwest wind is blowing so hard that I'm shivering. Do me a favor and help me warm up, will you?"

The woman cast him another sidelong glance:

"Got any money?"

Sun Xi shook his pocket so that the coins chimed. Grinning, Sun Xi asked:

"Did you hear that?"

The woman replied impatiently, "That's just bronze stuff." She patted her thigh. "If you want service, you'll have to pay me in silver dollars."

"Silver dollars!" Sun Xi cried out. "Just one dollar's enough to buy a woman for a lifetime."

The woman gestured toward the earthen wall:

"You see that? Know what it is?"

Sun Xi looked and said, "It's a hole."

"It's a bullet hole," the woman excitedly raised her eyebrows. "I risk my life to please you, and all you can offer me is some lousy bronze coins?"

"This is all I've got."

The woman spread her fingers in the air. "What you've got is just about half of what you'll need."

"Listen, sister. It's not like you have any other customers right now anyway. You might as well make a little money."

"Bullshit. I'd rather let it rot than sell myself short."

Sun Xi stomped his feet. "Fine. And I don't want to cheat you. Just let me do it half price. Half the time, half the way there. Is that fair?"

The woman thought for a moment, nodded, turned, and walked back into her room with Sun Xi in tow. She stripped off her pants and lay down on top of the bed. Then she splayed open her legs. Sun Xi stood motionless above her and stared. She yelled:

"Hurry the fuck up, will you?"

It was only then that Sun Xi, afraid that she would change her mind, hurriedly slipped off his pants and mounted her. Almost as soon as Sun Xi entered her, the woman slapped his shoulders and yelled, "Hey, hey! Didn't you say you'd just go halfway?"

Sun Xi chuckled:

"Yeah. The second half."

10

With the advent of fair weather, Wang Ziqing had a good mind to go out for a stroll, for ever since his son had been carried off by the Japanese, the weeping of the two frightened women of the house had driven him to distraction. The day before, as he had seen Old Master Ma off at the door, he had concluded:

"How could I not be worried? But those two women just make it that much worse."

The landlord usually frequented the Xinglong Teahouse in town. The upstairs room of the Xinglong had elegant red-lacquered tables, each of which was screened off from the others by a painted silk screen. Through the spotless windows lay a panoramic view of the dark blue waters of the lake. This was a teahouse frequented by distinguished patrons, patrons with whom Wang Ziqing shared common interests. But, what with the Japanese occupation of the town, the landlord felt it would be wiser to meet at a different venue.

Wang Ziqing walked through the warm winter sunlight wearing a woolen cap and a long silk robe. He held a walking stick in his hand, which tapped against the soft road with each step he took. The flattened weeds next to the road had recovered from the rain and now stood erect, plastered with dried mud. As the landlord walked through the barren, broad fields, breathing deeply of the cool winter air, his face gradually unfolded into a smile.

The Japanese had occupied Anchang Gate a few days before but had lingered there only one day. There was a good teahouse there that possessed the additional virtue of being the closest to town.

As soon as Wang Ziqing stepped through the door, he caught sight of the few old friends with whom he usually drank tea at the Xinglong gathered around a table. They were among the wealthiest men in town. Now they sat by the wall without so much as a wooden screen to seclude them from the rabble at the adjoining table. Even so, they looked quite cheerful despite the noise that filled the room.

Old Master Ma was the first to catch sight of Wang Ziqing:

"Everybody's here. We're together again."

Wang Ziqing bowed to each member of the party, repeating:

"Together again, together again."

It seemed that the tea friends of Xinglong Teahouse had, unexpectedly and unbeknownst to one another, gathered here at Anchang Gate. Old Master Ma said:

"I was going to send someone for you, but, what with the difficulty with your son, I thought it might be better not to disturb you."

Wang Ziqing thanked him profusely.

One member of the company leaned over the table and asked: "How is the young master?"

Wang Ziqing clasped his hands in thanks, replying:

"Let's not talk about it. That little bastard's just reaping what he's sown."

After Wang Ziqing had taken a seat, a waiter brought an earthenware wine pot and warmer in his left hand and a bronze kettle in his right. He set the pot down on the table and began to pour the boiling water from the kettle from somewhere well above Wang Ziqing's head. Steam poured into the air as the waiter sent a stream of water cascading down into the pot. Finally, without spilling so much as a drop, he broke the stream in midair three separate times as a gesture of respect. Wang Ziqing, duly impressed, congratulated him:

"Well done, well done."

Old Master Ma, helping himself to a cup of wine, added:

"The decor may not be all that it could be, but the service is extraordinary."

To Wang Ziqing's right sat the principal of the town school. The principal, gold-rimmed spectacles flashing, said:

"Remember Qi Laosan, the waiter over at the Xinglong with such fast, steady hands? I hear he got most of his head blown off by the Japanese."

Another guest corrected him. "No, it wasn't his head. They shot him right through the heart."

"Amounts to the same thing," Old Master Ma broke in. "If they get you anywhere else, you might have a chance, but if it's the head or the heart, you won't even have time to blink before you're gone."

Wang Ziqing picked up his cup between two fingers and took a sip of wine. "A good way to go. The best way to go."

The principal nodded in agreement, wiped his lips, and said:

"Mr. Zhang from just outside the south gate had both his legs broken."

Someone asked, "Which Mr. Zhang was that?"

"The one who's a fortune-teller. After they broke his legs, he knew he could never walk again, knew he was going to die. There was blood pouring down his legs, and it was just heartbreaking to hear the way he was crying. The worst thing is knowing that you're going to die."

Old Master Ma chuckled:

"That's right. One of my workers went up to him and asked him how he knew he was going to die. And he wailed, I'm a fortune-teller, aren't I?"

Another guest nodded seriously:

"He was a fortune-teller indeed. If he said he was going to die, then you'd better believe he was going to die."

The principal continued:

"When he died, he was so scared that he was crying and shaking all over, shrunken up in a little ball, just staring wide-eyed at everyone around him. And he stunk. He shit in his pants."

Wang Ziqing shook his head:

"Awful. What an awful way to go."

An itinerant performer making the teahouse rounds approached their table, holding a little stack of red paper scrolls:

"Gentleman Immortals. What I have in my hand are magic spells passed down through the generations. If you'd like to get rich, or to quit drinking, or whatever it is you'd like to do, you need only consult these secret spells. Two bronze coins for a spell. Just two bronze coins – a mere pittance for gentlemen such as yourselves. How about it? A magic spell for just two bronze coins?"

Old Master Ma said, "What kind of spells do you have?"

The itinerant flipped through the cards, saying:

"You're all affluent gentlemen, so I guess you won't be interested in the 'get rich' spells. But there's spells for laying off the bottle, too, and for curing impotence . . ."

"Hold on there," Old Master Ma cut in, dropping two coins in his hand. "I want to see the 'get rich' one anyway."

The itinerant handed over the spell. Old Master Ma unrolled the paper, smiled mysteriously, and slowly placed it in his pocket. The rest of the company could only gaze at one another in bemusement.

The entertainer continued:

"Flowers only bloom for a hundred days, and men can't last longer than a hundred years. Suffering and heartbreak are unavoidable in this world, and suffering and heartbreak can really wear a man down. When things are rough, food doesn't taste any good anymore. You can't sleep well. You start to worry that your days are numbered. But don't worry. I have here a spell expressly formulated to rid a man of suffering and heartbreak. Why doesn't one of you gentlemen get yourself a copy?"

Wang Ziqing put two coins down on the table:

"I'll take it."

Wang Ziqing took the scroll in hand and unrolled it. The spell consisted of just two simple words:

"Don't think."

Wang Ziqing could not help but chuckle. But his smile was rapidly superseded by a sigh.

Now, Old Master Ma took out the "get rich" spell to show the other guests. And once again, Wang Ziqing saw that there were just two words written on the scroll. "Work hard."

11

The weeds crawled down into the water. They were tangled in dense clumps on the banks, but as soon as they entered the water, they began to unfurl, to sway in the currents of the cold azure lake. The lake water was brilliantly clear and as tranquil as sleep, for there were neither frogs nor tadpoles to disturb the peace, only the gentle roll of the water as the surface of the lake filled with ripples like row after row of fish scales glinting in the sun. Wang Xianghuo watched the brilliant light reflected off these scales swell and begin to roll across the surface of the lake in the form of a wave. It was as if the lake itself was breathing. He could not see a single boat. The lake was as clean and empty as an unclouded sky. The tops of the bamboo enclosures stuck lazily out from the water, as if they had merely lifted their necks to gaze out across the water.

They had already crossed the last bridge. The wooden planks were nearly rotten with age, wind, and rain, and they had given off a muted crack like a popping bubble with each step across the bridge. This was the planks' swan song – no longer would they sound out underfoot. Toss them in the water, let them sink to the bottom to share the fate of the pebbles on the lake floor. Even if they rose to the surface

once more, it would be a mere curtain call, a final flores-
cence before the very end.

Wang Xianghuo looked suspiciously at the beams that
supported the wooden planks. After years under water, how
much longer could they possibly hold up? The long, long
bridge extended out toward the opposite shore in a slow,
egg-shaped arc, curving in order to fend off the tidal bore.

The opposite shore lay unfurled in the distance, but because of the sunlight reflecting across the water, Wang
Xianghuo's view of the bank itself was obscured. He could
see houses, but they seemed to float dim and lusterless on
the water because of the intense gleaming light. It seemed
that he could see a few figures in the distance as well, gathering by the shore like little ants.

One by one, the Japanese troops stood up and slapped the
dust off their uniforms. The officer barked out his orders,
and the troops fell hurriedly into two columns, rifles in
hand. The translator asked Wang Xianghuo:

"How much farther is it to Songhuang?"

You'll never get to Songhuang, Wang Xianghuo thought
to himself. He was finally standing on the muddy ground of
Orphan Hill. The hill was actually an island, surrounded on
all four sides by the lake. The hill was the beginning of the
end, and now the long wooden bridge was the only thing
that mattered. And very soon, that bridge would disappear.
He said:

"We'll be there soon."

The translator babbled with the officer for a moment,
then turned to Wang Xianghuo:

"Very good. The commandant is quite pleased. He says
you'll be rewarded when we get there."

Wang Xianghuo lowered his head and took his place at
the front of the two columns of troops. Their youthful and
energetic faces were coated with dirt, but weeks of hard
marching had failed to dent their spirits. There was an innocence to those faces that made a kind of pity well up in

Wang Xianghuo's chest. He began to guide them up a path that led away from the water.

The road was very smooth, perhaps because it had never been particularly well traveled. There was none of the bumpiness one might expect of a track footprinted and pitted by travelers after a hard rain. He heard the soldier's disciplined, obedient footsteps pounding behind him like a multitude of lobsters climbing up out of the water and onto the beach. A cloud of yellow dust rose above them and drifted to either side of the path in their wake. The barren winter trees stretched what looked like wounded branches toward the column of men, as if calling for help or perhaps casting blame.

The curves in the road seemed to lack any sort of rhyme or reason. They encountered no real obstacles, but the road was several times forced to curve around dense clumps of trees in order to continue up the hill. Soon, the road was covered with knee-high weeds so tangled that they seemed to be part of the same yellowed and lifeless creature.

Wang Xianghuo's progress across the island had by this point become completely random. If anything resembling a road continued to unfold before him, he followed it. The hill was quiet. There was no sound save the orderly crunch of their boots and, from time to time, a few murmurs passing between the soldiers. He glanced up at the sky. It was already late in the afternoon. Clouds were spread sparsely across the sky, and the pale sunlight shone through a featureless blue field in which Wang Xianghuo could not see even a single bird.

After a while, they came to a halt. The road had ended abruptly in front of an old thatched cottage. The cottage looked as if it were crawling across the ground with its thatched roof streaming unkempt onto the muddy ground below. Two rifle-bearing Japanese soldiers advanced toward the cottage and kicked in the door. Wang Xianghuo caught sight of a second door inside the cottage. The soldiers pushed open this second door with their bare hands. The road they were following took up where it had left off just past the second door.

The translator said: "Where the fuck are we?"

Instead of replying, Wang Xianghuo walked through the cottage and continued down the road. Propelled by force of habit, the troops mechanically began to follow behind him, while the translator glanced suspiciously around and muttered, "This is looking worse and worse . . ."

After a while, they seemed to have crossed the island and arrived once again at the shore of the lake. Wang Xianghuo hesitated for a moment before turning right so as to loop back around toward the wooden bridge. Wang Xianghuo saw the weeds crawling down into the water a second time. The surface of the lake was dark and shadowy now, but the waves rolling in the distance still glittered as before. A bank of clouds had blocked the sun. The clouds glowed like leaves shining under the sun.

He heard a Japanese soldier blow a whistle somewhere behind him. The whistle was followed by the poignant sound of a chorus of voices breaking into song. The voices dispersed across the shadowy surface of the lake. Wang Xianghuo turned to gaze back at the soldiers. The dirt-caked face of the soldier leading the chorus with his whistle was rapt with concentration. This young Japanese soldier had absently begun to whistle as he gazed at the water. He hadn't even realized that he was whistling the melody of a song from his native land. Gradually, the other soldiers had unthinkingly begun to hum along. Wang Xianghuo had marched along with these weary soldiers for days now, but this was the first time he had been able to move unaccompanied by the constant rhythmic thud of their boots. The deep, stirring hum of their voices raised together in song pushed him along the path like a hand at his back.

Now, Wang Xianghuo could see the dismantled bridge lying in the distance. The bridge was wreathed in shadows, fractured into little islands in the lake, like stepping stones scattered across a stream. About a dozen boats glided on the surface of the lake. The faint sound of sculling oars floated into his ears like a thread through the eye of a needle. The Japanese troops behind him erupted into a clamor of babble and opened fire on the boats. The boats turned, scudding across the water toward the opposite side before climbing the lake shore like clumps of tangled weeds. The sound of oars hitting the water was drowned out by machine-gun fire. Gazing at the shattered bridge lying over the broad surface of the lake, Wang Xianghuo laughed desolately.

12

When Sun Xi arrived at the shore across from Orphan Hill, the sun had just been obscured by a bank of clouds, the bright surface of the lake went dim, and Orphan Hill looked like nothing so much as an upended basin floating on the water across the lake.

The locals had begun to dismantle the bridge. A dozen small craft positioned themselves parallel to the wooden support beams as the men hacked at the piers and columns. The old wood gave way beneath the axes with a dull thudding sound. Sun Xi saw one man tumble from his boat when a weakened beam gave far more easily under his ax than he had expected. Spray cascaded in all directions, and when his head finally bobbed back to the surface, he hollered:

"I'm freezing!"

Another boat swayed over toward him, and he was pulled up onto the deck. His cotton robe clung to his skin, and he shivered so violently that he looked almost as if he were sobbing. A man on another boat shouted across the water:

"Take it off! Don't just stand there! Take off your clothes!"

The man stood gazing about him in shock and bewilderment, his arms wrapped tightly around his torso. The person next to him took forcible hold of his arms, unclasped them, and stripped off his robe. Finally, the man stood motionless on the swaying deck as he meekly allowed the others to rub his naked body with grain spirits.

Sun Xi found all of this tremendously interesting. He watched intently as they continued to hack apart the bridge as if it were so much firewood. Two boats had almost reached the opposite side of the lake, where they continued to work. The men on the side closer to Sun Xi's began to holler for them to get back to safety as fast as they could. But the men at work by the shore of Orphan Hill simply gestured for the others to join them, yelling:

"Come on over!"

Sun Xi heard one of the boatmen standing on a boat by the shore say:

"If the Japanese got hold of one of those boats, we'd be off to see our ancestors in no time flat."

Someone began to scream, his voice shrill and piercing like a woman's:

"The Japs are coming!"

The crew of the two boats closest to Orphan Hill fell into a panic, their craft colliding with one another as they frantically tried to turn their prows back toward the other side of the lake. Once disentangled, the two craft rowed madly for the opposite shore, rolling dramatically on the waves as if they might capsize at any moment. When they had reached the others, though, they were greeted with a burst of hysterical laughter. It was only when they gazed back toward Orphan Hill that they realized that they had fallen victim to a ruse:

"Motherfuckers! Where do you get off?"

Sun Xi laughed and called out:

"Hey! Is the young master over there?"

No one seemed to notice him. The bridge was already

wrecked. Stray beams drifted across the lake like flood flotsam. Sun Xi called out once more, and this time someone shouted back:

"Who are you asking?"

"You're as good as any. Is the young master over there? Did he cross over to the island?"

"Which young master do you mean?"

"The one from the Wang family outside of Anchang Gate."

"Oh." He waved his hands toward the island. "He crossed over."

Realizing that his mission was accomplished and he could now return home to report, Sun Xi wheeled around and walked toward the road that led to the right. The boatman shouted toward his retreating figure:

"Hey you! Where do you think you're going?"

"I'm going home," Sun Xi returned. "First to Hong Family Bridge, then Bamboo Grove."

"It's gone," the man burst into laughter. "We tore that bridge down."

"Tore it down?"

"Wasn't it your young master who said we should tear them all down?"

Sun Xi flushed:

"But what the fuck am I supposed to do now?"

Another man on the deck laughed:

"How should we know? Go ask your young master."

The first man continued:

"Try going to Baiyuan. If you're lucky, they won't have torn that one down yet."

Sun Xi turned left and began to sprint down the road to Baiyuan.

When he arrived later that afternoon, they had just finished dismantling the bridge. A few boats were paddling swiftly away toward the west.

Sun Xi began to scream at the top of his lungs:

"Wait! How am I supposed to get across?"

The boats were already too far away to have heard his plea, so he began to give chase, sprinting along the bank. But the boats were coasting quickly on the current, and Sun Xi broke into a string of curses:

"Wait up, turtle's eggs! Wait up, sons of bitches! Slow down, I can't keep up!"

When Sun Xi finally managed to catch up, he pleaded between gasps for breath:

"Brother, do me a favor. Brother, can't you give me a ride across?"

A man on the deck asked:

"Where you headed?"

"Home, Anchang Gate."

"You're on the wrong track. You should be trying to cross at Hong Family Bridge."

Sun Xi painstakingly spit out a mouthful of foamy saliva:

"That bridge's already gone. Come on, brother, do me a favor?"

The man on the deck told him:

"Then the best thing for you to do is keep on running. There's another bridge just up ahead. We're on our way to tear it down."

Sun Xi once again threw himself into a sprint, thinking as he ran: Got to get there before these goddamn turtle's eggs. Moments later, he caught sight of a bridge. He glanced toward the boats, made certain that they were well behind him, and only then slowed to a walk.

When he had made his way to the middle of the bridge, he stopped to watch as the boats rowed closer and closer. Then he slowly and deliberately made his way across the bridge and to the other side. Now completely assured of safe passage, he sat on the grassy bank for a rest.

The boats maneuvered under the bridge, and a few men stood and began to hack at the beams. One of the oarsmen glanced over at Sun Xi and called out:

"What're you doing hanging around here?"

Sun Xi thought: I can do whatever I damn well please. He was about to say something to that effect when the oarsman continued:

"You'd better run for it. They're gonna tear down the bridge from here to Songhuang any minute now. And then the bridge from Songhuang to Bamboo Grove too. You still wanna hang around?"

More bridges?

Sun Xi leaped to his feet in fright and sprinted into the distance like a mad dog.

13

Sensing that it was about time that Sun Xi returned, the landlord stood on the front steps fingering a string of cash.

Dusk was approaching, and the sky lit up incandescently red to the horizon, suffusing the winter evening with a sort of warmth. Wang Ziqing's eyes peered above the courtyard wall and followed the twists of the dirt path toward the horizon, where a tiny figure was outlined against hovering pink clouds. The landlord was pleased by the way Sun Xi sprinted down the path toward home.

He knew the two women were looking mournfully at him from inside the door. They had been waiting intently for Sun Xi's arrival, waiting for word as to whether the little bastard was dead or alive. They had finally come to an understanding of just how exhausting it can be to cry. Their tears had been for the landlord's benefit anyway. Now they no longer had the heart to cry the whole day through, and the landlord was grateful for the quiet that their new knowledge had afforded him.

Sun Xi, drenched with sweat, ran forward to meet him. He had originally planned to run directly to the water crock, but when he saw the landlord waiting, he hesitated, stopped, and prepared to give his report.

But before he could even open his mouth, the landlord waved him away:

"Go get a drink first."

Sun Xi hurried over to the water crock and sucked down two ladlefuls of water. Then he wiped his mouth and turned toward the landlord:

"Master, all the bridges are down. The young master took them to Orphan Hill, and then they tore down all the bridges. Even the bridges out of Bamboo Grove are gone."

He bit his lip and continued:

"I almost didn't make it back."

The landlord looked up and gazed expressionlessly down the path. The women burst into screaming sobs, their voices splashing like countless basins of water onto the steps.

Sun Xi stood awkwardly at the foot of the steps, eyes fixed on the string of cash clasped between the landlord's fingers as he wondered why he still had not been tossed his reward. In order to prod the landlord, he continued his report:

"Master, I'll go take another look."

The landlord shook his head:

"It's no use."

As he spoke, the landlord put the money back into his pocket and said to his disappointed laborer:

"You ought to be on your way home, Sun Xi. Take a sack of rice with you."

Sun Xi immediately strode past the landlord and into the house. At the same time, the two women emerged:

"Make Sun Xi go back and have another look."

The landlord waved his hand dismissively, stating:

"There's no need."

Sun Xi came out with a sack of rice, attached it to one end of a carrying pole, and halfheartedly attempted to lift the pole over his shoulder before setting it back down. He said:

"Master, one end of the pole's too heavy."
The landlord smiled faintly:
"Go get another sack then."
Sun Xi bowed:
"Thank you master."

14

"You can't get to Songhuang." Wang Xianghuo, who had been watching as the boats disappeared in the distance, finally turned and addressed the translator. "This is an island. Orphan Hill. They tore down all the bridges. Not one of you will be able to get away."

The translator flew into a panic and began to scream, waving his fist at Wang Xianghuo, before turning anxiously toward the Japanese officer and babbling a report.

A sort of astonishment washed over the faces of the young Japanese soldiers as they turned to gaze uncomprehendingly at the broad waters that surrounded them. After a moment, one soldier, perhaps having finally digested the gravity of their predicament, suddenly began to scream as he ran toward Wang Xianghuo with his bayonet leveled. His shouts ignited the anger of the rest of the troops, and within seconds what seemed like the entire brigade had besieged him with their bayonets. When the commanding officer bellowed something, the soldiers quickly pulled back their weapons and stood at attention. The officer moved toward Wang Xianghuo, brandishing his fist and squealing something in Japanese. Wang Xianghuo watched the officer's fist hover in front of him for what seemed like several moments before it finally slammed against his face. Wang Xianghuo collapsed on the ground beneath the officer's boots, and the translator landed a few hard kicks on his torso:

"Get up. Take us to Songhuang."
Wang Xianghuo pushed himself to his knees with his

forearms and then slowly stood to his full height. The translator continued:

"The commandant says that if you want to live you have to take us to Songhuang."

Wang Xianghuo shook his head and said:

"You can't get to Songhuang now. All the bridges are gone."

The translator slapped Wang Xianghuo across the face. Wang Xianghuo's head lolled back and forth as the translator said:

"Do you fucking want to die?"

Wang Xianghuo looked down and mumbled:

"You're all going to die too."

The translator's face went ash gray, and he seemed to be stuttering as he relayed this last conversation to the officer. The officer, too, seemed not to have come to a thorough understanding of his plight, for he told the translator to tell Wang Xianghuo to lead them away from the island. Wang Xianghuo said to the translator:

"You should kill me."

Wang Xianghuo gazed over at the rippling surface of the lake and said to the translator:

"Even if you knew how to swim, there'd be no way to come out alive. You'd freeze to death by the time you got to the middle. You should kill me."

The translator said something to the officer. The Japanese soldiers grew increasingly restive as they stared imploringly at their commanding officer, entrusting their fates to someone just as helpless as themselves.

Wang Xianghuo, standing to one side, told the translator:

"You tell them that even if they could get to the other side alive, they'd find that every bridge throughout the region has been torn down."

Then he smiled and somewhat sheepishly added:

"I was the one who told them to tear down the bridges."

The young soldiers began to shriek. One by one, they pointed their bayonets at him. The sight of their mud-spattered uniforms suddenly filled him with a kind of sorrow, for they reminded him less of soldiers than little boys. The officer waved a command, and two of the Japanese soldiers dragged Wang Xianghuo to an old withered tree, slamming him against its trunk with blows to his shoulders from the butts of their rifles. Wang Xianghuo bit his lips to stave off the intense pain. With his head lolling to one side, Wang Xianghuo watched the two Japanese soldiers discuss something. The other soldiers milled around in the distance, faces etched with anxiety, seeming hardly to notice what was about to happen. He saw the two Japanese soldiers stand shoulder to shoulder and advance toward him with their bayonets held at the ready. Suddenly, the sun emerged from behind the clouds and with it a wave of dizzying light that transformed everything before his eyes into a glittering, brilliant screen. One of the Japanese soldiers knelt down, rifle in hand, and took off his overcoat. Then he folded it over his knees and bowed his head toward the ground. Another soldier walked up to him and began to stroke his narrow, bony shoulder. The first soldier remained motionless, and the second stood by his side.

The two soldiers with bayonets retreated five or six meters and then stopped. One of them turned to glance at the commanding officer. The officer turned away from a conversation with the translator and barked a couple of clipped phrases toward the soldiers. Wang Xianghuo watched a few of the soldiers take off their caps and rub the grime from their faces. Fragments of the shattered bridge flashed in the sunlight.

The two soldiers came shrieking toward him. A few of the others turned to watch. The two shining bayonet blades looked as if they were sticking out of the soldier's chins as they hurtled toward him. The blades pierced his chest and his stomach. He felt them churn inside him, and he felt them being pulled from his body. It seemed that he had been disemboweled. Wang Xianghuo screamed:

"Pa, it hurts!"

His body slid down the tree trunk to the ground and lay lifelessly twisted in a pool of gore.

The officer barked out an order, and the Japanese soldiers immediately gathered into two neat columns. The officer waved his arm, and, boots thudding rhythmically against the dirt, the brigade began to march away. One of the soldiers took up the same tune on his whistle, and the rest of the brigade joined in low song. In the hours before their death, through the approaching dusk, the brigade sang a song of their native land as they marched across foreign soil.

15

After Sun Xi left, two sacks of rice squeaking on the carrying pole, Wang Ziqing slowly walked out of the courtyard, hands clasped behind his back, and moved through the gleaming light of the setting sun toward the night soil vat by the village gate.

The silver-whiskered landlord walked desolately across the barren fields. The withered trees, motionless even in the breeze, reminded him of corpses. A peasant approached and bowed respectfully:

"Master."

"Uhh."

He grunted and continued to walk until he reached the edge of the vat. He lifted up the edge of his robe, let his pants fall to his ankles, and squatted over the vat. He gazed at the path that extended into the distance, but it was empty of anything save gradually approaching darkness. Not far away, an old peasant was tilling the land, repeatedly slapping his hoe weakly into the mud. He felt his trembling legs begin to shake violently, tried in vain to steady himself by crouching down on the edge of the vat. He looked up at the mottled sunset sky, but the speckles of light only made him dizzy. He closed his eyes. With this tiny movement, he tumbled down beside the vat.

He watched the peasant walk up to him and inquire:

"Master, are you all right?"

He lay propped against the side of the vat, but when he tried to move, his body went limp, as if it were just a hollow shell. It was only with great effort that he lifted a couple of crooked fingers toward the peasant. The peasant immediately knelt next to him:

"Master, what can I do for you?"

He softly asked the peasant:

"Have you ever seen me fall before?"

The peasant shook his head:

"No, master."

He lifted up one finger:

"The first time?"

"Yes, master. The first time."

The landlord laughed quietly and waved the peasant away. The old peasant returned to his work. The landlord lay limply against the vat as the night spread around him like black smoke. The path in the distance was still pale with light.

He heard the sound of a woman calling for someone float toward him from out of the distance, and he trembled. It was the sound of his young wife's voice. She was calling for his reluctant little son to stop playing and come on inside. He closed his eyes and watched the endless waters of the lake swell across his chest. The pink clouds were much too low. They coiled across the surface of the water like wind. He saw his son move distractedly toward him, and he cursed under his breath: The little bastard.

The two women of the house, immersed in a sorrow that ebbed and crested throughout the day, suddenly realized with alarm that the landlord had not come home. It was well past dusk, and moonlight sparkled down from the night sky. The two women hobbled on their bound feet across the fields to the village gate, calling for the landlord. When no response came, they began to sob his name. Their voices flew across the field like the twittering sobs of night birds. By the time they had arrived by the side of the night soil vat, the landlord's body lay lifelessly twisted across the ground.

Predestination

The sun was bright that day, and wind whistled outside the window. Spring had arrived. Liu Dongsheng sat by the eighteenth-floor window of a high-rise building, listening to the blind cries of children playing in the schoolyard below. The songs of this innocent flock of children bothered him. He saw the soft green treetops lining the banks of the city moat, saw a jumble of taxis and trucks jockey past them on the avenue. In the distance, the Ferris wheel in the amusement park revolved slowly and almost imperceptibly through the air.

It was just then that an envelope, the return address printed in boldface type, landed in his hands, startling him from his reverie. There was no need to open it. The boldface type clearly and unmistakably told him that his best friend was dead. The corner of the envelope read: **Chen Lei Funeral Committee.**

The wealthiest of all his childhood friends had been murdered, and another old friend had organized a funeral committee for the millionaire so as to testify to the wealth and power that had been his before he was killed. The committee had posted an unsettling funeral notice all over the small town where they'd grown up. Apparently, this flurry of three or four hundred posters had blanketed the dull provincial town like a layer of snow. The people who lived there had never known passion and seldom been afraid. Suddenly to bombard them with hundreds of funeral notices was really a little cruel. The residential lanes where they lived were plastered with the notices. Posters were pasted to the fronts of their houses. Even their doors and windows were covered with the inauspicious news of his friend's murder. The poster was no longer a simple notice of his death. Instead, it seemed like an invitation – come on over to my place.

The indignation and alarm of the townspeople had naturally bubbled over into action. The night after they had been posted, every single one of the memorial notices had been torn down. But the people's torment wasn't over even then. On the day of the funeral, a sound truck snaked slowly through town, broadcasting funereal music at an appalling volume. The sound truck seemed more like it was advancing into battle than making its way toward the crematorium outside of town.

Over the next two weeks, Liu Dongsheng received a steady stream of letters from the committee three hundred miles away. Each of the letters contained updates as to the circumstances surrounding Chen Lei's death and the progress of the subsequent murder investigation.

Chen Lei had been the richest man in town. He had owned two factories. He had opened the fanciest hotel in town. Later, he had bought what had always been considered the most elegant residence in the area, the old Wang family house. When Liu Dongsheng had gone back to town for Spring Festival five years earlier, the old Wang house was being refurbished after years of unoccupied neglect. Liu Dongsheng had run into another childhood friend – now clad in a police uniform – and asked him where he could find Chen Lei. The man had replied: "You'll find him at the old Wang house."

Liu walked all the way across town, but when he should have arrived at a bamboo grove, he discovered that it had been torn down to make way for five new apartment buildings. He continued on alone to the old Wang house. The house was swaddled with scaffolding, and about a dozen workers were scattered across the property. As soon as he walked into the courtyard, a brick fell just in front of his feet, and one of the workers in the scaffolding yelled, "Are you trying to get yourself killed?"

The yell brought him to a halt. He stood and looked at the bits of broken brick around his feet. Then he carefully backed out of the courtyard and took a seat on a pile of neatly stacked bricks outside the door. He sat for a long time before he finally caught sight of Chen Lei riding toward him on a motorcycle.

Chen Lei stopped the bike, propped it up on its kickstand, fished for a cigarette from the pocket of his black leather jacket, and lit it. It was only then that he seemed to notice that someone was sitting on the brick pile. He turned and rapidly made his way toward the courtyard. A few steps later, he glanced back in Liu Dongsheng's direction. This time, his mouth twisted in a chuckle of recognition. Liu Dongsheng, rising from his perch on the brick pile, laughed with him. Chen Lei walked over to the brick pile, threw his arm around Liu's shoulders, and said, "Come on, let's go get a drink."

Chen Lei was dead now.

From the committee's letters, Liu Dongsheng knew that Chen Lei had been alone that night. His wife and children had left the old Wang house to visit their grandmother in a village about ten miles outside of town. Someone had beaten him to death with an iron hammer as he slept. He was riddled with little holes from his head down to his chest.

Chen Lei's wife had returned to the old Wang house two days later. The first thing she had done was to call the company office and ask where he was. The assistant manager told her that he had been wondering the same thing.

Startled and worried, she had made her way into the bedroom to look for clues. The pitiful sight of Chen Lei's battered corpse brought a stream of urine sliding down the inside of her pants leg and onto the carpet. There wasn't even enough time to scream. She fell in a faint.

Chen Lei had always loved collecting cigarette lighters.

When the police arrived at the scene of the crime, they soon discovered that nothing was missing. Nothing, that is, except his collection of over five hundred different kinds of lighters. The assailant had taken every single one of them, from the cheapest disposables to the rarest and most valuable works of craftsmanship.

Reading through the committee's letters at three hundred miles' remove, Liu learned that the police had been unable to come up with any leads. Even so, the letters overflowed with speculation. There were even descriptions of possible suspects. Although the letters didn't divulge the suspects' names, Liu Dongsheng could tell who several of them were. But he wasn't really interested in any of that. He had his own ideas about the death of the man who had been his best friend. He began to remember what had happened thirty years before.

THIRTY YEARS AGO

The flagstone pavement gleamed dark and wet in the sun after the downpour. So did the plastic tarps slung over the bamboo clotheslines. There were about as many feet walking on the flagstones as insects crawling across the tarps. The eaves of the houses on either side of the street seemed to be connected in an unbroken line. Sheets and clothes protruded out from under the open windows of the houses. Electrical lines ran above them. They swayed gently up and down when a few twittering magpies alighted on the wires.

A child named Liu Dongsheng leaned against a window, chin pressed against the whitewashed sill as he gazed down at the street. Finally, he saw a child called Chen Lei emerge from a house across the street. Chen Lei moved dejectedly between the legs of the grown-ups filling the street, glancing back and forth as he went. He stopped in front of a little grocery store a few doors down the street, fumbled in his pocket for something, and put whatever it was on his tongue. Then he walked over to the door of the blacksmith shop. A grown-up's voice emerged from amid the clamor of metal hammering on metal: "Go on. Get out of here."

His head turned helplessly back to the street, and he slowly ambled away.

It was the same every day. After he heard his parents click the front door lock resoundingly into place on their way out to work, Liu Dongsheng ran to the window to watch Chen Lei follow his parents out of the house across the street. Chen Lei always craned his neck to watch his parents lock the front door. And each morning before his parents left for work, they always yelled: "Don't go play by the river."

Chen Lei always gazed up at them without a word until one of them added: "Chen Lei! Did you hear me?"

Chen Lei replied, "I heard you."

By then, Liu Dongsheng's parents had already walked down the stairs and into the street. They glanced back up at him, scolding, "Don't lean against the window!"

He scurried away from the window. His parents continued: "And don't you dare play with fire inside the house!"

Liu Dongsheng muttered something in response. When he was sure that his parents were already well on their way, he once more took up his place by the window, but by then Chen Lei was already gone.

But this time, Chen Lei was still standing on a flagstone in the middle of the street. Suddenly, his body rocked violently to one side, pushing the edge of the flagstone into the soft ground underneath. A stream of muddy liquid squirted out from underneath the stone, soiling the pants leg of one of the grown-ups walking by. The man stopped and grabbed Chen Lei's arm with his outstretched hand:

"You little motherfucker."

Chen Lei was so scared that he squeezed his eyes shut and covered his face with his free hand. The bearded man released his arm and said in a menacing tone: "You better watch out, or I'll kill you."

The man swaggered off, leaving Chen Lei in a daze. Arms hanging limp at his sides, he stood and watched the grownups passing by until he was sure that none of them had noticed what he had just done. Then his little frame began to thread its way through the grown-ups until he had reached his own front door. He sat with his back pressed up against the door, stretched his arms out in front of him, and rubbed his eyes. He yawned. When he had finished yawning, he looked up at a window across the street. Another child was staring at him from the window.

When Liu Dongsheng realized that Chen Lei had finally noticed him, he smiled and called out, "Chen Lei."

Chen Lei's voice rang back in response, "How do you know my name?"

Liu Dongsheng giggled. "I just know."

The two children started to laugh. They looked at each other for another moment before Liu Dongsheng asked, "Why do your mom and dad lock you out of the house?"

Chen Lei said, "They're afraid I'll play with fire and burn the house down."

Chen Lei asked, "Why do your mom and dad lock you inside the house?"

"They're afraid I'll go play by the river and drown."

The children looked excitedly at each other.

Chen Lei asked, "How old are you?"

"I'm six," Liu Dongsheng answered.

"I'm six, too." Chen Lei said. "I thought you were older than me."

Liu Dongsheng laughed, "That's cause I'm standing on a stool."

The road stretched toward the next intersection, where a crowd of people suddenly surged together in a circle. A few people sprinted past the children in the direction of the crowd. Liu Dongsheng asked, "What's going on over there?"

Chen Lei stood up from his perch and said, "I'll go check."

Liu Dongsheng, head hanging out over the street, watched as Chen Lei ran toward the corner. The crowd of screaming people surged around the corner and down the next street, where Liu's eyes could no longer follow. Then Chen Lei disappeared around the corner in pursuit.

A moment later, Chen Lei came panting back and, in between gasps, yelled up toward the window, "They're fighting. One of their faces is all bloody. Lots of people's clothes got all ripped up. There's even a lady fighting, too."

A frightened Liu Dongsheng asked, "Did anyone die?"

Chen Lei shook his head. "I don't know."

Awed by this sudden outburst of violence, the two children fell silent.

It was only after a long time that Liu Dongsheng broke the silence with a sigh. "You're so lucky!"

Chen Lei said, "What do you mean?"

"You can go wherever you want to. I can't go anywhere."

"I've got it bad, too." Chen Lei replied. "I can't go inside when I get sleepy."

Liu Dongsheng continued, even more heartbroken than before, "I might not ever see you again. My dad said he's going to nail the window shut 'cause I'm not allowed to stand here in case I fall down and die."

Chen Lei looked down at the ground and traced imaginary lines back and forth across the ground. Then he looked up and asked, "Can you hear me from here?"

Liu Dongsheng nodded.

Chen Lei said, "I'll stand here every day and talk to you."

Liu Dongsheng smiled and said, "Promise?"

Chen Lei said, "If I break the promise then . . . then I hope to heaven I'll be eaten alive by a mad dog."

Chen Lei continued, "Can you see the tops of the houses from up there?"

Liu Dongsheng nodded, "I can see them."

"I've never seen the top of a house," Chen Lei explained, his voice tinged with a hint of sorrow.

Liu Dongsheng said, "The tippy-top of the house looks like a string. Then the two sides slant down to the ground."

That was how the friendship between the two children began. Every day they told each other about the things that the other child couldn't see. Liu Dongsheng would talk about things that came from the sky, and it was up to Chen Lei to describe anything that happened on the ground. This went on for a whole year. But, one day, Liu Dongsheng's father accidentally left a set of keys in the house. Liu Dongsheng threw the keys down to Chen Lei, who ran up the stairs and unlocked the front door.

That was the day Chen Lei led Liu Dongsheng all the way across town, past a bamboo grove, and onto the grounds of the old Wang family house.

The old Wang family house was the grandest thing in town, and over the past year it was the place that Chen Lei had spent the most time describing for his friend.

The two children stood outside the sealed-off wall of the deserted estate watching gusts of magpies hover above the arched tile roof of the mansion within. The whitewashed wall was still in one piece in those days, and it gleamed in the sunlight. The cylindrical roof tiles that stuck out over the eaves of the house were hollow, with all kinds of patterns carved inside them.

Liu Dongsheng, deeply absorbed in his contemplation of the mansion, heard Chen Lei say, "There are lots of swallows' nests inside those tiles."

As he spoke, he gathered a handful of rocks and started to throw them at the eaves. After several tries, he finally scored a bull's-eye. A little swallow emerged from the hollow tile and flitted back and forth through the air, twittering in alarm.

Liu Dongsheng picked up his own handful of rocks and began to throw them at the eaves.

That afternoon, they circled the house, rousting each and every one of the swallows from their nests. The uneasy cries of alarmed swallows continued unbroken throughout the afternoon. When the sun finally began to sink toward the horizon and the air filled with the shouts of peasants on their way home from the fields, the exhausted boys sat down on a little embankment across from the house, watching the swallows return to their nests. A few lost swallows, returning to the wrong nests and repeatedly ousted by the rightful occupants, circled dolefully through the air until bigger swallows came and escorted them home.

Chen Lei said, "Those big ones are their moms and dads."

As the sky gradually grew darker, the children, oblivious to the fact that they really ought to be on their way home, sat talking about whether they should try to climb over the walls and into the mansion itself.

"Do you think anyone lives there anymore?" Liu Dongsheng asked.

Chen Lei shook his head. "Nah, no one lives there. Don't worry. No one's going to chase us away."

"But it's getting dark."

As Chen Lei watched the darkness descend, his determination ebbed rapidly away. He fumbled in his pocket for a moment and finally put something in his mouth.

Liu Dongsheng swallowed and asked, "What are you eating?"

Chen Lei said, "Salt."

As he spoke, his hand fumbled once more in his pocket. Then he put a single grain of salt on Liu Dongsheng's tongue.

But, just at that moment, they thought they heard a child scream.

"Help!"

They were so scared that they leapt to their feet. They

stared wide-eyed at each other for a second before Liu Dong-sheng whispered, "Was that you?"

Chen Lei shook his head.

"Wasn't me."

As soon as his reply had faded into silence, a voice identical to Chen Lei's rang out once more from within the dark walls of the mansion: "Help!"

Liu Dongsheng went pale. "That was your voice."

Chen Lei stared at Liu Dongsheng, eyes wide with fear. After a second, he said, "It wasn't me. I didn't say anything."

When the voice rang out for the third time, the children were already running down the road through the swirling darkness.

Translator's Postscript

Yu Hua was born in 1960 and grew up in a small town near Shanghai. After working for five years as a dentist, he published his first piece of short fiction in 1984. In the ensuing years, he has produced a steady stream of shocking, innovative, and highly controversial short stories and novels that have earned him not only a place at the forefront of China's avant-garde literary scene but also (in the words of one prominent mainland critic) a reputation as "perhaps the foremost literary provocateur of our time."[1]

Yu Hua, of course, was not the only "provocateur" to have emerged in China in the second half of the 1980s. He is part of a new generation of young writers (including luminaries like Su Tong and Ge Fei) who rose to literary stardom in the years of intellectual and cultural ferment that preceded the Tiananmen Incident of 1989. This group – whose work has come to be referred to as "experimental fiction" – is separated by a very interesting and historically significant kind of generation gap from the writers who preceded them. That first generation of writers to cast aside the rigid strictures of Maoist ideological orthodoxy came of age during the Cultural Revolution, and they are now in their forties. Many of them were "educated youth" who were sacrificed at the altar of Communist Party politics and deported en masse from the cities to remote rural regions, where they spent much of the 1970s. These writers (and their work) are indelibly marked by their experiences of

---

[1] Chen Xiaoming, "Shengguo fufa: Juewang de xinli zizhuan: Ping Yu Hua *Huhan yu Xiyu*" (Overcoming the law of the patriarch: A psychological autobiography of despair: On Yu Hua's *Screams and Drizzle*), *Dangdai zuojia pinglun* 4 (1992): 4.

revolutionary disillusionment and internal exile. When they finally were allowed to trickle back into the cities from which they had come in the late 1970s and early 1980s, they gradually began to break away from the orbit of socialist realism and the revolutionary doctrines in which they had been schooled.

Experimental writers like Yu Hua, most of whom are still in their early thirties, began to write after that same orthodoxy had already crumbled. Yu Hua was still a child during the Cultural Revolution. By the time he was in high school, Chairman Mao was already dead. Yu Hua now lives and writes in a nation transfigured by economic reform and a freewheeling quasi market economy. This historical trajectory is captured nicely by the last story in the collection, "Predestination." Something of what it was like to grow up during the late 1960s — schools closed, parents absented from the home owing to unremitting political campaigns, the threat of political violence looming in the air — is suggested by the predicament of the two children portrayed here. Their adult incarnations are just as representative of the changes that have swept across China in the 1980s and early 1990s: Chen Lei becomes a wealthy factory owner and hotel magnate who lives in a renovated prerevolutionary mansion; Liu Dongsheng moves to the big city and works in a high-rise office building. As the conclusion of the story suggests, however, neither man (nor perhaps China itself) is able to shake off the specters of the past as easily as he might.

Another difference between the two generations is more purely literary. Growing up during a period in which the Chinese literary diet consisted almost entirely of the works of Chairman Mao, earlier writers had little or no access to world fiction in Chinese translation. The liberalized cultural policies of the 1980s, however, resulted in a flood of new literary translations. Like many of his contemporaries, Yu Hua was inspired to write by encounters with such modernist authors as Japanese Nobel Prize-winner Kawabata Yasunari,

Franz Kafka, Jorge Luis Borges, and by the French new novelist Alain Robbe-Grillet. These influences are in abundant evidence throughout this volume. We can see touches of Kawabata's cruel, incisive lyricism in stories like "World Like Mist." The narrator's absurd encounter with a truck driver in "On the Road at Eighteen" smacks of Kafka. The "labyrinth" that Yu Hua constructs in "The Past and the Punishments" is reminiscent of Borges' metaphysical narratives of time and space, necessity and coincidence. Throughout the volume, finally, Yu Hua's attention to the description of surface detail – at the expense of the inner life of the character – may well remind us of Robbe-Grillet's revolt against the tenets of realist fiction.

It would be a real mistake, however, to read Yu Hua's fiction as a derivative "replay" of these earlier literary monuments. A large part of what makes Yu Hua's stories so interesting (and, in the Chinese context, subversive) is his relentless experimentation with traditional Chinese narrative. "Classical Love" is a prime example. In crafting this haunting tale of romance and cannibalism set in premodern China, Yu Hua has mined a rich vein of traditional vernacular fiction (most of which dates from the Ming and Qing dynasties). Indeed, the story is a seemingly "postmodern" pastiche of traditional story types and time-honored motifs: romances between "talented scholars and beautiful maidens" *(caizi jiaren),* ghost stories and tales of resurrection from the grave, elegiac laments for fallen cities and ruined palaces. Even the horrific scenes of cannibalism are recycled from a Tang dynasty anecdote (which later became a notorious late Ming dynasty story called "A Filial Woman Sells Herself to a Butcher at the Yangzhou Market"). The difference here is that Yu Hua gives us the story in the absence of the moral imperative (filial piety) that made the original tick. What we are left with is the inexplicable cruelty and sheer horror of the grisly acts that Yu Hua so meticulously and unflinchingly portrays.

"Blood and Plum Blossoms" plays a similar trick. The story is based on a genre of popular fiction that remains wildly popular to this day: tales of knight-errantry *(wuxia xiaoshuo)*. At the heart of the vast majority of these martial arts novels (and the scores of kung-fu movies and television series that they have inspired) runs a single obsessional theme: a hero (or a group of heroes) wanders the "rivers and lakes" of an idealized traditional China in order to take his just revenge on some implacable enemy. Yu Hua's sophisticated retake of the genre has all the trappings of a proper revenge tale, but the moral center of the narrative mold has been hollowed out, casting the reader into an enigmatic world of chance, coincidence, and uncertainty.

While other stories are not as directly predicated on past literary models, they infuse contemporary settings with echoes of traditional beliefs and practices, to unsettling effect. The claustrophobic yet hauntingly sensuous world of "World Like Mist" is cobbled together out of such echoes, its intricate narrative mosaic shot through with Chinese ghost lore, death rites, fortune-telling, and (as is most apparent in the names of the characters themselves) numerology. The sudden eruption of the supernatural into a story of childhood friendship in "Predestination" is more than a little reminiscent of another classical genre, the "tale of the strange" *(chuanqi)*. Both "1986" and "The Past and the Punishments," finally, are predicated on yet another sort of textual tradition — ancient historical records that detail the punishments meted out to those who had run afoul of the social order.

Nor does Yu Hua shy away from taking on more recent traditions. Chinese readers born after 1949 grew up on stirring, brutally realistic novels of revolutionary insurrection against the rural gentry. A second, related genre was fiction eulogizing Chinese popular resistance to Japanese invasion. In these works of socialist realism, the world was very simple. Peasants were good. Landlords were bad. Revolutionary violence was heroic, and a Bolshevik hero would always rise up to lead the masses to victory, usually sacrificing his life in the process. "The Death of the Landlord" deftly combines these two genres and, in doing so, subtly undercuts them. Wang Xianghuo is neither a Bolshevik nor a patriot. Sun Xi, whose lowly background should by all rights make him a hero, is a knave. The violence and brutality of both sides is less glorious than grotesque. The old verities of war and revolution fall by the wayside, and, by the time we reach the conclusion of the story, we have traveled through an ethical and emotional landscape that is infinitely more complex and ambivalent than that of its generic forerunners.

What unites these restlessly innovative, willfully provocative stories is Yu Hua's almost obsessive preoccupation with the twin specters of Chinese history ("the past") and the human capacity for cruelty and violence ("the punishments"). These are preoccupations that he shares with other avant-garde writers of his generation, and they stem directly from an acute awareness of the incalculable suffering that was the consequence of China's entrance into modernity. The laundry list is long and bitter: humiliation at the hands of imperialist powers, Japanese invasion, protracted civil war, followed by a revolution the brightest ideals and noblest aspirations of which were crushed by an ever-deepening spiral of disastrous policies, senseless persecution, corruption, factional violence, and disillusionment.

It was only with the brilliant cultural efflorescence of the post-Mao 1980s that Chinese intellectuals began to explore this troubling legacy, to ask themselves what exactly had gone wrong. Much of this work was carried out by the generation of "educated youth" who had borne the brunt of the Cultural Revolution. Collectively, they launched movement after movement aimed at freeing Chinese artists and intellectuals from the shackles of their Maoist inheritance. Some of the more notable of their achievements include the "misty poetry" of Bei Dao and others associated with the 1979 Democracy Wall movement in Beijing, the new wave cinema of "fifth generation" directors like Zhang Yimou and Chen Kaige, and the "roots-seeking" fiction of writers like Mo Yan and Han Shaogong. What all these figures shared was a broad faith in the redemptive power of humanism, intellectual enlightenment, and democracy.

In this sense, they were little different from their counterparts of the 1920s, who had promoted an epochal cultural transformation usually referred to as the May Fourth movement. Indeed, many of the intellectual and artistic developments of the 1980s represented a resurrection of May Fourth-era ideals, ideals that were felt to have been betrayed by the vagaries of twentieth-century history, extremist politics, and the persistence of traditional, "feudal" Chinese culture.

It is only in this context that we can begin to understand Yu Hua and his contemporaries – because, more than anything else, their work represents a revolt not only against Maoism but also against the grand ideals that have sustained Chinese intellectuals and reformers since the May Fourth era. To put it simply, Yu Hua is in the business of knocking over idols, of undermining the traditional faith of modern Chinese intellectuals in the triumphal march of history and humanism.

A story like "The Past and the Punishments" suggests something of both the stakes involved in Yu Hua's critique of his forebears and the disenchantment from which it arises. In the "punishment expert," we have a scholar dedicated to compiling "a summation of human wisdom," a man who quite literally has taken possession of history. And, not unlike generations of idealist Chinese intellectuals, he firmly believes that he has spent his life in the service of progress, scientific knowledge, and humanity. Ultimately, however, he cannot see the blood of his victims dripping from his own hands. His tragedy, Yu Hua implies, may be that of China as well.

This radical distrust of all "totalizing ideologies" is, of course, not without its parallels in the West. Indeed, many Chinese critics have been quick to identify the fiction of Yu Hua and others like him as "postmodernist." In the Chinese context, however, it is probably more useful to discuss the way Yu Hua and others have abandoned the realist tradition in which they were reared. Ever since the pioneering work of Lu Xun, the most prominent of the May Fourth-era intellectuals and the "father of modern Chinese literature," realism has dominated the Chinese literary scene. Why? Modern Chinese literature has always been a literature of social and political engagement. By realistically portraying the darkness and oppression around them, writers like Lu Xun would enlighten their readers and, in doing so, write a new and brighter world into existence. The time of realism – not unlike that of historical narrative – is linear. And its primary concern is humanity – the portrayal of individual psyches in relation to their social, political, and natural context. These qualities made it uniquely suited to intellectuals whose overriding concern was to refashion China's historical destiny by means of a progressive literature of social and political enlightenment.

Yu Hua has largely abandoned these conventions. His stories seldom unfold in a specific time and place. Time does not always flow inexorably forward from some specific starting point. Instead, his narratives fragment, overlap, loop back on themselves. Linear history disperses like so much mist into the air. In Yu Hua's world there is no such thing as progress – only relentless change. Nor is there anyone remotely resembling a hero. We are almost never given access to a character's inner world. Indeed, as Yu Hua himself has commented in an essay on his own work, "I am far more concerned with a character's desires [than with his or her personality], for it is desire rather than 'personality' that represents the value of someone's existence. . . . Nor do I believe that characters should be any more important than rivers, sunlight, leaves, streets, or houses. I believe that people, rivers, sunlight, and so on are all the same: just props within the fiction. The manner in which a river flows manifests its desire, and houses, though silent, also reveal the existence of desire."[2]

This passage, I think, goes a long way toward explaining the disturbing power of Yu Hua's fiction. Yu Hua offers us a textual world in which humans are walking ciphers and ordinary objects are invested with an enigmatic and menacing radiance. It is a world that asks us to move beyond the ethical, political, and stylistic truths of realist fiction and challenges us to make sense of a disorienting, but at the same time enormously suggestive, landscape.

The extreme violence of Yu Hua's fiction demands comment. To journey through his fictional universe is to subject oneself to a harrowing series of depictions of death, dismembered bodies, and acts of extreme and seemingly gratuitous cruelty. Reading Yu Hua is not easy; indeed, it can be gut-wrenching. As a translator, I have often grappled with the ethical dimension of this work. Is it right to loose these sorts of representations on an unsuspecting world? How can one reconcile the violence of these stories with the literary virtuosity with which that violence is sometimes portrayed? If we find ourselves enjoying Yu Hua's fiction, are we somehow guilty of complicity with his aestheticization of violence?

[2] Yu Hua, "Xuwei de zuopin" (Hypocritical writings), preface to *Shishi ru yan* (World like mist) (Taibei: Yuanliu chuban gongsi, 1991), 21.

These are difficult questions that are beyond the scope of this introduction. Each of Yu Hua's readers will have to face them in his or her own way. And, in fact, much of the power and provocation of this work derives from the way in which it forces us to confront just these kinds of issues.

Part of the reason that Yu Hua's fiction is so very grisly, no doubt, has to do with his own psychological makeup. When I first met him, I could not help asking why it was that his fiction was so liberally littered with corpses. He told me that he had grown up in the hospital where both his parents worked as doctors. On hot summer afternoons, the coolest place he could find to take a nap was the morgue in the basement. "So," he concluded, "things like that don't really bother me."

This biographical detail may well help explain Yu Hua's authorial sangfroid, the matter-of-fact lyricism with which he sets about the task of describing things that most of us would rather avoid. It does not tell us (and ultimately I am not convinced that we really need to know) just why Yu Hua is both haunted by and determined to confront the horrors of cruelty and violence in his fiction.

That this violence is somehow linked to the horrors of recent Chinese history is made clear in a story like "1986." In this tale, the terror of the Cultural Revolution returns to haunt a town caught up in the blissful historical amnesia of the post-Mao economic boom. It would be easy to read the piece as a narrowly political allegory. Easy, but misleading. The madman, after all, is treated rather nicely by the Red Guards. His madness goes deeper than mere historical circumstance. Instead, it represents a meditation on the ways in which history, culture, and language collaborate with our seemingly innate capacity for brutality and callousness to create political violence.

Like all good literature, Yu Hua's work asks more questions of its readers than it answers. In this sense, Yu Hua's fiction places its readers in a predicament not unlike that faced by the townspeople in "1986." We can choose to ignore the terror and brutality depicted here. We can nervously laugh such things off as the handiwork of a madman or a charlatan. We can stand around and enjoy the spectacle. Alternatively, we can respond to Yu Hua's implicit challenge by attempting to make sense of these texts in allegorical terms: what do they tell us about history, politics, culture, contemporary Chinese literature, China in the 1990s? All these responses are valid. But it is only when we ask what reading these difficult and beautiful stories means to us on an ethical, and ultimately human, level that they come into their own.

A NOTE ON THE TRANSLATION

"To translate," the conventional wisdom reads, is inevitably "to betray" the original. Translators are inexorably trapped between the demands of fidelity and readability, between the tasks of conveying the literal sense of a literary work and capturing its essence. Early on in the project, I asked Yu Hua what sort of translation he felt would be most suited to his work. His response was short and simple: "If you can get the images and the rhythm of my language down on paper, everything else will follow." While these instructions may well have been overly optimistic, I have tried my best to reduplicate in English something of the experience of reading Yu Hua's fiction in the original Chinese, to create a rough analogue of his utterly distinctive style, without sacrificing its sense. Experience, of course, is necessarily subjective. And, in this sense, my translations can never aspire to represent a perfect or authoritative representation of Yu Hua's fiction. They are, instead, interpretations springing from my own encounters with these complex and illuminating stories.

ACKNOWLEDGMENTS

This book would never have reached its readers without the cooperation and assistance of many friends and colleagues. Li Tuo, one of the earliest and most influential supporters of experimental fiction in China, first inspired me to read and write about Yu Hua's work when he was a visiting professor at Berkeley. Yu Hua willingly and enthusiastically entrusted his work to the hands of a young and inexperienced translator. I am grateful for his faith in me and in this project. Howard Goldblatt helped make sure that my translations would reach their intended audience. Cherry Chan provided the space in which I could successfully complete the project. Sharon Yamamoto, finally, was an extraordinarily thoughtful and unfailingly helpful editor.

Many others — including Lydia Liu, Jing Wang, Chris Hamm, Franka Jones, and the two anonymous readers for the Press — read sections of the manuscript and offered encouragement, criticism, and suggestions for improvement. Many of my original mistakes and misinterpretations have been weeded out thanks to their help. Those that remain are entirely my own responsibility.

Editor's Note

The stories in this collection were originally published in Chinese in literary journals and subsequently were anthologized in different collections both in Taiwan and mainland China.

Literary journals. —— "On the Road at Eighteen" (Shiba sui chumen yuanxing); "The Past and the Punishments" (Wangshi yu xingfa); and "Classical Love" (Gudian aiqing) first appeared in *Beijing wenxue* (Beijing literature), 1:1987, 2:1989, and 12:1988, respectively. "Blood and Plum Blossoms" (Xianxue meihua) and "Predestination" (Mingzhong zhuding) first appeared in *Renmin wenxue* (People's literature), 3:1989 and 7:1993. "1986" (Yijiu baliu nian) and "World Like Mist" (Shishi ru yan) first appeared in *Shouhuo* (Harvest literary magazine), 6:1987 and 5:1988. "The Death of a Landlord" (Yige dizhu de si) first appeared in *Zhongshan* (Bell mountain), 6:1992.

Anthologies. —— *On the Road at Eighteen* (Taipei: Yuanliu, 1991) includes "On the Road at Eighteen" and "1986." *World Like Mist* (Taipei: Yuanliu, 1991) includes "World Like Mist" and "Classical Love." *Summer Typhoon* [Xiaji taifeng] (Taipei: Yuanliu, 1993) includes "Blood and Plum Blossoms" and "The Past and the Punishments." *Shudder* [Zhanli] (Hong Kong: Boyi chubanshe, 1995) includes "Predestination" and "The Death of a Landlord." In addition, all of the stories are included in a comprehensive three-volume collection of Yu Hua's short fiction entitled *Yu Hua's Collected Works* (Yu Hua zuopin ji), Beijing: Zhongguo shehui kexue chubanshe, 1994.

The English translation of "On the Road at Eighteen" appeared in slightly different form in *The Columbia Anthology of Modern Chinese Literature*, edited by Joseph S. M. Lau and Howard Goldblatt (Columbia University Press, 1995). The English translation of "The Past and the Punishments" appeared in slightly different form in *Chairman Mao Would Not Be Amused*, edited by Howard Goldblatt (Grove Press, 1995).

About the Translator

ANDREW F. JONES is the author of *Like a Knife: Ideology and Genre in Contemporary Chinese Popular Music.* His writings on Chinese literature and popular culture have appeared in the journals *Modern Chinese Literature* and *positions: east asia cultures critique* as well as in *Spin Magazine.* He is currently completing his Ph.D. in East Asian Languages at UC Berkeley.

Production Notes

Composition and paging were done in
FrameMaker software on an AccuSet
Postscript Imagesetter by the design
and production staff of University
of Hawaiʻi Press.

The text and display typeface is Garamond 3.

Offset presswork and binding were done by
The Maple-Vail Book Manufacturing Group.
Text paper is Glatfelter Smooth Antique,
basis 50.